The Man in the Middle

His name is Nicholas Arden. He has, in his lifetime,
been a slave worker in Nazi camps, and when the
novel begins he is working as an interpreter. He
is possessed of secret information that, should
it be divulged, would spark off the fuse for
World War Three. *He cannot be allowed to live!*

Hugh Atkinson's powerful and moving novel,
like his bestselling novels *The Games* and *The
Most Savage Animal*, is passionately involved with
the confused and dangerous world of today.

'A tautly-written political thriller with an
all-too-plausible plot . . . ingenious, and very
nasty denouement . . . masterly.' *Liverpool Daily
Post*

The Man in the Middle

Hugh Atkinson

Mayflower

Granada Publishing Limited
Published in 1975 by Mayflower Books Ltd
Frogmore, St Albans, Herts AL2 2NF

First published in Great Britain by
Hart-Davis, MacGibbon Ltd 1973
Copyright © Hugh Atkinson 1973
Made and printed in Great Britain by
Cox & Wyman Ltd
London, Reading and Fakenham
Set in Linotype Times

For Phoebe

CHAPTER ONE

BRANDISHING their package tour suntans, lumped with hand baggage and the motley of compulsively bought souvenirs, parents prodded their children up the ramp, already resentful of another year's routine, of the rain swirling on the windows, the difficulties of hands and passports, the bureaucratic obstacles to be endured between the aircraft and the cram of the coaches.

The tall dark man walked almost cruelly through them, as though this impediment was not human, sheep or goats to be forced aside.

At Passport Control he waited, remote and indifferent, his gaze above the clerk's bent head.

'Will you be staying long, sir?'

'A few days only.' The accent was hard, grating.

The clerk considered the man against his photograph, stamped the visa.

'Business or pleasure, sir?'

'Business.'

The clerk barely proffered the passport, holding it between two fingers. The visitor took it without a glance.

In the baggage hall he skirted the crush around the turntables, the porters weaving their trolleys, the disordered traffic towards Customs, his isolated, unadmitting progress a seeming refutation of the reverberating terminal and all who moved in it. He carried the small hard black leather case before him, absorbing on that any unavoidable human contact.

The customs officer noted the man's diffidence. The badly cut lightweight suit, the savagely thin dark face and spiky, cropped hair.

'Anything to declare, sir?'

'Nothing.'

The officer sought the other man's eyes.

'No other luggage, sir?'

'No.'

For an instant the officer debated.

'Would you mind opening your bag, sir?'

He heard the locks click, looked up and was startled by the hostility that burned in the eyes that had avoided him.

There was almost nothing in the case. Two shirts, a cardigan, toothbrush and paste, the corner of something hard. The officer edged the shirts aside and removed it. He leafed through the book, recognizing the language in which it was printed. He could feel in his mistake and discomfort the unseen eyes burning at him.

'What's this, sir?'

He had to wait on the reply, a deliberately studied contempt.

'It is the Koran.'

He replaced the book, almost absurdly, as he had found it, under the shirts.

'Thank you.'

The locks clicked shut. The officer watched the Arab go, still oddly discomforted. 'That's a right one,' he told himself.

The taxi turned off Exhibition Road into Prince's Gate, the driver straining across the seat, steering with one hand.

'Somewhere 'ere on the left, is it, guv?'

His passenger gestured a hand, said nothing.

The driver craned farther across the seat.

'Musta passed it. We're in the sixties 'ere.'

He braked and reversed, stopped at the corner, craned again to check the numbers.

'That's it, then.'

His passenger got out.

'How much money?' he asked.

'Three fifty, that little lot.'

'Three pounds, and a half pound?'

'That's right, guv.'

The passenger paid him exactly, looked briefly at the tall, creamy white building, turned and carried his bag up the steps.

The driver examined the money in his hand, then the plaque on the building.

'Bloody wog,' he said loudly.

A few rugs were scattered on the parquetry-floored lobby. A man stood beside a reception desk near the back wall. There were no chairs. Three posters captioned in Arabic bore the likenesses of Colonel Gadaffi, President Sadat, President Nimeiry. The red and green of their colours had faded, edges split, attached to the wall with scotch tape.

The big room had windows looking out to the green of a small garden. The stout man who rose from behind the desk was in shirt sleeves, collar button undone, tie loosened. He smiled.

'*Salam-alekum*,' he said, and added the Arab word for brother.

The tall Arab left his case on the side table.

'And on you be peace, Brother.'

An English girl in a mini-skirt, with a tray of cakes and coffee, had followed the visitor. When she had withdrawn and shut the door the two men talked quietly, sipping at their cups. This hospitality observed, the stout man searched in his drawers, frowning, before he found the file.

'This is your hotel reservation, Brother. A comfortable place close by. This is the name and address of the man selected, some notes on his proficiency and the organizations that employ him. This is a copy of the advertisement he takes in the Personal Columns of *The Times*. He lives quietly, with his wife and child. Is there anything else you should know?'

The tall Arab read the few sheets of typed paper, folded them neatly, took his passport from the inside pocket of his jacket and placed the notes between the covers.

'It is enough,' he said.

They took their leave of each other.

The August rains had done little to relieve the heat that sweltered London. In the intervals of its falling the sun continued to beam, steaming the streets and pavements, incubating the growth in the parks.

Nicholas Arden sat at his dining table in shirt sleeves, writing on a large pad with an old-fashioned fountain pen. Loose sheets, booklets and sagging dictionaries lay before him. The air in the room was humid and congested. The rain had ceased, but a gusting wind blew at the window and whistled beneath the door.

The terrace of small houses had been built in the early sixties, a profitable speculation of the cheapest materials, already hurrying to its ordained end as a pine and plaster slum. The suburb was new, there were trees about and a broad heath near by. The surroundings were clean, the roads not greatly trafficked. Nicholas took satisfaction in it as a favourable place to bring up his son. When the first cracks had appeared in walls and ceilings, doors shrunk in their jambs, he had accepted it with resignation and a twinge of old defeat.

The fountain pen scratched slowly and loudly. Footsteps occasionally sounded above him, hardly muffled, the creaking of floorboards distinct.

He heard her rattle down the stairs and enter the kitchen. Something crashed. She was for ever dropping things, chipping cups, being dismayed by boilings-over.

'Nicholas! For goodness sake, it's almost four o'clock.'

He leaned back, rubbed his eyes and stretched.

She paused as she entered from the kitchen.

'The air in here is like soup.'

Quickly, she crossed to the window and opened it. The loose sheets leaped above the table, whirled and blew to the floor. She stood there, looking out, slightly bent, the discreet skirt lifted on her strong, handsome legs, the perfectly cupped hollows behind the knees, the rounded swell to the thighs. Her bobbed, dusty-coloured hair fanned about her ears. The curtain flapped. She held it back, leaned farther out.

'I can see him. He just turned the corner.'

She partly shut the window, swung around.

'Quick, now. Do clear up. Nicholas?'

He rose from behind the table, holding the blown papers.

She asked, 'How do I look?'

She was almost very pretty in this girlish excitement which saddened him. But the thin chest and meagre shoulders mis-matched the generosity of legs and hips. The clean oval of her cheeks and chin were mismatched by the blunted tip of nose. There was something uneven in the expression of her eyes, so faint as to be beyond identification, almost beyond notice, affecting others with a wisping unease for which they could seldom furnish reason.

'You look very handsome, Cora.'

She snapped her fingers and dashed for the kitchen.

'I forgot to put on the kettle.'

A much-used briefcase was slumped against the chair. It somehow announced that it had never held documents of im-portance, no details of mergers, annual statements, directorial secrets. Sandwiches perhaps, and a newspaper, a change of dry woollen socks.

He cleared the table, filled the briefcase and carried it upstairs. In his son's room, at a small desk and chair bought for a birthday, he laid out his things, unscrewed the fountain pen and put it beside the pad.

The bell rang. He went to the bedroom door and closed it against their voices.

He tried to resume his work but his thoughts had wandered. He did not really mind the priest's visits, or resent his own exclusion on these weekly occasions. He thought the priest a gluttonous bore, braying a laugh or being suddenly unctuous, poking scones and cakes into his wet, pink mouth with his soft pink woman's fingers. It was sad that it should mean so much to Cora, dressing for the father and preparing for the father as a girl might do for a suitor. Possessive of him, lowering her voice to discuss Church dogma on contraception, or the ancient and special privilege of their Eastern-Rite brethren to ordain married men. Cora was fierce about the twin sins of contraception and abortion, untroubled in her conscience about these by the saving grace of an hysterectomy.

He went absently to the window, looking down to the small square of garden, repeated in equal dimensions behind each identical house. It was these 'desirable plots' which had encouraged the developers to name the estate Belmont Park.

A few shrubs and flowers struggled there. Others had died in apparent recognition of the lack of faith in which they had been set in the ground. He did not have Green Fingers, disliked exposing himself there to the chat or observation of neighbours. Green Fingers. It was odd that the expression had no equivalent in Russian or Arabic. Rorstoy perst, perhaps. Meaningless. Fingers dipped in green paint. Akhdargnine. Meaningless.

He continued to muse. His marriage was something like that garden, a clumsy planting on inhospitable soil. The resentment that Cora bore within her was a corrosion beyond his correcting.

She resented the forced circumstances of her marriage and the sin which had been its condition. She resented her father's suicide, and the sin of that. She resented her mother's contented vulgarity, the comfortable house in Leeds into which she took paying guests and the knowing, confident, proprietorial air of different boarders down the years. Their camouflaged glances, the night-time creaking of floors and doors, and the shame and the sin of that.

Cora was always worse after a visit to her mother. She would fling off her hat.

'It was miserable. There's a new Number One boarder. She refers to him as "Dear Mr. Casey". He eats like a pig and picks his teeth behind his hand. I wouldn't talk to him, I just wouldn't. Nicholas, where's she getting the money? You should just see her wardrobe. She thinks nothing of going out and spending thirty pounds on a dress. She's got colour television, think of it. It makes me seethe. Never an offer of help for us. "I bought a present for Bobby!" she says. Do you know what it is? A wooden train, with the price sticker on it. Fourteen shillings. Four-teen shillings!'

Cora's father had embezzled money from the insurance company in which he had worked as a supervising clerk. He had not spent it on women or racehorses. He had invested it in stocks and shares. Three months after he had shot himself in a panic, Cora's mother discovered the scrip. Most of it was worthless. That year an Australian nickel holding boomed. The widow sold the shares for twenty-two thousand pounds.

Cora had made her religion a wrapping comfort, and catharsis of the confessional a let for a catalogue of frustrations. In the ritualized anonymity of the box, hushed between vaulted stones, she vented in small made-up sins the needs which other women expend in gossip.

He left the window, sat and picked up his pen. I don't begrudge her, he thought. Perhaps it is sad. So much is. He himself had no God. He had seen God die. He had his son and in the boy lay both his resurrection and redemption. The little boy who was at once his father's image and image of his father's father. Straight, olive-skinned, dark-haired and dark-eyed, the nose already beginning to beak a little on the bridge. It seemed that his father and his father's father had got reborn in the boy, using Cora's womb and a less tormented country as a convenience in which to try again.

The fountain pen began to scratch.

The rat-tat of the high heels his wife had worn for the priest disturbed his concentration, a tattoo of irritation on the thin boards of the stairs. He raised his head and waited. The door banged open.

'Really! Were you expecting a visitor? What an inconvenient time to call.'

12

'No. I expected nobody. Who is it?'

'How do I know? Do get rid of him, Nicholas. And don't stand talking in the door. It has begun to blow again.'

He recapped the pen, wondering who it might be, hearing her go, more carefully now to make her entry below.

There had been market survey people in the suburb recently and canvassers for a by-election. It had irritated Cora that he found it so hard to dismiss them.

He went downstairs quietly. She had shut the front door.

Opening the door, he said, 'I'm sorry. The door must have slammed,' and hesitated, looking at the man. Deep lines carved his cheeks. The wind ran through his cropped hair, flapped at the skirt of his jacket. The hot eyes and the distaste about his mouth only slightly relaxed.

'*Neharkum sa'id,*' he said.

'*Neharkum sa'id we mubarak.*'

Nicholas smiled at his automatic response, the correct exchange of greetings between a Muslim and a non-Muslim. He was puzzled as to what the man could want, his fierce, alien expression.

'Do you speak English?'

'Well enough.'

'What can I do for you?'

'You are Nicholas Arden?'

'I am.'

'I wish to make a talk with you.'

Nicholas remembered the open door, the wind blowing inside.

'I'm afraid it's not convenient. My wife – we – are entertaining. If you could tell me what it's about.'

'It is private. A matter of some importance. Furthermore, my time is small.'

Again the wind gusted, flapping the priest's top coat on the hall stand. He could not dismiss the man nor could he stand longer in the doorway.

He said, 'Please come in,' and stood aside.

They bumped in the tiny hallway. It was difficult for Nicholas to introduce a stranger into the intimacy of his son's bedroom. There was only the one small chair. He made a formal apology in Arabic for the lack of hospitality, and sat tentatively on the bed.

The Arab looked at nothing, they might have been seated on

13

an empty desert. He took a paper from his pocket, unfolded it.

'This is yours?'

Pasted on the yellow sheet was a cutting of the advertisement Nicholas sometimes put in *The Times*.

He felt relief and a small, unaccountable disappointment. The man's burning, unyielding eyes, the strange authority about him, had communicated something unexpected, even the possibility of something absurd.

'Take my card,' the Arab instructed him.

On the cheap yellow board Nicholas read:

Yusef Kemal
Director,
Trans-Arabia Projects

'You would like me to translate something for you?' He had a need now to quickly get rid of the man.

The Arab gestured.

'No, not translate.'

He gave no further help, his eyes watching with a grip unwarranted by the small concern of this meeting. Nicholas felt suddenly irritated by the Arab and his intrusion. Why had he not answered the advertisement to his box number?

'You speak Russian – fluently?'

Nicholas wondered at that, and refused the involvement of small talk.

'Yes. Now, exactly what do you want?'

'My company is making important business. We need a man fluent in Russian and Arabic. Not to make paper translation, to interpret, to interpret a business meeting.'

Nicholas looked up in some surprise. A Russian Trade Delegation was visiting. There had been photographs and notes in the newspapers. Old things stirred within him.

'I see.' He looked away to the window. 'I don't know. I am busy at present. I've not worked as an interpreter. It can be difficult, sometimes impossible, to transpose technical terms. It can be difficult to interpret for an accent one isn't familiar with. Are there not professional interpreters in these languages?'

The Arab ignored the question, watching, jigging his crossed leg.

He said, 'My company will pay one hundred English pounds a day.'

Nicholas felt his breath catch. The words reverberated in his head. He felt compelled to stand, walk to the window.

'For how many days would I be . . . required?'

'Three days. Four days. Initially.'

When he was able, he turned.

'I would need time to study the business of the meetings. To familiarize myself with any special terms.'

Three days, four days – initially. Three hundred, four hundred pounds!

'The terms of discussion will be simple,' the Arab said. 'There is nothing to study.'

Nicholas sat on the bed. It seemed unreal. The man watching him seemed unreal. He had become withdrawn, the dark emaciated face brooding, the long thin leg in the flapping trousers jigging as though in spasm.

'When would you want me?'

The Arab uncrossed his legs, leaned forward.

'Tomorrow, Mr. Arden. I presume you hold a passport?'

The wait had been agonizing. Nicholas had moved from the bed to the chair, from the chair to the bed, had walked the room, sat, got up and walked again. Twice he had gone to listen at the sitting-room door, hating the priest now, who must have long ago stuffed himself and drunk his sherry.

'You spoil me, Mrs. Arden. I don't mind if I do.'

How many times had he heard it? Always with the same inflection, the same anticipatory shift of bulk in the chair.

At last the priest was gone, a blessing bestowed in the doorway.

She had carried the tea-tray to the kitchen. Water splashed in the sink. Her back was turned. She reached for an apron.

'Cora?'

'Would you wipe up for me, Nicholas?'

He had rehearsed the news he would give her.

'Cora, I have something to tell you.'

She wasn't listening, crashing the cups and plates into the wash.

'I had such a pleasant afternoon. Father Francis agrees with me that the mass isn't the same without Latin. He used the most beautiful phrase for the old form. I memorized it. As dark and cool and articulate as cathedral stones, he said.'

She paused on that, her hands in the sink.

15

'Cora, leave the dishes for a moment.'

She turned her head frowning.

'What is it?' and then, 'Have you seen Bobby? It must be getting late.'

He crossed from the door, took her arm.

'Cora, leave the dishes. I have something to tell you.'

She took her hands from the sink, slowly wiped them on the apron, looking up at him.

'What is it? What's the matter?'

'Come,' he said gently.

In the dining-room she asked again, 'What is it?' a mixture of impatience and curiosity.

He put his hands on her shoulders and smiled, quite changing the high-nosed gravity of feature he had got from his father, his warm skin and eyes glowing in the evening light.

'Would you like to own a car, Cora?'

He cocked his head. 'Not a Rolls-Royce, mind. A good small used car.'

'What in the world are you talking about? We barely make ends meet.'

'That man who came to see me.'

'What about him? I didn't like his look.'

'He's a business man, Cora, an Arab. He wants me to do a job for his company.'

She closed her eyes and expelled a breath.

'Translating!'

She shook her head.

'I don't know what flight of fancy you're having now, but I've got things to do.'

'Don't go,' he stopped her with his hand. 'It isn't translating. It's interpreting. An important business meeting. Very important, apparently.'

That it should be important restrained her as much as had his hand. She saw the difference in his face, and wondered at it.

'So?'

'The fee, Cora. The fee is one hundred pounds a day.'

The wind quite went out of her. She could find nothing to say. And then, 'I don't believe it.'

'It's true. The meetings will be over three to four days – initially.'

'He must be mad. He looked mad.'

'No.'

16

'My God!'

He had to laugh, for his victory and the disarrangement of her face, then he remembered.

'Cora, the meetings are to be held in Libya.'

Nicholas could not forbid the excitement which still revelled in him. When he went up to kiss his son goodnight the boy had been standing at the little table where he ran his electric train. He had picked up the locomotive and replaced it to run in the reverse direction. Nicholas watched before he spoke, moved as always by this small body which appeared so vulnerable to him, in pyjamas and at the edge of sleep.

It had been like that. As though he himself had been arbitrarily lifted and put down on a strange new course. He ruffled the boy's thick, wild hair.

'It's late. Into bed with you.'

The dark, slightly slanted eyes considered him in the utmost gravity.

'I don't like you going away, Daddy.'

'What? Not even for a few days?'

'No. I will miss you.'

He felt again the familiar pang for this small life so dependent on him.

'You will have to be the man of the house, and look after your mother. I will be back before you know it. I will bring you a surprise.'

'A surprise,' the child said, 'that would be nice.'

His father bent and kissed him.

'Sleep well,' he said.

At dinner and afterwards they had to discuss it all again. Cora had been quite unlike herself, attentive that he should have more lamb, pouring them sherry from the priest's bottle. She found it unbelievable that he should be going abroad, flying off with paid expenses to deal with foreigners, in foreign places. Arabs and Russians. It was much too confusing. The faint, uneven expression of her eyes became quite dislocated at the thought.

He said gently, without hope, 'They are people, like us. You forget that I too am Russian.'

She did forget and he knew that she had also cast it out, as one might rid oneself of the memory of an indecency or a painful public embarrassment. There could be no appeal for the

17

godless, barbarian Russian stereotype which had been impressed on her mind. In a flutter of anxiety she sought quickly to dismiss it.

'Nonsense. You were only a child. You've hardly lived in the place. Nobody would guess that you aren't English.'

Perhaps not, he thought. Even I don't know what or who I am. Nicolai Fydorovich Dzontenvili ... Nicholas Arden. He saw his mother dressing her long black hair with mustard oil, plaiting the heavy braid she wore over one shoulder, singing the songs of her people to defy his officer father, horrifying him when he discovered the old, forbidden Koran which she had for so long kept secret, as the only memory of her parents, a world and a childhood obliterated almost without trace, except there in the faded pictures in her mind.

'Nicholas. You're not listening.'

He brought himself back with an effort, frowning. There was much he did not wish to remember.

'I'm sorry. What can't you understand?'

'I can't understand why this is all being left till the last minute. What if you'd not been able to go, or not held a passport. It doesn't seem at all businesslike.'

'Kemal explained that. The interpreter they were going to use fell ill.'

'Even so. This man knocks on the door one day, without a word of warning. And the next he has you going abroad.'

Abroad. Nicholas had smiled at her repetitions. The words were talismans to her, reinforcements of each other. It was sufficient that he should be engaged on something of importance. But important, and abroad!

'And why the secrecy? Why can't I tell anyone? That toffee nosed Mrs. Parker, always going on about whatever her husband does in the Ministry of Housing, why can't I tell her you're going abroad to interpret at an important international meeting?'

It was international now.

'Cora,' he said, 'you're getting yourself in a stew. It's really quite simple, even if it is – abroad. Business agreements can be very confidential. Don't you remember those television programmes about commercial espionage? If Kemal's company doesn't want us to talk about it, we don't want to do so and perhaps prejudice future work, do we?'

'Oh, Nicholas,' she said. 'Will there be future work?'

He put his hand on hers in sudden understanding. She was like a child now, waiting on a birthday, or Christmas. In the routine he had come to accept, in the resignation of his marriage, somewhere he had failed her. Had he been different, more ambitious perhaps, had he been more forceful, had they married out of romantic love or even the illusions that passed for it . . .

There were so many had-there-beens in his life. His entire existence seemed to be composed of things which should not have happened. Everything had been taken from him. His name, his country, his family, his future hopes and freedom. It had made an animal of him, unable to feel, care, know or think beyond survival. And yet, he had survived. He had endured the horror and the terror. What they had now did not perhaps seem a great deal to Cora. But he had known times, many times, when this room, this house, this meal, had been impossible aspirations.

He said, his hand still on hers, 'Let's not jump ahead. Kemal did suggest that there could be further work. We will have to wait and see. For the present let us just enjoy our little stroke of good fortune.'

In the kitchen, excitement tingled him again. It would be such a release. Such a change. There would be so much to enjoy. The travel, eating meals on the aircraft, seeing England drop away, the landing in a foreign place. Being met, and escorted. Taking his seat in some unimaginable room. The focus there of all the strange faces. Nicholas Arden, the interpreter.

The palms of his hands dampened. He would be among people of his own for the first time since boyhood. Why did it make him feel like this? An unpent kaleidoscope of emotions that churned in him like a sickness. He drank from the cup and refilled it, composing himself.

Inside, making a grimace for the magnitude of the mistake he had almost made, trying to be light, he asked: 'Did you know I almost chased him away?'

'Kemal?'

'Yes. He was rather – arrogant. I had thought he only wanted something translated and resented him coming to the house. I was about—'

Then he stopped. She had been looking up at him, and saw the change in his face, everything there arrested. She waited for him to continue.

19

'Well?'

'Oh, nothing.'

'What is it?'

'It doesn't matter. Something just struck me.'

She got up.

'I'll take my coffee upstairs. I'm going to run a bath.'

'At this time?'

She said, close to him, 'I want to make myself sweet, and pretty.'

He could not properly indulge the surprise of that, or his wonder at it. The other thought had possession of him.

He had believed it was translating work the Arab wanted. It had irritated him that the man had not written to the box number given in the advertisement, that he had instead presented himself.

But Nicholas did not use his name or his address in these advertisements. How had the Arab known?

The bedside alarm had at first failed to wake him. He heard it as a muzzy, undifferentiated presence in the confused rousing to consciousness. Then he opened his eyes and became aware. The alarm gave a last dying whir. Yesterday, last night, today, all crowded at him. He sat up. She was deep in sleep, turned towards him, her face emptied of any expression, like a room that had been stripped of its furniture. The covers about her had been thrown back, the nightdress bunched about her sprawled hips in that mismatched opulence of flesh. He covered her before calling her awake.

The public messenger arrived almost punctually, shortly after nine o'clock. Nicholas signed for the envelope, opened it at the dining-room table. It held his air ticket, his passport, ten pounds in notes and a typed message on yellow paper.

'On arrival please wait to be met in the main lounge near the bookstall.'

She called down from his packing.

'Who was that?'

'The messenger. I've got my air ticket. There was ten pounds in the envelope.'

'It's true then,' she called.

It made him realize that he had himself somewhere provided for it not being true.

CHAPTER TWO

DAVID LAWRENCE ordered an Arak, added iced water and swirled the glass. He drank the local spirit because he preferred it, not for reasons of economy or snobbery. He seldom suffered from it and had reason to believe in the drink's aphrodisiac effects.

He had walked to the Hotel Phoenicia in the hope of a sea breeze on the Rue Minet el Hosn, in which he had been disappointed, and arrived grateful to be air-conditioned again, wiping at the run on his forehead and inside the neck-band of his shirt.

There were few others in the Underwater Bar at this time, watching without great interest the bare, writhing legs of the women bathers in the pool behind the glass. A mermaid swam down and put her face there, rolled, turned her neat bikini-ed bottom, opened her legs wide and bubbled out of sight. Lawrence had observed how seldom men used this side of the pool. He thought it characteristic of the female's sexual egotism, the inborn need to flaunt and exhibit, even the plainest and dullest of them somewhere convinced they carried a holy grail between their thighs. It bored him.

He had finished his drink and was checking the time when Max Morrow arrived.

'All set?'

'Yes,' Morrow said. 'It's been a bit of a run-a-round. I made a call at the Embassy, that put me behind. Then I couldn't find my air ticket. It was in a jacket I had packed. It's hot out there, Character. What are you drinking?'

'Arak.'

'Order two. I'm going to the little boys' room. Watch the bag.'

Lawrence took the glasses and the attaché case to a table. His chief would come out of there washed, cologned and combed. He'd have given himself a hot towel and have had a cloth rubbed over his shoes. It wasn't vanity, or the need to impress. It was the outward and visible sign of a permanently mobilized mind.

He would probably have shaved leading the mad dash to Hechingen, to capture the German scientists who had been experimenting with uranium and thorium, declaring to the burgomaster in small towns that the Eighth Army was at his heels, which it was by no means, and ordering him to telephone the burgomaster of the next town to surrender when Morrow arrived.

The French got there afterwards, with the armies, on the same fateful mission. It was their zone. They had lost.

He would have been urbane in Persia, helping plot the coup which ousted Mossadeq, and with the OSS in Egypt tracking down German agents. Lawrence treasured every story he could glean about his chief. Particularly, and with reason, one anecdote. Morrow had briefly been a recruiter for the OSS. An applicant with special skills, but lacking in formal education, had turned in a massive IQ score. Later, it was discovered he had contrived to cheat. 'All the better,' Morrow had said, 'that's just the kind of character we want.'

He had picked Lawrence that way, and not because he knew the family, after Lawrence disgraced himself at Princeton.

Morrow returned, cool and kempt, took a long pull at the Arak, unlocked his case from a key pouch and felt for his glasses.

'Haven't got used to the need for these yet.'

He began to study a file, speed-reading the pages.

'I don't like any of it. There's something coming off, Character.'

David Lawrence sipped his drink and waited.

'This man you've got in Tripoli, the Italian. Is he likely to be given the push?'

'No. He's in his sixties, married to a Libyan woman. He runs a restaurant in the Souk. He's got two grown-up sons in the Civil Service. He's into the woodwork, and he's clean.'

'There were a lot of Italians into the woodwork before the revolution. It didn't stop sixteen thousand of them being given the push.'

'They weren't married to Libyan women, Max. They weren't self-employed. They've been letting a few back lately, in any case.'

'There's too much activity. How do you read it?'

'I think it's another price hike. A united front this time. Pay up and like it or we will all nationalize our oil.'

22

Morrow pushed down his glasses and looked at Lawrence over the lenses.

'It could be. It could be, Character.'

'How do you read it?'

Morrow thought. 'Let me tell you a story. It's attributed to an Alexandrian Greek, possibly one of Aesop's descendants. A frog was crouched on the banks of the Sweet Water Canal about to swim across, when he heard a voice behind him. It was a scorpion. The scorpion asked the frog to ferry him to the other side, where his wife and family were waiting.

'Well, the frog wasn't that mad. "If I let you on my back," he said, "you would sting me to death." The scorpion laughed, or whatever scorpions do. "If I sting you to death," he said, "then I shall drown." The frog thought about that. "Very well," he said "climb aboard."

'Half-way across the Sweet Water Canal, the scorpion stung the frog. The dying frog looked back. "You've killed me," he said. "And now you will drown. Where's the sense in that?" '

Morrow took off his glasses. Lawrence was smiling.

'So?' he said, 'where is the sense?'

'That's the point, Character. The scorpion answered the frog that they were in the Middle East.'

They were quiet.

Lawrence said, 'So you don't think all this activity makes sense?'

'On the contrary. When Arabs get together, there's cause to watch out.'

'Your friend Nasser got the Arabs together. The United Arab Republic didn't last.'

'Gamal was a revolutionary, with no money and his own troubles. Gadaffi is a revolutionary with an oil income over two billion dollars a year, and he's out to make trouble.'

Lawrence thought about it.

'If it is another price hike, Max, with the Arabs getting together for that, isn't that enough trouble, all across the board?'

Now Morrow was thoughtful.

'That's a different kind of trouble. That's commercial trouble.'

'Then what kind of trouble do you expect?'

'Quote,' Morrow said, 'Arab unity, Socialism, rights of in-heritance, the place of women in society, the destiny of the

23

planet after the invention of the atom bomb – all is there for the man who can read the sacred Koran. Unquote.'

'Gadaffi?'

'Gadaffi. He's a zealot. More than Gamal ever was. He sees himself as a divine, chosen instrument.'

'Of what, Max?'

'Of whatever. I've got time for another drink, Character.'

When Lawrence returned to the table, Morrow was watching the near naked girls who had swum down to ogle at the glass.

'Very pretty. The one on the right is probably American. Our girls get bigger every year.'

'And our men probably get smaller.'

Morrow swirled the new drink.

'You're prejudiced.'

'Not really. Ambivalent, perhaps.'

'Are you keeping your nose clean, Character?'

'The soul of discretion,' Lawrence said.

'Your mother worries about you. It's been two years. You should pay a visit.'

'Mother has never worried about anyone but herself in her life. She did worry when Dad died – about how much money he'd left. I shan't pay a visit. Beirut suits me very well.'

Morrow studied the young man.

'There's a very unpleasant streak in you, Character.'

Lawrence tried to dismiss it.

'It's only the way God made me.'

'Cop out!' Morrow said.

He checked his watch.

'Well, that's it. Time to go. Which clients are getting this report?'

Lawrence told him.

'You'd better let City Bank have one.'

David Lawrence drove home as prayers were being chanted. He found it agreeable in the theoretically unlawful din of car horns. He had accustomed himself to Arab music too and, like Arak, had almost come to prefer it.

He had not much looked forward to this evening. Barbara's cosmopolitan friends, the extravagance of their manners, seldom offered more than surfaces. Occasionally he picked up something useful among them. He was ready for the evening now, a little suspended and lonely, as he always felt after Max's rushed visits. The older man's vitality, his wry, uncritical acceptance of most human foibles comforted Lawrence. There had been something between he and Lawrence's mother. It could have been an affair. It gave him satisfaction to imagine his mother with Max Morrow. She, enthralled by her own pink and gold beauty. Never less than faultlessly groomed at any hour, unable to receive a child's embrace without dismay at the ruin to her make-up.

Max would have accounted for her damn make-up. Her precious person and egregious self-love would have suffered a man's assault.

Lawrence turned right into the Rue Weygand, changed down and accelerated past a crawl of Mercedes, Buicks and Cadillacs. Outraged drivers honked at him.

'Go screw yourselves!' he shouted.

He could see the mountains ahead, tipped with snow on the crowns. He would take a nap before he bathed and dressed.

The Casino du Liban was set on a cliff, outside Beirut on the coast road. Civilizations had flourished on this Mediterranean littoral six thousand years ago. In bygone times the cliff had been inhabited by gods.

Many of those who now came to the cliff shared that other omnipotence. The old gods had been custodians of retribution and justice. The new gods cared only for the miracle of money.

These were the oil millionaires, the manipulators of the unrestricted currency markets, affluent spy-masters, the international speculators protected by official banking secrecy, the death dealers who armed revolutions. It was Lawrence's job to move among them, to be Max Morrow's ears.

From his Beirut listening-post Morrow serviced the interests of commercial conglomerates whose Middle East operations figured in billions. On special assignments he drew a personal fee of one thousand dollars a day.

The Casino du Liban mirrored the men who used it. A dazzling extravagance only limited by the acres it occupied. Antique mosaics were set in the oriental ceilings of the gambling casino. Banks of floodlit water displays spumed in the pools and lakes outside the ballroom.

Max Morrow had said, 'You see before you, Character, a world at the end of its tether.'

Lawrence had overslept, which he attributed to the Arak. He had missed the pre-dinner drinks in the old palace on which Barbara Barse had spent a fortune. He dressed in some irritation. There would be little opportunity at the Casino du Liban to fossick for interest among the guests.

Michael, the Casino's oleaginous greeter, bowed as Lawrence entered. Michael had given himself the title of Prince and the claim to Russian estates lost to his family by the revolution. The pose was a patent pomp. He was obviously Mediterranean, swarthy and short, with blue jowls discreetly powdered. Lawrence guessed that Michael had learned his worldliness as a waiter in a good Parisian restaurant.

'Mr. Lawrence, what a pleasure to see you again. Miss Barse has asked me to apologize for her. The party has gone in.'

'Is it a big party, Michael?'

'No, sir. A party of fourteen.'

'Anybody you know?'

'Mostly strangers, Mr. Lawrence. Off a yacht, I understand. Two young lady house guests and the Japanese sculptor who was modelling Sheikh Raschid.'

The guests appeared to have ordered and sat chatting over aperitifs. Lawrence stood behind Barbara Barse while she finished what she was saying.

'I call it my Husband Apartment. It has absolutely everything a man could want, even a sweet little gymnasium and sauna bath. Tiki, that's my new decorator, has had the most wonderful water mattress made for it. Have you tried one? They're divine. One just floats and floats off to sleep.'

'But Barbara, darling,' one of the women said, 'you have no husband at present.'

Barbara clutched her brow in one hand.

'Have I not? It's so confusing, the way they come and go. In any case, I make it a policy to be prepared.'

Those closest to her laughed. So like Barbara.

Lawrence bent and kissed her cheek. She was wearing a representative collection of her celebrated jewellery.

'I'd have thought you'd have had a champagne mattress, Barbara. Water is plebeian.'

She pursed her mouth.

'Where have you been, you naughty boy? I needed you at the drinks.'

'Max has been in town,' Lawrence said.

26

'And he didn't come to see me? How revolting of him.'

She tapped her glass with a fork.

'Everybody, this is David Lawrence. David, this is everybody.'

She pulled him down by the sleeve and whispered.

'You are to sit next to that stunning brunette. She has just divorced her brute of a husband. I want you to be very attentive and witty and interesting and not say cynical things. Do you hear?'

She slapped him on the bottom. The chatter rose again. David took his chair and smiled greetings.

The girl said, 'Well, hello, Mr. Better-late-than-never.'

David saw that she was already tight. He guessed her to be about thirty. She had been beautiful, but a mask had hardened on her face, as it can on women who cheat too much, and drink too much, and abuse trust and love too often. The essence of her femininity had departed or become non-negotiable.'

'Hello, yourself,' he said. 'I understand you've just been divorced and I'm to be attentive to you, witty, and not say cynical things.'

'Well,' she exclaimed, 'that will do for starters.'

Most of the guests were agreeably flushed when Barbara Barse announced that Feddie had invited them to a moonlight cruise on his yacht. Kate Durrell, the girl Lawrence partnered, had drunk heavily and looked a little wild and disordered. There had been strange exchanges of signals between she and Barbara Barse, which Lawrence could not interpret.

As the cars were brought he decided not to go. Once on the yacht he would be captive. They could decide to cruise all night, or for days if it took Barbara's fancy.

The chauffeur opened the car door. Barbara stamped her foot. 'But I want you to come. Kate must have a companion.'

'Barbara, I'm whacked. You know what it's like when Max hits town. I've got a lot of work tomorrow.'

'Work. Work. Why must everyone work?'

Kate Durrell said, 'I don't much feel like cruising either. Where do you live, David?'

'I have a place at Yarze.'

'What a coincidence,' she looked at Barbara. 'That's where I live. You could run me home.'

'Kate, really!' Barbara said. She looked worn now. Face lifts often failed her after too many parties.

27

Kate Durrell clapped her hands.

'Goodie, goodie,' she said, and turned a pirouette. 'Home to bed.'

'You'll do no such thing,' Barbara told her.

'I will. Ohhh, yes I will.'

'This is going too far.'

Kate took David's arm, making a moue and looking up.

'It isn't too far, is it, David?'

'You shouldn't run out on the party,' he said, to help Barbara and himself. 'It's a beautiful night to be on the water.'

'I'm not running out,' she said, 'I'm driving out. You are driving me out of the party.'

'You're being impossible, Kate,' Barbara said.

'I'm not impossible. I'm very, very possible.'

'Very well. On your head be it.'

Barbara got into the car and slammed the door.

In the car park, hugging a stole about her shoulders, Kate Durrell asked, 'Which is your car? Is it that Cadillac?'

'It's that Porsche,' David told her and unlocked the door.

Driving out, he asked, 'Whereabouts in Yarze are you staying?'

'I will show you,' she said. 'I will show you when we get there.'

Driving fast on the road above the sea, the wind rushing in the windows, she suddenly shivered.

'Are you cold?'

'No. The wind is making me sober. How unpleasant.'

David turned the radio on. After a silence she roused herself.

'It is my command that you should point out places of interest to me. Remember, I'm a tourist.'

'Very well,' David said. 'We'll begin with the mental hospital. That's it over there.'

She flounced.

'I don't believe you. You're being cynical again.'

In the winding climb to the foothills the car filled with cold.

'Brrrrr,' Kate said and wound up her window.

Lawrence concentrated on the curves.

'It must be blowing off the snow.'

She said, 'Your hair. It looks so dramatic with those light streaks running through it. Do you do that deliberately?'

'I've been ski-ing. It's sun-bleached.'

28

'I think blond men are most attractive. Truly blond men, like you.'

'What colour was your husband?'

'I don't want to talk about him. I want to talk about you.'

'What do you want to know?'

'I already know quite a lot.'

'Barbara?'

'Barbara.'

'What did she tell you?'

'That you're clever – and spoiled. She said you're too good looking by half and utterly amoral.'

'I see. That's a rather mixed recommendation.'

Lawrence had changed down as the grade steepened. They were conscious of each other, the sharp turns sometimes pitching them together, the heat of their bodies a subtle familiarity in the close confines now sealed against the chill.

'Barbara says your villa is beautiful. It must be. She hates admiring anything she doesn't own or can't buy.'

'It's not really a villa. It was originally a hunting lodge, a place to sleep overnight. The owner had it reconstructed from seventeenth- and eighteenth-century palaces.'

'It's not yours?'

'Unfortunately not. It belongs to a cousin of the Sheikh of Kuwait. There are a good many antique brasses however, which I do own.'

They were almost at the top of the climb.

'Now. Whereabouts is it you're staying?'

'Oh,' she said and leaned forward, her hands between her knees. 'Let me see, where are we?'

Lawrence told her.

She said, 'Do you know what I'd like?'

'What?'

'I'd like to see your brasses.'

From the outside the lodge was singularly undistinguished. Old stones set among trees, a small cube of a building, its crenellations the only touch of romance. The arched door of old, studded timbers had a great brass lock which had come from the keep of a harem.

Lawrence said, 'I'll get the key.' And thought, 'Damn the woman.' For manners' sake, or for Barbara's sake, he would give her a coffee. He wondered with whom she could be staying.

'That's a key?' Kate Durrell asked.

The key that matched the lock had a flourished loop of handle bigger than his hand.

'As you can see, not quite the thing for a fob pocket.'

He pushed the door open. The entrance to the lodge was also its main room.

Nothing minimized the impact. Lawrence had put on the lights from outside. Multiple stones in ancient mosaic, on heavy pink and black pillars, arched the first room. Geometric patterns of marble set the floor, around a small splashing fountain. The light came from the ceiling, which was slightly vaulted and closely beamed with mosaic. The three walls beyond the farthest arch were set with low sofas, cushioned in extravagant silks. Coloured glass panelling to the outside bent the light there to a diffused, cathedral glow. Old brass shone in wall niches and on low, square tables as dark and remorseless as ebony.

Lawrence waited. At last she exclaimed with a little gasp, 'What a pad!'

The incongruity, the vulgarity of the remark, amused him.

He led her to the sofas, took her wrap.

'Coffee?'

'I prefer whisky, on the rocks.'

He opened an inlaid wall cabinet.

'Would you care to help yourself?'

Small arched doors, almost hidden in the patterned walls, led off to other rooms. Lawrence excused himself. He took off his coat and tie, went to the bathroom, refreshed himself with hot and cold water and swallowed vitamin tablets. It was not much after twelve. He could be in bed by one. He poured himself coffee from the automatic percolator and carried it in.

Kate Durrell was at the cabinet, topping up her drink. She must have bolted the first one. He lit them cigarettes.

'How long have you known Barbara?'

'For ever. She's a friend of the family. She was my heroine when I was little.'

'Not,' he observed, 'the most favourable model for a young girl.'

'Well! Listen to who's talking.'

She stretched herself on the cushions, bold and appraising, already affected by the drink.

'Meaning?'

'You're no boy scout yourself, are you?'

30

'I see.'

Lawrence felt a flush of hostility. 'Beirut has the reputation of being a city of intrigue. I sometimes wonder if it was that way before Barbara came to live.'

'It's a small community.'

'It's a small community, of smaller minds.'

'I shouldn't have thought you'd care for anybody's opinion.'

'I don't. I merely protect myself against boredom.'

She leaned back on her elbows. Her bare brown arms and shoulders were perfectly formed, with a hint of masculinity.

'Do I bore you?'

'Yes. A little.'

She decided not to contend.

'Thank you, sir. And may I ask why I bore you – a little?'

'You're predictable. A type.'

There was heat now under her skin, eyes narrowed. She tossed back her drink.

'For a Princeton man you're rather crude. In which of your pigeon holes have you put me?'

'Under Diana,' he said.

'Go on. Explain.'

'Damn, the huntress.'

'Explain further,' her voice was cold.

'Oh,' he said, tired of this, 'you're a predator. Most women are, in their way. Served meat doesn't much interest you. You need to stalk it and kill it yourself.'

She got up and poured another drink. Her hand shook slightly.

She said, meanly, 'And where did you learn all about women? I understand we're not much in your line.'

He could have struck her for a bitch. Instead, he put down the coffee, butted the cigarette.

'It's late, Diana.' He held out her wrap. 'Come, I will drop you home.'

She turned, hard and arrogant, but strangely apprehensive too.

'It's a long way. I'm staying with Barbara.'

For a moment he could not understand. Then small pieces collected, rushed together. The signals between she and Barbara over the dinner table. Barbara afterwards, frowning at the car.

'Kate, really!' And, 'This is going too far.'

31

They had made a joke of him. Humiliation, bitterness and rage surged in his ears. He could have strangled them. He felt despair too, as he used to feel with his mother.

She looked quite frightened now, and suddenly sober. Control continued to evade him, while he laboured. And then the mist passed, leaving a sharp, hard, white clarity.

He dropped the wrap and stepped towards her. She backed away at what she saw.

'No . . . don't . . . what is it?'

He said, 'Get your clothes off.'

'No! I don't want to. I've been silly. I'm sorry.'

He said, 'There's no help for you here. Not now.'

She put the glass down, shaking.

'David, it was only fun. I was tight. Please let me go.'

He put both hands on her breasts, pulled the low neck of her evening gown wide.

'Get your clothes off.'

Her breath gushed on his face. Absurdly, she said, 'You don't have to, you don't have to, David.'

He needed to tear at her. The material of the gown burst. She looked down at her ruin and sobbed. Coldly, calmly, he began to unbutton himself. Sobbing, almost mesmerized, she stepped her long brown legs out of the garment, put her hands back to the brassière.

He left in the light between night and day, colours shafting through the panelled glass. She was sprawled in a mess of cushions. Mascara stained and streaked her cheeks. Only the lacquered mouth, which he had not kissed, remained as it had been.

Lawrence showered and dressed and left, putting a note beside her. He drove mindlessly back to the city. Lay mindlessly on the office couch, and shut his eyes.

Noises in the next room woke him. Instantly, as his eyes snapped open, he remembered the night. He had no remorse, or self-reproach. In the humiliations he had adventured on her he had been justly purged of his own.

Lawrence went to the small bathroom and plugged in the electric razor. His blond hair was tumbled, waved across his forehead. The whites of his blue eyes were clear, the skin beneath them puffed and sooted. He considered his reflection, almost in mockery, and smiled at it, as between conspirators.

He opened the office door. The Lebanese secretary was drinking coffee, and jumped.

'Meester Lorens. I deed not know you are here.'

'I came in early, Freni. Run down to Angelos and get me a pizza, would you?'

He went back to his room and dialled a number.

'Has Miss Barse come home, Simone? I don't doubt she's sleeping. This is David Lawrence. Your house guest, Miss Durrell, is at my place, at Yarze. Would you send out the driver for her – now. And Simone, pack her some day clothes.'

There was little or nothing likely to surprise Barbara's personal secretary. He wondered what Kate Durrell would tell her heroine. She might even tell her the truth.

Lawrence operated this branch of Max Morrow's consultancy with Freni's help, the services of a confidential male typist retired from army signals and several outside specialists whom Morrow had retained from earlier, more buccaneering days. One of these was Freni's father. 'He's not very bright,' Morrow had said, 'but I like to keep things in the family.'

The small room off the main office housed the Telex to Morrow's Washington office, a France-Presse and a UPI teleprinter. Freni had prepared the signals.

Most of the dispatches were routine.

'The Beauty of Britain is threatened not only by industrial development, urbanization and traffic, but also by dereliction, litter and waste, an expert said in London today. The creation of a desert is growing at the rate of ten acres every day of every week . . .'

'Last chance to make peace in Vietnam . . .'

Chief Justice Warren Berger . . .'

'Spanish police expel hippies from Ibiza. Shopkeepers are being stolen blind, a spokesman said. People are locking their doors for the first time. Because of the excessive use of hashish, LSD, mescalin and over-the-counter drugs . . .'

'Two senior American officials were given the cold shoulder at Cairo airport today. No one from the Egyptian Foreign Ministry was at hand to receive them. The presence of Donald C. Bergus and Michael Sterner in the Egyptian capital signalled a new U.S. push for a Middle East settlement. In Washington and elsewhere, optimism has given way to a sinking feeling that time is running out for a negotiated solution to the tangled Arab–Israeli conflict. It is believed that if Cairo shows a continued interest in an interem Suez plan, U.S. Assistant Secretary of State Joseph J. Sisco would then be sent on a follow-up mission to pursue the matter with Jerusalem. Despite pressures from other Arab capitals for more direct action against Israel . . .'

Lawrence made notes on the long message and put it aside for further study.

'COUP IN MOROCCO FAILS.'

'For the third time, King Hassan of Morocco has narrowly escaped an attempt on his life. Journeying from his seaside residence at Skhirat to the palace in the capital of Rabat, the King's limousine, bearing the royal flag, was blown up by a landmine apparently exploded electronically from a distance. All four occupants were killed. The King was travelling in a closed army vehicle, some distance behind the royal car.

'No arrests have so far been reported, although suspects are being rounded up and interrogated.

'The King's moderate foreign policy, his close ties with the U.S. and his refusal to aid Arab states in the war with Israel, has stirred the wrath of the revolutionary Moroccans, many of whom are believed to be in close contact with Colonel Gadaffi, the Libyan leader, whose calls for a Holy War against Israel are well known.

'As one expert put it, "In this part of the world, American policy is often just one bullet away from disaster . . ." '

Lawrence read through the message again and checked his watch to calculate Washington time. Max Morrow would be dialling his confidential sources, flicking switches on his squawk box. Summarize all client interests directly and indirectly concerned in Morocco. Flick! Check status reports on Morocco for anything hard on possible disaffection. Flick! Get your ass down to the press club and see what you can pick up. Flick! Flick! Flick! Ernest, this is Max. Did you guys at State have a pipe into Hassan's party?

Max Morrow had personally arranged a three-million-dollar deal for a client to put cash registers and calculating equipment into Morocco. He had told Lawrence, 'The calculators I can understand. Why they want cash registers I don't know. The King and two or three families own all the money there is.'

He'd be worrying about that. Final payment on the contract was not due for another six months.

34

Lawrence sat in his office, files for months back about him, drinking coffee and breakfasting on the pizza. This was a bad one. Hassan's last clean up had been frighteningly thorough. He'd seemed secure. Lawrence needed to turn up something in the past reports with which they could cover themselves. A few lines would do, with which to make something.

'The Consultancy refers your attention to Para. 4, page 8, status report H/M/125: Further irrational action in Morocco by extremists cannot be eliminated from forward thinking ...'

Max would expect him to find a face-saver. He didn't like black eyes. Lawrence began making notes.

The St. Georges Hotel bar on the Rue Minet el Hosn had long been a rendezvous of the Press Corps. The Lebanese mezze, a wildly varied and extended hors d'oeuvres, was good there. A man could make a meal of mezze and Arak for a few dollars, or dine pleasantly and economically on the terrace over the sea.

A senior editor of *Newsweek* was on his way to interview Hassan. Lawrence moved about buying drinks, asking questions, listening. A huddle at the bar's farther end opened up. A tall, bearded man in a rumpled and stained safari jacket, with quizzical eyes and a bent nose, had been the centre of attention there. He winked across, pushing peanuts into a small mouth that chomped on them like a locust at a leaf.

David had met him at one of Barbara's parties and had afterwards invited him to Yarze. He wrote as great journalists used to do and expiated a spectacular and private compulsion to hazard the security of his shambling frame as an itinerant Boswell to wars, famines, revolutions, floods, pestilences, erupting volcanoes, earthquakes, Everest climbs, around-the-world yachtsmen and rocket journeys to the moon, when that could be arranged.

'Harvey,' Lawrence said. 'This is a surprise. Where have you come from?'

'Been out at the 'Nam. I'm working up a theory on the place.'

He chomped at the nuts, quizzing Lawrence down his nose.

'Tell me about it,' Lawrence said.

The only way you can explain it, the South 'Nam government, Thieu, Ky, the generals, the civil service, they're all Viet Cong. Kissinger is the Cong's man in Washington. Maybe Ellsworth Bunker has gone over too.'

He chomped more nuts.

'How does that grab you?'

Lawrence laughed.

'I suppose it makes as much sense as anything. How long are you staying?'

'A day or so. It's a lay-over. I'm waiting an assignment.'

'Morocco?'

'Maybe.'

'Have you got any theories on that?'

'It's routine. A part of the new revolutionary wave. Today, Islam. Tomorrow, the world. Nationalism is the only policy the Arabs have got. When they get down on those prayer mats, they should thank Allah for Israel. That fight is all that keeps any of them together.'

Lawrence said, 'That fight is what could pull us all apart.'

The correspondent tipped his head, mocking.

'Come on! Your government and the Russian government have a secret agreement that neither of them is going to let World War Three start in the Middle East. The Russkies have backed themselves into a corner. Islam is more anti-communist than the Pentagon. The Russkies are shit-scared of Arab nationalism. And it's got out of their control.'

'What's the scenario, Harvey?'

'Ride the tiger,' the correspondent said and wiped his mouth. 'Ride the tiger, Davie boy.' He waved his goodbyes. 'See you. I'm going up to siesta.'

Max Morrow telexed in the mid-afternoon. Morrow expected the ruthlessly authoritarian Moroccan interior minister to be given control of the administration. A programme of repression in the country was virtually assured. 'Hassan is a bone in the throat of Arab Nationalism,' Morrow had signalled, 'next time they'll cough him out.' As a market for investment capital Morocco was to be classified as: 'very short term, speculative'.

'David?'

Immediately he heard her voice, the summary demand she could invest in a word, he knew he'd been expecting her call.

'Hello, Barbara. How was the moonlit cruise?'

'Moonlit,' she said. 'Distinctly moonlit. I wish to have a talk with you David.'

'I'm working, Barbara.'

'Nevertheless. I will pick you up outside the building in ten minutes.'

She must be telephoning from her car.

'Very well, then. I spoil you, Barbara.'

Lawrence lit a cigarette, went to the window and looked out. At this late hour the bay was still busy with small craft and water skiers. He wondered what the damned girl had said. He did not want, and could not afford, to have trouble with Barbara Barse.

The Bentley had been custom-built. The chauffeur bade Lawrence good evening, knocked on the tinted glass and opened the door. Barbara Barse was smoking. She patted the seat beside her.

'I haven't much time. Tiki is taking me shopping. Now, exactly what happened last night?'

Lawrence sat, gave her his profile and considered.

'We dined at the Casino du Liban. I was late, for which I apologized. I ordered oysters on the half shell, to be followed by—'

She smacked his knee.

'Stop that. I'm really quite concerned. Kate has kept to her room all day. She didn't come out to lunch and doesn't want to talk. It's altogether unlike her. What happened between you?'

Lawrence indicated the cabinet in the back of the front seat.

'Can I give myself a drink?'

'Do. You won't find any of your beastly Arak.'

He made a whisky and soda, said wearily, 'Look, Barbara, dear Barbara, it's none of your goddamn business.'

'You think not?'

'I think not.'

'I'm responsible for that girl.'

Now he looked at her. 'Yes. Responsible, too, for her coming out here.'

'I was not,' she said indignantly, 'I tried to stop her.'

'Your joke got out of hand, Barbara.'

'Joke? What joke?'

He was disappointed in her, feeling disgust now at everything, and a surge of melancholy. He looked away.

'I was the joke, Barbara. Isn't it an awful waste, that handsome brute going with Arab boys? I'm sure deep down he's normal. He only needs the right woman to bring him out. It could be you, Kate, or Sheila or Robin or bloody Hortense. I'm sick of it.'

He turned on her. 'I'll tell you, in my judgement I'm a damn sight cleaner than your precious Kate. And an Arab boy from the bloody bazaar can be a loyal friend.'

Lawrence threw his head back.

'Hell!' he said, and was silent.

Barbara Barse sat paled in her corner. She looked out the window, smoothed the material of her skirt. A little nervously, she lit another cigarette. 'However! I would like you to assure me that you did not, in any way – abuse – my house guest.'

Lawrence did not move, or open his eyes.

'If it will satisfy your feminine curiosity, I rode her down. I rode her down like a great big hairy heterosexual.'

He did not see her sudden desolation, the stab of something distant that mourned about her mouth. When she spoke her voice was very soft.

'Finish up your drink, now. Tiki will be waiting.'

Lawrence swallowed and put the glass back in the cabinet. They looked at each other. 'Friends?' he asked.

'Friends. Which does not mean that you're not impossible. I banish you for a month. It would be undesirable for you and Kate to meet again.'

'Until she leaves, then.'

Barbara Barse nodded, still a little absent. Lawrence got out.

CHAPTER THREE

NICHOLAS ARDEN pushed the belt through the buckle and pressed the button to erect his seat. He had been without company since Rome. The two elderly ladies had disembarked there. He had drunk several whiskies, encouraged by the steward. 'You'll go dry in Tripoli, sir. Allah doesn't approve of drink.' The joke was a whispered confidence to the non-Muslim passengers, a conspiracy between superiors.

There had been much for him to think about. In the delay before take-off he had felt the severance from home and family and routine. In the savage surging rush that lofted them into the sky, miniaturizing houses, traffic, and landscape, reducing the belch of factory chimneys to cigarette puffs, more than the earth was left behind. In the aircraft's tilting thrust through wet grey streams of cloud, to emerge into the unlimited sunlight above them, everything else fell away.

He leaned to the window. Squat buildings shone as white as spun sugar in the evening light, scattered among tufted date palms, eucalypts and onion-domed minarets. Orange groves in severe geometric patterns spread distantly across the plain. A wide carriageway beside the sea streamed with cars and trucks. He felt the wheels bump down. The engines noisily throttled back, pressing him into the seat.

'*Neharkum sa'id.*'

'*Neharkum sa'id we mubarak.*'

'Your flight? It was good?'

'Very smooth,' Nicholas said.

The Arab was altered in his own country. Less wary, at ease, his eyes and person less contentious. He wore a green, pocketed bush shirt. With his short spiky hair it gave him a military appearance.

Nicholas said, 'I think we should speak Arabic,' and smiled. 'I need the practice.'

The Arab nodded.

'Come then, Brother.'

Outside the terminal, cabs and coaches were loading. Policemen leaned on the walls. The Arab raised his hand. An old

Chevrolet drew out of the shadows and double parked. The Arab opened the door, took Nicholas's bag and put it through the front window. In Arabic he said. 'Please enter and be comfortable, Brother.'

There was little to be seen on the short drive to the city. The evening had pitched into darkness, the abrupt Mediterranean snuffing of last light that falls with the weight of a curtain.

'Much is new,' Nicholas said, glimpsing farms and settlements.

'There is much to make new, Brother,' the Arab answered.

The car stopped for the passage of loaded camel carts, crossing the concrete into fields. The Arab grunted with impatience.

Nicholas said carefully, 'This form of address: Brother. Is that new?'

'Yes, it is since the revolution. Even the President is addressed as Brother, by the most lowly. All Arabs, everywhere, are brothers in Islam. It was so in the days of our glory. The Imperialists who divided and oppressed and exploited us feigned to forget the fact that since olden times this people have offered sacrifices on the altar of freedom, Arabism and Islam. We and our brothers will go on offering sacrifices on the altar of freedom, honour, Arabism and faith until Doomsday.'

Nicholas said, again carefully, 'I was surprised at the number of Americans on the flight. I thought Americans were no longer welcome here.'

'They come,' the Arab said, 'if we wish it. They come as guests now, and equals. The Americans are building a great tourist city on the coast, in partnership with this people. It was falsely alleged in the American and Western press and radios, that after the departure of the Americans and the British from the bases, bases which the people were even forbidden to draw near despite the fact that they were erected on the sacred land for which the people's blood and souls were sacrificed, the Russians would replace them in these bases. In reply we told them that if the freedom of the people could not be safeguarded, nor their independence realized without Russian protection, then, let this people go to hell. And should the peoples of the world, this people being one, fail to fill the void, or fail to exist without American influence, let this people go to hell.

'Imperialists everywhere should know that this readiness for sacrifice is not confined to one generation or to a certain period of our history.

'All previous generations have sacrificed their souls and valuables for the sake of freedom.'

In the dim light from the instrument panel, in the dashed light from street lamps, the Arab sat forward, his eyes wide and burning. He seemed to have forgotten Nicholas.

'We claim that the Imperialists are unable in any corner of the world to succeed in confronting a nation that seeks death so as to be granted life. This was the lesson we drew from our fathers who sought death and were granted life. In this part of the world we shall continue inculcating the same belief in our future generations.'

Nicholas felt the Arab's fervour communicated into his own person, and fleetingly wished that he could be one of them, to be possessed by something above and outside one's self. To escape from the tyranny of self into a brotherhood of resolution and purpose. He sensed the conflict and flux about him like a sudden stirring and odour.

Peace be on you, Brother. And to you, peace, Brother. What kind of peace did they wish each other from hearts so visionary with violence?

The streets had condensed. The car bumped into a maze scarcely wide enough to permit passage. Flat-fronted houses were about them, gates in their walls. Copper beaters and hawkers filled the car with their din. Dyed materials in fierce, vivid colours hung about tiny shops. Cabin trunks as bright as parakeets were displayed against the walls. Pedestrians avoided the car and stared their dark faces in the windows, wrapped from head to foot in a single cloth that reminded Nicholas of a blanket.

'This is the Souk,' Kemal said and gave the driver an instruction.

Nicholas unbuttoned his jacket. It was hot in these airless confines, dense with the smell of cooking spices, urine, drains and bodies.

They entered a wide, new area, silent and almost deserted.

'Where are we now?' he asked.

Kemal made a gesture.

'New city. So the Italians call it. It is a monument to shame.'

41

There were many big shops, stridently empty, the vacant glass of their fronts blind and dismal.

The car turned, bumped down a long cobbled gut and emerged into a wide area of walled villas. There was no street lighting. The moon was in its last phase and lay clear and languid on the white sandstone walls, on the white buildings behind them, on the abundant green of trees and creepers and vines.

The car turned and entered an almost identical street.

Kemal said, 'This is given the name of Garden city. It is close to your work, Brother.'

At the end of the long street, at the last walled villa, the driver stopped. Kemal turned.

'You are welcome here. This is your house. In it you are master.'

An attendant unlocked the wrought-iron gates and bowed them inside. A short gravelled path led through the garden. Shadowed figures rose on the verandah behind an arch, called greetings and sat down. There were other figures in the entrance who mumbled and stepped aside. At the end of a corridor Kemal opened a door.

The room contained a sagged sofa, two lounge chairs, a small dining table, a television set and a sideboard. Kemal went to a door at the end of the room and beckoned Nicholas to precede him. Behind the door, a large brass bedstead with a tall flourished end occupied most of the space. There was a chair beside the bed and opposite it a desk, furnished with pads and paper. Kemal opened another door and put on the light.

'This is a bathroom,' he said.

Nicholas had expected to be quartered in an hotel. He did not know whether to be pleased or disappointed. Constraint pricked uncomfortably at him, and a curiosity about the house and the men there.

He said, 'It is very comfortable. You do me too much honour.'

'You can be quiet here and at peace,' Kemal said. 'There are fresh fruits in the garden. Do you wish to take food, or drink? Permit me, in your house, to illustrate.'

He led the way back to the sitting-room, opened a cupboard and put out a bottle of whisky and a glass.

Nicholas said, embarrassed, 'That is not necessary. I hardly drink alcohol, ever.'

42

'That is for your conscience,' Kemal said.

He took up a brass bell which Nicholas had not noticed.

'With this you will call attention for your wants. To take food—' he rang the bell. 'For coffee—' he rang the bell. 'If you wish to read—'

The door opened. An arm pushed Nicholas's bag inside and disappeared.

The savagely thin face watched him, almost with concern.

'Is it enough, Brother? Is there anything further?'

'It is enough,' Nicholas said.

'Then, until tomorrow morning. I will come for you at ten.'

They wished each other a night of peace.

Nicholas wandered uncertainly in the rooms. For occupation, he unpacked his clothes. He parted the bedroom curtains and looked out on the green of the gardens. He could not identify in the moonlight the fruit that hung there. He opened a window for air and decided to bathe.

He put his shaving gear in a cabinet above a glass shelf. There were towels folded on a table, but no soap in the tray. In the next room, self-consciously, he lifted the bell, and rang it.

Almost immediately, the door opened. A fat middle-aged man in trousers and singlet stood there. Nicholas asked for soap. He nodded and withdrew, without speaking.

The bath plug did not fit. He found a grimy cloth and packed it until it wedged tight, adjusted the taps and let them run. The water trickled very slowly into the bath.

The silence oppressed him. He put the door ajar and listened. Faintly, from somewhere in the house, he heard voices murmur, and a shuffle of slippers.

The television set stared at him. Experimentally, he twisted a knob. Light edged the screen and slowly filled it.

The newsreader sat at a table before a painted backdrop of the flag.

'—if America is intimidating the world with its CIA and its octopus that extends throughout the world, with its bases and with its power, our answer is that she cannot intimidate us. She was unable to intimidate us in the past because we managed to raise our voices high on the first of September, despite America, her bases and her intelligence services. We managed to oust America out of this base. Now we can say that was the result of this people's belief in their right to live and their readiness to fall martyr for the sake of freedom.'

The reader looked up, turned a page.

In the newsreader's pause Nicholas was aware of breathing. The fat man stood at his shoulder, watching the set, a used bar of soap on a glass plate. His heavy, wheezed breath bore the smell of food and dental decay.

'—It is now time for the Arab man to raise his head high and to express his will in the way he likes. The time is ripe for the masses to be liberated and for the people to shape its fate for itself, and to put down what the enemies have had set up. It is time for the masses of the Arab people to march in a holy and armed procession on Palestine, for the Arab people to revive its old glorious heritage, for the call of "God is great" to be raised . . .'

Nicholas stood up and took the plate. The fat man did not remove his attention from the set.

'Soon,' he said, 'food will come.'

Nicholas left him there and went to the bedroom.

Later, he had eaten. A dish of kebab and rice with hot sauce, fresh bread, goat cheese and melon. He had sipped at a drink he could not identify, too sweet and perfumed for his taste.

Now he arranged himself on the mattress of obtrusive lumps and holes and looked into the moonlight through the curtains he had partly drawn. He felt secure now, under covers, in the dark. He was too spent to consider tomorrow with any apprehension, had tested himself at the television after dinner. There had been some words and structures strange to him, colloquialisms he could only guess at. He would ask Kemal to keep the Arabic formal.

The landscape, the minarets, the old palace they had passed, had revived forgotten things in him. He did not feel a stranger here, he felt almost familiar, at home.

In Baku there had been a palace like that, in the old city inside its crumbling walls. He had often walked there with his mother, the plait over her shoulder, his hand in hers, listening to her stories. The Shah of Shirvan had built his palace and the mosque in ancient, better times. He remembered the circular court of justice and imagined again as he had as a child the Shah in jewels and great white beard, sitting with his officials around the walls. He had used to laugh at the idea of the accused men standing in a crypt to be tried, with their heads sticking out of the square hole in the middle of the court of justice.

44

Often, her voice almost dreaming, her hand fondling his head, his mother had told him the story of the Maiden's Tower. The Shah of that time had set his heart on a beautiful young girl. She knew herself to be his daughter by one of the harem, but the Shah would not believe her. When he asked what she wanted as a wedding present she pleaded for a tower near the sea, taller than any building in the city. When the tower was built the girl climbed to the top and jumped off into the Caspian.

He remembered, smiling, how his mother would say proudly, 'Her name was Sameera Al-Din, as mine was, Little Cabbage Ears, before I married your wild father.'

In the dark his breath clotted with sleep. He moved and jerked on the lumped mattress. The nations of The Book . . . The time is ripe for the masses to be liberated . . . It is said Thou Shalt find the Jews and infidels bearing the bitterest grudge . . . There is much to make new, Brother . . . Abroad . . . An important business meeting . . . I can't find my needles, the white shirt needs buttons . . . The Book . . . One hundred pounds a day . . . I will miss you, Daddy . . .

The iced water in the vacuum flasks had been sweetened with lemonade powder. In the Russian's pause to shuffle again in his papers, the heavy fall of his heavy hands, the set of his big, jowled head still unrelenting, Nicholas filled his glass, trying to still the tremor in his hands. Only the picture of Lenin on the opposite wall seemed not to avoid his eyes. The two other Russians at the big table kept their heads bent, scratching patterns on their pads. The Arabs were blanked behind dark glasses, the impenetrable lenses turning the most ordinary movements of their heads into an awkward, blinding questing. In the silence Nicholas could again hear the chair at his shoulder in which Kemal sat, its joinery rubbing and squeaking as he jigged his leg.

The lemonade cut the musk in his mouth. He swilled it back into his teeth, gulped at the long cold fall into the pent muscles of his stomach. The leavings of the earlier disruption still curdled in the room. The squeaking chair behind him began to sound as loud in his head as drums.

They had not wanted him here. He had not been expected. He could not properly identify the grievous offence represented in his person. The surprise of the Embassy gate, the refusal

45

there while Kemal went savagely to the telephone in the small box inside, had begun the unreality. He had only been able to think that he was on Russian soil, shocked by the symbol of that into a convulsion of emotions. Savagely, Kemal had returned, shouldered the guard aside, savagely slammed the car door.

Nothing had prepared him for the grim, contentious faces that served for reception, the outbreak of questions in the crowded entrance to the villa. There had been no greetings. A short Russian with a Georgian accent had pushed to the steps, demanded Nicholas's name and then turned to Kemal. He spoke placatingly, in perfect Arabic.

'It is not the fault of the guards. They were only obeying instructions. You gave no warning, Brother. There should have been discussion.'

The big Russian had almost pulled Nicholas aside, against the wall of the lobby, his voice disturbed and urgent.

'Are you Russian?'

'I am Russian born.'

'When did you leave?'

'I was taken by the Germans.'

Nicholas heard Kemal's raised voice, 'We will do anything we like. This is our business, not yours,' and momentarily, over the big Russian's shoulder, caught the fierce flash of Kemal's eyes.

'Why did you not return?'

'I had nothing to return to.'

'What was your family name? Where did you come from?'

Kemal, with the younger Russian at his shoulder, interrupted.

'What are you saying, Brother? What are you being asked?'

Reluctantly, the big Russian withdrew his pressure.

Nicholas said, 'My name. Where my family come from.'

The young Russian drew the older one aside, his voice low and urgent. Another car stopped at the entrance to the villa. More Arabs entered, another Russian appeared. Nicholas was lost in the confusion about him.

The young Russian said, 'There has been a misunderstanding, Comrade. It would be best if you waited in this room.'

He opened a door. From the wall Kemal nodded. The young Russian had almost pushed Nicholas inside.

The room was small, with chairs and a table, the walls bare.

46

The furniture looked like a heavy-handed interpretation of something Scandinavian. There were newspapers on the table. It could have been the waiting-room of an English doctor or dentist with a prosperous practice. Nicholas grasped at the familiarity, feeling now in this isolation the heavy beating of his heart. He sat down and sought to make order of his thoughts. In the lobby outside, the voices briefly grew louder and then hushed. Feet shuffled past.

He had not been expected. That was why the guard had refused him admittance. It was really an ordinary matter. It was understandable that he should be questioned. This was an Embassy, Russian soil. Into these alien acres the government of Soviet Russia, the supreme Presidium, reached out of the Kremlin. Nicholas could feel Russia beat at him from the walls. Absurdly he put out his hand and laid the palm against the stone, suddenly engulfed in a nostalgia that filled him like swallowed tears. A nostalgia and a bitterness and a mourning. He sat with closed eyes, his palm against the wall, and surrendered, in submission to the great plaque on the gate, the flag over the entrance lobby, the Georgian accent which had been his father's . . .

The big Russian looked up, directly at Nicholas, the toleration forced upon him by whatever consultations had been taken before Nicholas had been fetched from the small room, still advertised in his voice and eyes.

'If the interpreter is ready, we will continue,' he said, his chin drawn into his collar, bulging the dark jowls.

Nicholas put down the glass.

'I am ready, Comrade Chairman.'

'In summary, all these studies indicate that the desired results can be achieved in each designated area and that the plan can be successfully prosecuted.'

The Russian waited while the Arabs at the table moved in their chairs, bending their blinded glances at each other.

'We will briefly examine the position in each designated area. In Area Red there is no special problem. It is comparatively remote and the carry is over very long distances. Unskilled teams, under instruction, can achieve the objective here with flexibility and speed. Logistically, Area Red can be operated at short notice and with little strain on resources.'

Nicholas hesitated. He could think of no equivalent in Arabic for logistics. The young Russian with the Georgian accent suggested 'In the matter of supply . . .'

'In the matter of supply Area Red can be operated . . .'

It was the first time he had fumbled. He must empty his head of every thought except these words which must be transposed.

'In Area Blue . . .'

The air-conditioning unit clicked in and out, readjusting the temperature, interrupting the steady, consoling note of the fan.

'—a detailed survey of all transport needed, in each designated area, including types and location points . . .'

'—in Area Green . . .'

'—the hydro-electric engineers . . .'

Once, for a few minutes, the meeting was adjourned for the relieving of bladders. Nicholas remained seated as the others moved out, hearing again the unremitting agitation from the chair behind him. Nicholas turned. Kemal was leaning forward, his examination like a grasp.

'Is it well?' Nicholas had to ask.

Kemal nodded.

'Yes, it is well, Brother.'

Relief and satisfaction flooded in Nicholas.

Kemal said, with his grasping intentness. 'Do you understand our business, Brother?'

He felt that he would be expected to understand, but really did not, and said unsurely, 'I don't understand the reference. Isn't it something to do with irrigation or water recovery?'

Kemal smiled. It almost startled Nicholas, this revelation that curved the sunken cheeks and softened the eyes.

'Indeed it is. There is much to be reclaimed, Brother.'

He looked away, smiling. 'There is much to be reclaimed.'

In his relief Nicholas had been struck by the ebbing of tensions, the confusion and disruption that had preceded the meeting, his being in a Russian Embassy, the resentment of his person and presence. He felt wrung by it all, tired by the long effort of concentration. The breath went out of him. He rubbed his face.

Kemal said, 'It will finish soon.'

The door opened. Chairs scraped back. Nicholas fixed his attention on the big portrait of Lenin and waited.

In the procession down marble stairs to the lobby, the change

48

from the air-conditioned meeting room was immediate, the air almost too thick to breathe, charged with a humidity that infested the lungs and clotted respiration. They were too many for the confines of the passage, the Arabs in groups, exchanging words in low voices, adjusting their loose gowns. Nicholas felt sweat start in his armpits and on his chest. Kemal had gone to the entrance and now returned.

'The car is waiting, Brother. I will join you later at your house.'

The young Georgian looked over, then nodded at Nicholas and smiled. It was absurd that such a simple act should give him this pleasure.

The old Chevrolet pulled out into the circular drive. There were handball courts in the shrubbery, a glimpse of other villas and from somewhere hidden a calling of children's voices. The guard saw the car coming and went to the meshed metal gate.

Nicholas lay on the old brass bed and closed his eyes. He had taken off his shoes and jacket, unbuttoned his shirt. The ceiling fan made a clicking, unbalanced sound, stirring the sluggish air. He wriggled his toes, feeling the damp run between them. He had been ridiculously unprepared for a climate like this and felt a dart of distaste for himself, for the sheer stolid stupidity of the serge suit and the underdog's woollen socks.

It seemed inexplicable to him that it had been only days since he had opened his front door on Kemal. It was as though the evidences which he had accepted as his identity had been capsized like an iceberg, to surface with a different tip. He felt a change in ways he was unable to understand, a change at once unknown yet familiar, like a long-forgotten room in which one is haunted by remembrances of the furniture.

His skin began to dry under the fan. He resisted this otherness which had thrust itself on him, summoned up his wife in exorcization. But he couldn't focus Cora's face or her voice or her person. She seemed dwindled, almost disappeared, behind screens of gauze.

'There is coffee.'

The surprise and intrusion bumped his heart. He swung his stockinged feet to the floor. The fat Arab stood wheezing in the doorway, holding things on a tray.

'Soon food will come,' the man said, and left on his silent bare feet. Nicholas sat on the bed, rubbing his face.

49

He had no appetite for the spiced food that was brought before he had finished with the coffee. Curds of fat floated in it and edged the rim of the plate. He had wanted to bathe but had not lest Kemal should arrive, but had lain again on the bed under the clicking fan and dissolved into a restless doze. Voices and a clatter of plates in the next room woke him. He put on his shoes. His head ached with a heavy, muzzy throb. His tongue felt thick and sour.

Kemal dismissed the servant.

'Did you sleep well, Brother?'

Nicholas wondered how long he had been there and looked at his watch.

He said, 'I must have done.'

There were several typed sheets of yellow paper on the table, neatly arranged alongside a thin leather envelope.

Kemal said, 'Would you read this for me, Brother?' and touched the sheets with his finger. 'It is in the Russian language.'

Nicholas sat at the table and began to study the first sheet. He ran a finger down the page, frowning.

'What is this? It is nonsense.'

Kemal's face tightened.

'Nonsense? Why do you say that, Brother?'

'It is gibberish.'

Kemal said again, 'It is in the Russian language.'

Irritation flared in Nicholas. He pushed the paper from him.

'It is meant to be Russian. Some of the words can be understood. The rest is . . . gibberish, like something a child has overheard and tried to write down.'

Kemal leaned forward.

'Read me the words you understand. Try to make sense of it, Brother.'

Reluctantly, Nicholas again studied the pages. The muzzy ache in his head beat louder.

'Danger,' he said and puzzled. 'Dangerous adventure . . . the projects ad . . . ministration must be . . . satisfied . . . unreliable . . . red . . . America . . . blue . . . status . . . Arab . . .'

He stopped.

'It is impossible to make sense of it.'

Kemal said, as though he were persuading a child, 'Try a little more, Brother. Perhaps it is a puzzle and you are trying to work it out. Think of it as a puzzle.'

'Nationalism ... the forces ... the forces of nationalism ... timing ... reaction ... the project's administration ... the Sudan.'

Kemal interrupted.

'The Sudan Brother?'

'The Sudan ...'

'What of the Sudan?'

'Nothing. It is one word among the gibberish. Area ... Area red ...'

Nicholas sat back.

'It is impossible. I can't help you. What is it?'

Kemal said, his eyes hot, 'It has been badly done?'

'If it is meant to be Russian the man who wrote it is deranged. It sounds like something someone has tried to write down phonetically. Someone who doesn't know Russian.'

'It has been badly done,' Kemal said, and shook his head.

'It is something to do with your irrigation project. It mentions some of the designated areas.'

'That is true, Brother.'

Kemal put the papers in the leather envelope and zipped it shut. He looked taut again and brooding.

The mish-mash typed on the yellow sheets had unreasonably irritated Nicholas. It reminded him of the scene in the Embassy, another thing badly done.

He said, 'Why was I not expected this morning? Why was I questioned like that?'

Kemal guarded his eyes.

'Our friends like to do things their way. In this country, this people, we do things our way. Never again will we put this people in another people's hands. When our friends come to do business in this country, they must do it in our way.'

Nicholas said. 'The young Comrade, Kapitsa, has fluent Arabic. He could have interpreted.'

Kemal knocked the table with his knuckles.

'That Comrade is *their* interpreter. In this country you are *our* interpreter. It is we who decide such things here. Besides,' he said, brooding, 'there are other matters of the Russian language for which we need your help.'

Nicholas said, 'I want to go out, Brother.'

Kemal snapped his attention from the window.

'What do you need, Brother? Tell me what you need.'

'I don't need anything. I want to go out, look around, buy presents for my family.'

Kemal said, 'It isn't safe, Brother. There are those who cannot forget the humiliations this people have suffered. You might come to harm. You might lose your way. Are you not comfortable in your own house?'

Nicholas said, 'Kemal, I am grateful for this house of my own, in which I am comfortable. But tonight I wish to go out. I would appreciate a little money, with which to eat in a restaurant and do some shopping.'

'Very well, Brother,' Kemal said. 'It would be wise to have a guide. A guide who will see you are not cheated over prices. You are the guest of my company. You must only take away from this people the best and the happiest of memories. I will send a guide to your house. It will be his pleasure to pay for anything you buy.'

'It is appreciated,' Nicholas said.

Kemal got up.

'We will meet again in the morning. Our friends now understand that in this country we do things in our own way. You will not be made little again, Brother.'

Nicholas tested the cold water from the bathroom tap on the back of his hand. It was cool enough now. During the day it had been uncomfortably hot, the pipe that ran the water exposed somewhere outside to the sun. The system that heated the hot water supply was barely adequate. When he had considered bathing earlier in the afternoon he would have had to reverse the usual order to obtain a tolerable temperature. Nicholas felt quite excited to be going out and was amused that it should be so. Everything is upside down, he thought, even the water from the taps. To get a cold bath in the morning he would fill the tub and leave it overnight.

He was restless, waiting, after he had bathed and changed. He felt cooped in the rooms and oppressed again by the silence. For company he switched on the television set. Tractors rolled across the screen. Soil spilled from plough blades. Water gushed from pipe heads. A man holding a plan pointed into the distance. Workers, bent to harvest a ground crop, looked into the camera and giggled.

'In the Jefara Plain a further twelve thousand hectares of land will be reclaimed. One thousand two hundred water reservoirs and six hundred farm houses will be built. Researches for underground water are being carried out by the United Arab Republic Underground Waters Company. At Augla the British Geological Studies Institute is carrying out similar work and in the Ghadames area further surveys are being made by French companies specialized in this field.'

Huge machines rumbled and bumped over flat lands of low scrub, tearing at the growth.

'Within the new soil and water conservation schemes a number of contracts were signed. In Misurata ten wells are to be built, two wells at Jefren and two reservoirs completed near Agedebia . . .'

It pleased Nicholas to have a small part in this making, when so much everywhere was being ransacked and destroyed.

'—In Area Red . . . the logistics problem in Area Green . . . there is much to be reclaimed, Brother.'

When Kemal used that phrase all the challenge of these undertakings, the great flux on the screen, was there in his dark broodings. It meant more than business to Kemal. He was making war on the desert. Nicholas grew absorbed. Behind him the fat Arab said, 'It is for you,' his eyes on the screen, wheezing his foul breath. The card of cheap board was the same as that used by Kemal. TRANS-ARABIA PROJECTS was printed across it. Pencilled in English, BASHIR MASOUD.

Nicholas moved out of the other man's range.

He asked, 'Are you a camel?'

The fat Arab shifted his dull eyes, scratched at his armpit and tried to understand.

'I have no camel.'

'I asked are you a camel,' Nicholas said. 'One who has no hands to knock on a door. One who is without manners.'

A spark flared in the fat Arab's eyes, he scratched at his nose and grew dull.

'Do you wish me to knock at your door?'

'Yes, Brother,' Nicholas said.

The man dropped his head and shambled out. Nicholas went to the bathroom and got his coat off the back of a chair, wondering at himself.

The young man was alone on the arched verandah. He wore a clean suit, an open-necked shirt and white shoes. He introduced himself gravely and informed Nicholas that he had merely to express a wish to have it fulfilled.

53

Kemal's car and driver waited at the gate. Bashir Masoud opened the door for Nicholas and seated himself in the front.

'I know some little English,' he said, turning. 'I am making study in that language. Would you prefer it if I make English speaking?'

Nicholas had no wish to be conspicuous.

'We will use your own tongue,' he said.

The young man nodded.

'First, with your permission, we will make a small tour. There are certain places of interest.'

Nicholas settled back. The night was wonderfully clear, moonlit and stirring. A light breeze had reduced the humidity. The headache left him.

Walking in the Souk, his guide following discreetly, Nicholas was several times greeted by loungers and the shopkeepers in their doorways. In an alley a boy begged baksheesh from him because he was rich, a great sheikh. He had expected some curiosity about his person, even the hostility of which Kemal had warned. There had been nothing. He was ignored and accepted as he would have been walking in London.

Nicholas looked up from a tray of brass trinkets into a mirror advertising hair cream. The olive of his skin was darkened in the murky light. Fine black hair, dark eyes, a strong nose beaked on the bridge. He studied the man next to him, the others along the wall, the card players in the coffee shop behind the mirror. He could have been one of them, out of a different class. Here in the Souk, he had passed as an Arab. Watching again he searched the faces about him to find himself in them. What desert bloods had made their immemorial claim to stamp his father's face, which he had given to his son and which his son had now given to his. Truly, Nicholas thought, each man is a mosaic.

Masoud said, 'Would you like to take food now, Brother?'

'Yes. Where do you recommend?'

'There is a restaurant owned by an Italian these many years. Once, there were many foreigners taking food there. When tourists come, they often go to this restaurant.'

Nicholas said, 'Then let us eat in this restaurant.'

'I have already taken food, Brother,' Masoud said. 'While you eat I'll fetch the car.'

The restaurant was at the corner of a wide street off the Souk. It made little effort to recall its glory. In the further room beyond an arch, stacked chairs and tables mourned their disuse in darkened quiet. Four smartly dressed young Arabs ate at one table. Two middle-aged men and a dowdy woman conversed in French at another. The restaurant was otherwise empty.

Nicholas seated himself at the window, to watch the street. An elderly man in a clean white apron, with thin black hair carefully brushed across his scalp, came out from behind a bead curtain.

In Italian he bade Nicholas good evening and handed him a menu enclosed in plastic.

Nicholas said, in Arabic, 'You must excuse me, I don't know Italian,' and wondered wryly if he could also pass as one of them.

In Arabic the old man excused himself and said it was cooler this evening, that there could be rain about. A good storm, he said, would lay the dust.

Nicholas ignored the Arab dishes, he had a poor palate for spices, accustomed now to Cora's bland café cooking. Suddenly hungry, he sought without success for something he could recognize.

'What is this?' he asked, pointing.

'It is a savoury,' the Italian said, 'of semolina.'

'And this?'

'Bistecchine di Vitello alla Milanesa,' the Italian read, 'it is fillets of veal with macaroni and tomato.'

He wound his hands. 'Very good. Although, alas, the veal is frozen.'

'That will do very well,' Nicholas said.

The restaurant had two entrances. The one Nicholas had used, on the wide street, the other from the corner behind him. He recognized Kapitsa's Georgian accent immediately, it was like his father's, like Stalin's voice on the radio, a thick, burred Russian, as a highland Scot might speak the Queen's English. Something knotted in his stomach. He had been thinking of the Russians he had met, the nostalgia which had engulfed him in the Embassy, his sadness that these, his countrymen, should prove so distant, so alien.

'I noticed you from the street,' Kapitsa said. 'May I join you, Comrade?'

Nicholas said, 'I would be glad of your company, Comrade,' and thought, he did not notice me from the street. I would have seen him.

55

Kapitsa sat down and smiled. He did not look Georgian, he was fair, a tiny down of hair on the broad mould of his cheekbones.

He said, 'Let me congratulate you on your work today. You know Arabic very well.'

'My accent is not good,' Nicholas said. 'And I am not familiar with idioms. I am more accustomed to working on paper. There is more time to think.'

Kapitsa nodded, considering.

'Do you do much work – on paper?'

'I am a translator.'

'As,' Kapitsa said. 'You are a translator,' and offered Nicholas a cigarette.

'Where did you learn Arabic, Comrade?'

'From my mother. Afterwards, as a study.'

Kapitsa looked surprised.

'From your mother?'

'She had been born a Muslim. She was one of the Ingushi people.'

Kapitsa said quickly, 'The Ingushi? Are you then from Azerbaijan.'

'From Baku,' Nicholas said. 'Do you know Baku?'

Kapitsa said, 'No I don't, Comrade.'

Nicholas looked away in disappointment.

'You must forgive us,' Kapitsa said, 'for your reception this morning. The Arabs had not advised us that they would bring their own interpreter. In an Embassy one must observe procedures. You will understand that.'

'It is understandable,' Nicholas said.

'The Arabs,' Kapitsa smiled, 'are good fellows. But their revolution is very young. They are an excitable people, sometimes not easy to deal with.'

Nicholas sat back while his food was laid. The Italian put down a pitcher of iced water and a glass from the tray, polished a knife and fork on his apron.

Nicholas said, 'It was strange for me, being in a Russian Embassy,' and now he smiled at Kapitsa. 'I thought of it as Russian soil. It was strange – and rather childish. Have you eaten?'

In Arabic, Kapitsa asked for coffee. When the Italian had gone, he said, 'Have you ever thought of going home, Comrade? There are many posts for a man with Arabic.' He became earnest. 'Much business is being done with the Arab world. There are posts in our Embassies and Trade Departments and Special Missions. There are well-paid posts in the People's Publishing Houses with high rank and privileges. You could render much valuable service.'

Nicholas could feel something in him going away, a dwindling that panged him with sadness.

'No, Comrade,' he said saddened further by that word which could mean nothing to him. 'It is too late for me. It has been too late for a long time. There is no home for me to return to. My home is now in another place.'

Kapitsa said, leaning forward in emphasis, 'There is only one home for a Russian, Comrade. On his own soil, among his own people, on the sacred soil of Mother Russia.'

It reminded Nicholas of Kemal. There seemed to be so many sacred soils. He wondered by what grace or claim this or that earth became sanctified.

'How old are you, Comrade?' he asked.

Kapitsa looked surprised.

'My age? I'm thirty-two.'

'Thirty-two.' Nicholas considered. 'You would have been three years of age during the Siege of Stalingrad. My father was a Georgian, like you. One of the dark ones. He was a regular officer, with General Rodimtzer's 13th Guards, and died with his back to the Volga. I, and other boys like me, with old men too weak to fight, crawled over the Volga ice pushing food and ammunition before us. Sometimes the new ice cracked and broke and the children and the old ones and the boxes disappeared in the dark.'

Nicholas looked over his untouched food at Kapitsa's strained face.

'When our armies at last launched the counter attack on November nineteenth of that year, cutting the Germans off, we children and the women had been sent out, to the south. There were many hundreds of us and a few of the old men. We looked back on what seemed to be the world's end. It was my birthday. I was fifteen years of age. The retreating German column took us. I was among the boys they kept.'

Kapitsa said, quite pale now, 'What did they do with you, Comrade?'

'I was taken to Germany, as a slave labourer. The Americans liberated us.'

'And your mother?'

'I don't know.'

Kapitsa said, 'You don't know? She could be alive, Comrade.'

'Could she?' Nicholas said. 'The Germans destroyed everything behind them in the Caucasus. My mother had remained in Kaku.'

'But she could be alive. If you were to return home you could search for her.'

Nicholas said, 'Comrade Kapitsa, what the Germans did not destroy Comrade Stalin did.'

Kapitsa held still, his cigarette poised.

'In 1944 Comrade Stalin liquidated the Muslim autonomous republics. Did you not know that? You would have been ... sixteen when Khrushchev told about it in his speech. Oh yes, they were all deported to Siberia. The Chechen, the Ingushi, the Karachai and the Balkar; men, women and children. You see, some Muslims had collaborated with the Germans. Stalin liquidated all their nations in reprisal. We prisoners in some way heard about it at the end. That is what I would have returned home to, Comrade Kapitsa. I would have been deported with my mother's people ...'

The young man's face struggled to reject the simple words. Nicholas watched him in detachment and then added, '... to the sacred soil of Siberia.'

He began to eat his food, which had cooled, to spare them both any further. Kapitsa poured more coffee, lit another cigarette.

The elderly Italian returned to the table to ask if Nicholas had enjoyed the food and suggested other dishes with which he might follow. A street photographer, in a dirty cotton shirt with KODAK lettered on it, startled them with the sudden dazzle of a flash bulb, and extended a card. Kapitsa knocked it quite violently from his hand. The photographer backed away and went to the table where the French diners sat. Nicholas declined further food and ordered coffee.

When they were alone, Kapitsa said, in the brisk impersonal voice of a clerk making out some bureaucratic form, 'If you give me the particulars, Comrade, I will institute inquiries about your mother.'

'It is useless,' Nicholas said. 'I did what could be done, long ago.'

Kapitsa unscrewed a Parker pen and took a notebook from his pocket.

'Allow me to try,' he said. 'It would be a privilege to be of service to one who has suffered in the patriotic war.'

Nicholas felt himself tempted, tried to put it from him.

'There are some things it is better not to know.'

'I have some little influence,' Kapitsa said. 'Times have changed. Who knows?' His voice almost wheedled, full of anxiety to please. 'Who knows, Comrade? What was your father's name?'

Nicholas said dully, 'His name was the same as mine. Nicolai Fydorovich Dzontenvili. He had the rank of captain.'

'And your mother's name? Before marriage.'

'My mother's name was Sameera Al-Din.'

'And where do you now live, Comrade? Something may come of this. Who knows?'

'My address is 17 Belmont Park, London NW18.'

The elderly Italian stood in front of the beaded curtain, Kapitsa signalled him and insisted on paying the bill.

Too much had happened. Too many old things, mercifully asleep, had been aroused. The weariness that now settled on Nicholas was in his mind and his body like weights. His thoughts moved and stuck in the rusted disorder of something mechanical. He wasn't accustomed to having things happen to him, that was all in the past. He had a home and a wife and a son, his pen, his pads and his dictionaries. Nicholas Arden, translator. Nicholas Arden, safe and secure in a safe country, with his wife and his son and his pen and his pads and his garden in which some plantings lived. Nicholas Arden . . .

Masoud's clean suit was crumpled, his hands stained with grime.

'Forgive me, Brother,' he pleaded, 'I could not come to you sooner. The motor car expired. The innards of that car are very old and worn. It is hard to find a mechanic who is knowledgeable about these innards. Have you taken food? Have you been comfortable in this restaurant?'

'I have taken food, Brother,' Nicholas said, 'and I have been comfortable. There is no occasion for distress. If the car is working now I am ready to go home.'

Nicholas lay on his back in the dark. His hands gripped the sheet that covered him. But the weariness that was in his mind and body like weights would not surrender to the unconsciousness he craved.

They had fired the towns and villages on the line of retreat, the sky had been livid with the flames. Those left had burst out of their houses and buildings as timbers crashed in spark flares, some in flames themselves. The helmeted and bayonet-carrying men prodded and herded them into the trucks. The execution squads cut out the old ones, clipped fresh magazines to their weapons.

'. . . Army Group Centre will apprehend forty to fifty thousand youths from the age of ten to sixteen and transport them to the Reich. It is intended to allot these juveniles primarily to the German trades. This action is not only aimed at preventing a direct reinforcement of the enemy strength but also as a reduction of his biological potentialities.'

In the long trains of box cars the stiffened dead rolled and rode with the living in the stench and muck of human excreta. The babies born in blood and screams on the boards were small enough to be pushed out through the traps that served for air.

In the camps they wore sacks with holes for their arms and legs. Lice, fleas and bugs tortured them. Those without shoes staggered on frozen stumps in the winter.

At Nogerratstrasse the inmates lived for half a year in dog kennels, urinals and old bakehouses. The dog kennels were three feet high, nine feet long and six feet wide. Five men slept in each of them. They crawled in on their hands and knees. There was no running water in the camp.

'. . . Directive: the farm workers have to labour as long as is directed by the employer. There are no limits to the working time. Every employer has the right to give corporal punishment to his farm workers. They should if possible be removed from the community of the home and they can be quartered in stables, etc. No remorse whatever should restrict such action. There is no claim to free time. Sexual intercourse with women or girls is strictly prohibited. Special treatment (hanging) is requested. It should not take place in the immediate vicinity. A certain number, however, should attend this special treatment.'

At Kramperplatz there were ten children's toilets for the one thousand two hundred slaves. Excreta contaminated everything. The Tartars and the Kirghiz were first to die. They fell to the earth like sprayed flies.

60

'. . . Plenipotentiary General for the Allocation of Labour;
Directive: Foreign workers are to be treated in such a way as to
exploit them to the highest possible extent at the lowest conceivable degree of expenditure . . .'

He had passed through some camps where there was no shelter at all. They lay under the open sky during rain and snow.

'. . . Directive: Russian prisoners of war are to be branded
with a special endurable mark. The brand is to consist of an
acute angle of about forty-five degrees with one centimetre
length of side, pointing downwards on the left buttock, at about
one hand's length from the rectum.'

The ceiling fan clicked overhead. Nicholas lay stiffened on
the bed, his eyes wide and unseeing.

They were insane. Monsters out of a preposterous nightmare.
They had dragged Vasili from his machine, beaten him to death
on the floor. A group had chosen Andrei for a victim, had
beaten him every day for a week, and then tired of it. There had
been a room off one factory floor into which many were taken
and ordered to choose a whip. When the lashing was over they
would be sent back to work, soaked in their blood, sometimes
twenty or thirty in a morning.

He had endured it. He had survived. There had been much
strength in his body. The treachery of remembrance had to be
cut from his mind. He was Nicholas Arden, translator. He had
a wife and a son and a house and his pen and his pads and
his . . .

Nicholas forced his thoughts towards Moscow. Why had Kapitsa sought him out? He had not seen him from the street, as he
said. How did he know where to find him? Why had he wanted
to?

'—our hydro-electric engineers . . .'
'—in Area Red . . .'
'—there is much to be reclaimed, Brother.'

The ceiling fan clicked towards oblivion.

CHAPTER FOUR

'DAVID?'

The peremptory tone was unmistakable. Lawrence checked the date on his wrist watch. It had been a month, exactly.

'How are you, Barbara?'

'I have a beastly cold and feel miserable.'

'That's what comes of living in a palace. Too many draughts.'

'Don't be silly,' she said. 'I am telephoning to announce that your banishment is lifted. I want you for a party on Saturday.'

'I'm off the social circuit, Barbara. Max is coming in from Kuwait this afternoon.'

'How that man gets about. Poor Helen. It must be like being married to a commercial traveller. You must bring him with you. I insist.'

'I can't promise. You know how Max is.'

'Indeed I do. I'll expect you both at eight o'clock. Tiki is going to cook us one of his sukiyakis on those funny little stoves the Japanese use. We will all take our shoes off and sit on the floor. I've got rice wine, and kimonos for everybody.'

Lawrence said, 'I'll do what I can.'

'Where will Max be staying?'

'He has a suite at the Phoenicia.'

'I will call him there. I've not forgotten that he didn't come to see me on his last visit. Until Saturday, then.'

Lawrence went back to collating his reports. There had to be a good reason for this swing Max had done through the Gulf states. Max had ordered that every agent the consultancy used should report to Beirut on the slightest deviation from normal.

Max Morrow came out of the bedroom in a silk robe and Muslim slippers. His thick, greying hair was wet and tousled. He slumped into a chair, pushed out his legs.

'That feels better. It was hotter than hell in Kuwait, sand blowing. I got caught on the way to the airport, I was stuck all over with it, like a goddamned emery board. Fix me a beer, Character.'

He bent and scratched absently at the dark calf of his leg. Morrow was always tanned. He took a sun lamp twice a week after working out in his club's gymnasium. Lawrence thought his chief looked troubled. Morrow tasted the beer, drew a pattern on the frosted glass.

'I can't figure it,' he said. 'Our people in Washington can't figure it. The oil companies can't figure it.'

Lawrence said, 'Is it the same in Kuwait?'

'It's the same all over. Russians everywhere. Delegations, tourists, historians, journalists, engineers, agricultural experts. The only cover they're not using is front men for Billy Graham. In Saudi there are two teams out in the desert, under canvas, claiming to be archaeologists. What the hell is there to dig up in Saudi? There's been nothing but sand out there since Adam.'

'It could be legitimate, Max. The Russians are pushing hard with their economic and cultural co-operation programmes.'

'What the hell culture is there in those places to co-operate about? I don't believe any of it. In one place, yes. In two places, perhaps. But not all over, and not all at the same time.'

He got up and looked for cigarettes.

'The oil companies are jumpy, the State Department is jumpy and I'm getting to be jumpy.'

Morrow sat down. Lawrence leaned over and put a lighter to his cigarette.

He said, 'I don't see how an increased Russian presence in the oil states can be tied into another price hike. The Arabs know they can only go so far. They've just signed a new agreement. They're not about to kill the golden goose.'

'They can make the goose damn sick,' Morrow said. 'They've got the whip hand and they're beginning to know it.'

'The Arabs are as much dependent on the oil revenues as we are on their oil. The companies used to have it all their own way. It is inevitable that with the rise of nationalism there's going to be a levelling out. It happened in South America. We can't stop it happening here.'

Morrow said, 'It's our job to stop it happening. Or at least to call the shots. That's what our clients pay for.'

He squinted at Lawrence.

'It's about time you learned the facts of life. The technological societies can be headed for a smash-up worse than over population or pollution. In another twenty years we may not have enough energy left to pollute your grandmother.'

He stood up and began to pace.

'The Western world is over an oil barrel. There's not a government that isn't worried stiff. In the next ten years, at today's rate of consumption, and the index is leaping every year, the world will consume more fossil fuel than it has done in the last century.'

Morrow paused. 'There's a conflict ahead that is going to make racial differences and religious differences and cold war differences look like spats in an ever-loving family. The developing countries can't develop without energy. Their demands rocket every year. The developed countries need energy to develop further. The U.S. with only six per cent of the world's population, already consumes thirty-five per cent of the world's fossil fuel. You studied political science. Work that out on your slide rule.

'In another thirty years, if the undeveloped countries reach today's standard of living in the West, the world-wide level of energy consumption will be one hundred times the present figure. We can't produce that kind of energy. We don't have it on the planet.'

Lawrence moved uneasily.

'That's being a bit Malthusian, isn't it? We do have nuclear power.'

'So we've got a few nuclear power stations, a few nuclear-propelled vessels. We've also got about one hundred million motor cars and heavy transport. We've got a few million aircraft, a half million locomotives and I don't know how many million ships in this world. Nuclear power stations take a lot of money and time to build. Some of us don't have the money and maybe none of us have the time.'

Lawrence said, feeling shaken, 'But thermo-nuclear fission would be some kind of feasible energy alternative?'

'It would be – in a very limited way. Nuclear power can't get technology off the hook of being hostage to oil. We can't make steel without it. Derivatives of crude make up a bulk percentage of modern industry. There are all the chemical by-products. The whole goddamn plastics industry depends on oil. That suit you're wearing, most of the stuff in this room, is synthetic. I could make you up a catalogue of oil-based products bigger than the New York telephone book. Paint, detergents, artificial fibres, toiletries, medicines, stock food, containers, ball bearings . . .'

Morrow stopped pacing and topped up his beer.

'Arab oil accounts for eighty-five per cent of the world's exports and a third of the world's production. In the last decade, three quarters of all the oil discovered was in their areas. The Arabs own almost three quarters of the world's known reserves.'

Lawrence pushed his hair back. Reduced like this, to a few figures and projections, it made a chilling consideration.

'But this isn't new, Max,' he said, for comfort. 'This situation must have been known.'

'There's a difference between knowing a situation generally and getting down to the specific of facing it. What is new is that the Organization of Petroleum Exporting Countries – the OPEC – has been learning fast. That was a very tough nego-tiation they gave us after Algeria nationalized the non-French companies. The OPEC is getting sophisticated, and learning to stand together. The West has depended on Arab differences to beat the price hikes. It's a new ball game. We don't have the clout any more. Independence and nationalism have changed the political framework. With the Russian influence now in these areas we can't apply the old political pressures. And we can't, repeat can't, afford to pay for another price hike.'

Lawrence said, 'And we can't, repeat can't, afford *not* to pay it. Is that the picture?'

Morrow stubbed his cigarette, rubbing it hard into the tray.

'That's where the Arabs could have us all. Up tight over the oil barrel. Right now, the best we've got is a five-year mora-torium. Iran, some of the other signatories, are too short of foreign exchange to renegue. The Kuwaitis, the Libyans, they have the reserves. It would only take one to renegue and there goes the moratorium.'

Morrow felt his hair to see if it had dried. Thoughtfully, he poured the last of the beer.

'The crusades. Two world wars. A thousand battles that shaped and destroyed civilizations. The Semitics. Jesus Christ. Mohammed. Why does it always happen here? What in the hell is this navel of sand that pulls us all back by the umbilical?'

To be practical, David Lawrence said, 'Where do we fit into all this, Max?'

Morrow roused himself.

'I want to know what the Russkies are up to. I don't believe they're historians and tourists and archaeologists and experts on the chick-pea wilt. There's an infiltration going on and none of us can figure it out.'

Lawrence said, 'I had a few words with Quale last month. The time of the Moroccan trouble.'

'Quale?'

'The correspondent. In his opinion the Russians are shit scared of Arab nationalism. If there is this infiltration, couldn't it be an extending of influence? An attempt to hold things down? Even to collect information?'

Morrow rubbed his face.

'You could be right. Maybe we're getting jumpy. There's enough at stake out here to give anyone the jumps. You know the Russians are still hurting all over from their losses in the Six Day War. They're not looking for any part of a repeat performance. We know they want that Canal reopened. It has been a political dream of theirs since the Tsars and before to have access in and out of the Mediterranean.'

He was thoughtful again.

'It's got to where Israel is a burr under everyone's saddle.'

He got up and checked his watch.

'Freshen your drink. I'm going to dress. I've got an appointment with the Ambassador. You staying in town tonight?'

Lawrence shook his head.

'There's a courier coming in this evening, from Bellini. An Alitalia steward. I always meet him at the Lodge.'

'Bellini?'

'That Italian in Tripoli we inherited when Middle East Research folded.'

'The old guy with the restaurant? The one you said was into the woodwork?'

'That's the reference MER gave him.'

'Well,' Morrow said. 'I wonder what Bellini's cooked up?'

He raised his eyebrows at Lawrence.

'No? Bellini ... restaurant ... cooked up. I'm trying, aren't I?'

From the bedroom he called, 'If you're going home you can drop me off.'

Lawrence had forgotten to have Freni collect his dry cleaning. He took a short cut from the Embassy, through back streets, and wound up his window against the stench. Somewhere, the sewers had overflowed again. Off the main boulevards much of Beirut was revoltingly squalid and filthy. He was fortunate to have his place in the hills. Lebanon meant white. On the slopes even the snow was dirty yellow. At last he was out of it, the pine stands around the Hypodrome clean and green ahead.

Max had several times mentioned the State Department. He must have been conferring with his old colleagues. It was unlike Max to confess to being jumpy. Whatever worried State now worried him.

Lawrence recalled the piece he had filed that morning off the UPI service from London.

'. . . If Arab oil were to be priced upwards again, particularly at this time of critical balance-of-payment deficits, then Britain and the rest of Europe will suffer a catastrophe. It would be impossible to fill the gap from Iran, Venezuela, the U.S. and Nigeria. Rationing of the most rigorous kind would be inevitable in all the consuming countries of Western Europe, and the effects of the crisis would be crippling for a long time after it was resolved.'

It was their job to call the shots. That's what the clients paid for. How do you call the shots on a volatile people like the Arabs? The only thing predictable about them was that they could not be predicted.

The Porsche whined into the twisting climb off the flat. Lawrence continued to gnaw at it. Suppose the Russians were infiltrating some of the oil states. How could you speculate about that when all you had to connect it with was a heap of other speculations?

The photograph was post-card size. Lawrence put it opposite him on the desk, with the single sheets of ruled paper torn from a child's exercise book. He was bent, searching in his drawers for a magnifying glass, when Morrow entered the office.

Lawrence pointed. 'On the desk.'

Morrow sat down and arranged his spectacles. There were only a few sentences on the paper, scratched with a bad nib.

He said, 'I hope Bellini speaks Arabic better than he spells it.' He raised his eyes. 'An Arab fluent in Russian, sitting with a member of the Russian Embassy.'

There was a date on the report.

'First seen on the eighth. That's more than a month ago. Why didn't we get this earlier?'

'Bellini wouldn't have thought it urgent. It would have come with the usual bits and pieces had you not ordered all our contacts to report.'

Morrow continued to read the ill-written script.

'Next seen on the thirtieth, and followed. Housed in Garden City. Twice seen with unidentified Arab entering the Russian Embassy. A good man, your Bellini.'

Lawrence said, 'MER believed him to be working for Italian Intelligence.'

Morrow picked up the photograph. 'Which is the mystery man?'

Lawrence said, 'The one in the middle. He's arrowed, the other is the Russian.' He found the magnifying glass. Morrow took it.

'Uh – huh,' he said. 'That's Bellini in the apron. He looks a shrewd old cuss. The Russian's a bit hard to make out. It's a good picture of the man in the middle. He's not one of the dark Arabs. That shot was taken with a flash, judging by the lighting. They all look a bit startled.'

He put down the glass and lit a cigarette.

'I wonder how Bellini got it?'

Lawrence said, 'Would you like coffee?'

Morrow nodded, and called for Freni.

'What do you make of it, Max?'

'It could be anything – or nothing. An Arab with fluent Russian is unusual. There are a few in Egypt. There are almost certainly none in Libya. The educated class there hardly makes a quorum. This guy must be out of Egypt.'

Lawrence felt a rise of excitement.

'Couldn't that confirm your own feeling? That it isn't by accident that the Russians are interested in the oil states? If the pattern in the Gulf is being repeated in Libya, it must mean organization.'

Freni served the coffee. Morrow sweetened his with saccharin, returned the small tube to his pocket. He glanced again at the photograph.

'It's a good likeness,' he said. 'If this man's a Russian expert he's going to be highly placed in the Federation. He shouldn't be hard to identify. They would probably know him at State.'

'I had a feeling last night that this might mean something. I sent a message to Bellini asking for a detailed check out.'

'When will he get it?'

'Tomorrow. Our Alitalia man is on that run for the next few weeks.'

'An Arab with Russian,' Morrow said. 'You run our Cairo files through the machine. I'll see what they've got at the Embassy.'

He poured himself more coffee and pushed his chair back.

'You know, Character, this whole Middle East foul-up needn't and shouldn't have happened. Gamal liked us. He wanted to be friends. We reorganized the entire Egyptian Civil Service for him. He liked us and he trusted us, in the main. The Russians should never have got their noses into this part of the world.'

'Aswan,' Lawrence said.

'Aswan. One lousy power play that handed the ball to Russia. When State renegued on the agreement, that loan, it left Gamal without pride, prestige, place or position. Had he not turned to the Russians his officers would have hung him up by the heels. That dam represented everything the revolution said it stood for.'

He picked up the photograph.

'An Arab out of Egypt, with Russian.'

Suddenly Morrow slammed the table and tossed his head back. He blew a raspberry at the ceiling.

'What is it?'

Morrow rubbed his face.

'I must be getting old.'

Lawrence waited, his expression intent.

'We've been working on this curiosity of an Arab in Libya who speaks Russian. Why? Because Bellini assumed it. Why couldn't he be a Russian with Arabic? There are any number of those. They're spilling all over the goddamn place.'

Lawrence looked away. Why had such an obvious possibility not occurred to him? How many times had Max instructed him never to take anything for granted?

He said, in explanation, 'I'm the one who must be getting old,' regretting the haste of the telephone call with which he had summoned Morrow. 'I'm sorry, Max.'

Morrow stood up.

'We can't be sure. Put the Cairo file through the machine

69

anyway.' He looked at his watch. 'I've got a call booked to Washington for mid-day. That gives me time to take a massage.'

Lawrence needed to distract attention from his failure.

'Have you had a call from Barbara?'

Morrow shook his head.

'She's having a sukiyaki party tomorrow night. She asked me to invite you.'

'Are you going?'

'That depends on whether you need me.'

Morrow pocketed his glasses, thinking.

'What's the name of that professor at the American University? The tall one who heads up the language department?'

'Morecombe.'

'Could you get Barbara to invite him?'

'If it's a request from you, yes.'

'See what you can do about it, Character. He just might be able to tell us something.'

The records in the consultancy and those in the American Embassy had produced nothing to identify the man photographed in Tripoli. The one Egyptian whose description might have matched was already known to Max Morrow.

The cold Barbara Barse had complained about to Lawrence had become a streaming misery. Out of consideration for her discomfort the guests took an early leave, their extravagant commiserations exchanged for Barbara's extravagant apologies.

The night was oppressive with heat and cloud, the pressure of the impending storm almost palpable. Lightning quaked on the sky line. Splatters of rain drove against the windscreen. Lawrence switched on the wipers.

'Barbara should go home,' Morrow said. 'Breed horses or take up good-works. This business of the kimonos and sitting on the floor, that whole goddamn palace is like a child's make-believe. She's being destroyed by boredom, thinking up things to do.'

'She'd probably be equally as bored in the States. Was Morecombe any help?'

'He was very definite that the Libyans don't have any Russian linguists. Definite in that authoritarian, academic fashion which can't conceive of being wrong. In this instance I accept Morecombe's law. He spent some time at a language conference in Tripoli last summer.'

Morrow wound up his window.

'We're in for a squall. Did you know that one of the university's faculty was arrested for discussing the Arab–Israeli problem in a restaurant? He was discharged, of course, when he established who he was.'

'There's a spy mania on,' Lawrence said. 'Having a border with Israel makes the Lebanese very nervy. It's understandable. Beirut is only a few minutes' flying time from the advanced Israeli airfields. Our mail is being opened again, by the way. They hardly bother to restick the envelopes.'

'Everyone's jumpy,' Morrow said. He put his head back, rolling an unlit cigarette in his lips. Lawrence dipped the headlights as gusts of wind-driven rain struck the car, limiting vision. Max Morrow remained silent, and then shifted in his seat.

'Something's been worrying me. I can't pin it down. It came up when you showed me the photograph. It was something you said.'

'Something I said?' Lawrence tried to recall. 'The photograph and Bellini's note were on the desk. I was looking for the magnifier . . .'

'Uh – huh. What did you say?'

'What did I say?' Lawrence had made no observation that he could remember. He had felt that this might be a lead, but he had not said so.

'You asked why we had not got the signal earlier, and I . . .'

'No! It was a phrase. I picked up the photograph . . .'

'You asked me which was the mystery man—'

Morrow slapped the car door.

'That's it. That's it, Character. You said: the man in the middle.'

Lawrence snapped his eyes off the road.

'That's right. He was arrowed.'

'The man in the middle.' Morrow shook his head in deprecation. 'And you say I'm not getting old?'

Because he didn't understand, Lawrence asked with exasperation, 'What are you getting at?'

'It was a kind of code. We used it during the war at the Allied conferences I was at with security. You know these press photographs you've seen of meetings of heads of states? There's always one man out of focus in the background. The man in the middle. The interpreter. He can be a grade two clerk in the Foreign Office, an academic like Morecombe, a linguist out of an Embassy, anyone at all. He can be going about with secrets in his head that could blow up the goddamned world. There was a Summit Conference interpreter who knew the dates of D-Day, the landing places of the main force, the areas where feints would be made, the navy stations, the plans for air cover, and he got lost in a fog outside Dover. Drove into a ditch in a country lane and almost killed himself. It was four days before he was located in a hospital. The Allies almost called off the war.'

Again Lawrence felt the unreasonable lift of excitement, like a promise or forewarning, something already in preparation. He had felt it on the instant he shook the photograph from the packet. Lawrence could close his eyes and see the strong, gentle face, the fall of the man's dark hair, with a clarity come to life, as though the image breathed. He again heard Morrow's voice.

'So if he's a Russian who speaks Arabic, we've got nothing. If he's an Arab who speaks Russian, and he's out of Egypt or somewhere else, we should be able to trace him. If he's with the Organization of Petroleum Exporting Countries there's something coming off with the oil. If he's interpreting in those languages, the Russians are giving it their support. You know what that could mean? How it could tie in with all these Russians moving about?'

Lawrence did not wish to make a mistake.

'I think I can guess.'

'The big one,' Morrow said, 'the reason I've had this bad smell up my nose. These Russians could be oil technicians using cover. It could be, it just could be, a general nationalization. Expel the Western technicians, put the Russians in, and there goes the ball game. They could bring it off in twenty-four hours. There wouldn't be a thing our companies or governments could do.'

Morrow lit the cigarette he'd been playing with and blew a long, introspective puff of smoke.

'First thing tomorrow I'll work out a likelihood report. You can type it and make the Xerox copies. I'll arrange to send them out in the Diplomatic Bag. If they're opening the mail again, we don't want any hot and burning Arab getting sight of this one. I want a dozen copies of that photograph. Telex the Washington office that I'm staying on. Call me at the hotel immediately you get an ETA from Sam Hodges.'

Lawrence turned off the coast road into the city, trying to fix Morrow's continuing instructions in his mind.

Sam Hodges was in his seventies, a big man, heavy in the bones. He sat with his knees wide apart to accommodate the belly which seemed to have sagged out of long use and wear, the way the bottom can sag in a sack, the way the lids had sagged over his eyes until they could only be seen as glints.

He had brought in his first Texas well forty years ago, and wild-catted that start into a fortune which had become fabulous. Hodges liked to say, 'I started out as a rough-neck in the fields. I'm still a rough-neck. Any man who crosses Sam Hodges had better believe it.' As President of Peninsular Oil the old man still looked over his operations on the ground.

They sat in the annexe off Lawrence's office, the V.I.P. room usually kept locked. The old man's favourite bourbon and branch water had been put out on the antique brass table. He had listened without a word to Max Morrow's long summing up, chin on his chest, his big fists in his lap, as though he might be napping.

Morrow finished and topped up his drink. He took the glass and sat back.

'I know it sounds wild, Sam. But wilder things have happened.'

The old man lifted his head.

'If one of 'em nationalizes, even two of 'em, maybe we could wring their necks. This other thing, I don't know.' He squinted at Morrow. 'You really think the A-rabs could bring off that kind of operation?'

'If they're going to get Russian help, Sam, I don't see what's to stop it.'

'So we starve 'em out. Like we did in 'fifty-one in I-ran.'

Morrow said, 'It's not the same picture. When Anglo-Iranian got their judgement in the International Court upholding their agreement, it gave them the clout to sue anybody who bought or sold the nationalized oil. Iran had an established and powerful middle class and that three year lock-out squeezed them dry. In Libya, Kuwait, the Gulf, there's no vocal group to pressure the governments. And they've got the money, Sam. They could hold out a lot longer than we could, no matter what order The Hague handed down. There's enough oil money in Kuwait to roof over the whole goddamn place and air-condition it.'

The old man lowered his voice, against all the years that had passed, the security of the room they sat in, the shared and secret knowledge, as though it mattered still.

Almost whispering he said, 'You guys got rid of Prime Minister Mossadeq. You brought the Shah back from Rome. You set those revolutionaries flat on their asses. Maybe that's what we need here now, boy.'

Morrow looked at his old man whose power at home reached into the White House. In changing times nothing had changed for Sam Hodges.

'Those days have gone, Sam. We can't put back the clock out here. These people don't need us any more. And we can only buck the Russkies so far.'

The old man said, with a sudden vicious swishing of the ice in his glass, 'When we had the bomb, and they didn't, was the time to buck the Commies. We lost our guts back there. Those pinks and liberals . . .'

Because of the need to say something, to establish himself in some small measure, Lawrence asked, 'Isn't it true, Max, that Russian influence in the Arab states is on the decline? I mean the Russians are having to go along with the Arabs, rather than the reverse.'

'You could be right, Character.' Morrow decided that Lawrence should enter the conversation. It could be useful if he made a good impression. He said, 'Give us your view on that.'

Lawrence searched his mind. He had only spoken to be heard. 'I think the reality lies in the religious issue. Gadaffi is a Muslim zealot.' He tried to remember something Morrow had said. 'Back to the Koran. Today Islam, tomorrow the world. That kind of religious fanatic will only truck so far with a state that's officially godless. He's already making serious overtures to the French. In Egypt his influence increases every day. Sadat gets fifty million sterling pounds a year from him. We sometimes forget that none of the Arab states have a domestic communist party. There's great suspicion everywhere about the Russians. In the event of—'

'Young fella,' the old man interrupted, raising his hand, 'there's only one kinda politics. That's money. Money is the power. Let me tell you why the A-rabs are keeping a weather eye on the Commies. After Suez, when the A-rabs put an embargo on oil sales to France and Britain, those countries would have been disrupted had the Commies not stepped up their oil outlets to the West. They turned a nice profit on that. If the A-rabs nationalize and we get another international judgement against 'em, how do the A-rabs know the Commies won't replace their oil again? I know many ways that could be done. The West would be glad to pay 'em four times as much as they're paying for A-rab oil. It costs them that much now for Venezuelan crude. The Japs would pay the Commies any price they ask. They're importing six million barrels a day, every day, out there. The Commies could make enough in a coupla months to finance the next Five Year Plan.'

There was no question of disagreeing with Sam Hodges. Lawrence said, 'I see what you mean, sir. That's very interesting.'

He'd been given his say and now Morrow returned to the issue. 'It would be for your legal department to check out, Sam, or maybe your friends on Capitol Hill, but the risk area here is whether an international court ruling would stand up in these circumstances. Iran was stopped because their production was made up out of Saudi, Iraq and Kuwait. If Arab oil went national I don't know that Europe and Japan could hold out long enough to make a ruling effective.'

Hodges put down his glass. His eyelids rose briefly on very pale blue eyes.

'Maybe, maybe not. One thing's sure, we're not about to sit still for anything like that. When are you going to have this report of yours ready?'

'Tomorrow. In the morning.'

'You get a copy to me. I'll read it on the plane.'

He got up and nodded at Lawrence.

'Goodbye, young fella.'

In the outer office the two waiting men closed about the old man. Freni opened the door.

In the other room, Morrow smiled a little. 'Well?' Lawrence shook his head.

'He's everything I've read about him. He frightens me. What do those two ugly brutes do for him?'

Morrow said, emphasizing it, 'I would think anything he tells them, Character. Anything he might tell them.'

Lawrence felt a momentary chill. 'There's something evil about him.'

'He's no rose, I agree,' Morrow said. And then briskly, 'Right. Let's get to work.'

The copies made of the Tripoli photograph were distributed through the American Embassy. Morrow's Washington office telexed a negative identification after inquiries in the State Department and at CIA headquarters at Langly. After dispatch of his likelihood report, via the diplomatic bag, Max Morrow left for Morocco to negotiate the security of the one and a half million dollars still to be paid on the sale of cash registers and calculating equipment.

Ten days after David Lawrence had sent his request for further details on the man in the middle, his courier arrived with a second photograph and a note on a sheet from a child's exercise book. Morrow returned from Morocco the next morning.

The second photograph was indistinct. The man Morrow believed to be an interpreter was crouched to enter an old model Chevrolet. A tall Arab, in three-quarter profile, with cropped hair and a very thin face, held the door open.

Morrow put down the magnifying glass.

'It's a poor identification. The guy getting in the car could be anyone. All I can make out is his ass.'

Lawrence said, 'It's the same man, Max. I'd recognize him anywhere.'

It seemed an odd thing to say. Morrow narrowed his eyes and tapped the print.

'From this?'

'It's the same man,' Lawrence insisted. 'There's something about his face that you remember. He's – distinctive.'

'Not to me.' Morrow sat back. 'This guy flew out Libyan–Arab Airline on the Rome flight. If he's from Egypt, or maybe Syria, what's he doing flying to Rome? I've got something up my nose about this. There's only one satisfactory way to handle it.'

Freni brought the coffee. She looked very bright and pretty, very liberated in the fashionably short skirt in which she was careful not to stoop, putting down the tray with a little bob like a curtsy. Morrow smiled his thanks and took out the saccharin tablets.

'The next time he shows up in Tripoli, if there is any next time, you get out there. When he flies out, you fly out. Get a seat next to him. There are no reservations on these flights. They give you a seat number as you leave the terminal. If you're next to him there, you'll be next to him on the aircraft. Then, Character, you'll have to do as best you can.'

Lawrence could not account for his breathlessness. The sudden flush that stung his cheeks. In protection he put up his hand and pushed at the blond hair on his forehead. Something in him had leapt in acceptance and then hesitated, as at an exciting prospect cautioned by risks.

'How would I know when he leaves?'

'You wouldn't. There'd be only three or four Libyan–Arab Airline flights out of there each week. You can check that here, on their timetable. You'll have to wait at the airport on each flight until your man turns up. On each flight you make a provisional booking.'

Lawrence asked, rather shakily, 'Do you think my Arabic is good enough?'

'It's a damn sight better than your Russian. You don't have any of that.' Morrow pushed the new photograph over the desk. 'Have more copies made of this. The man at the car door is carrying a briefcase. He could be a member of the talks. Where's your passport?'

'It's in the safe.'

'The Libyan Embassy is out near the Hippodrome, isn't it?'

'Yes. Just off the Rue Ouzai.'

'You get yourself out there. We don't know how long they may take to issue a visa. Tell them you're taking a short holiday. That you're interested in archaeology and want to see Leptis Magna. That ruin has been drawing quite a few tourists.'

The visa application had been unexpectedly simple. The clerk, slow and sleepy, as though roused from bed by the counter bell which had jingled so loudly, found Lawrence a form, his protuberant teeth and nose sniffings adding an effect of stupidity to the slow motion of his movements. If Lawrence would return – in an hour. And then looking to the hard bench against the wall – or if he would prefer to wait. The clerk sniffed, the passport laid on the flat of his hand like some intolerable unimportance.

Lawrence walked for a long time in the unfamiliar streets, the face of the man he could meet, sit alongside in an aircraft, the strong, gentle face which had affected him so strangely, vivid again on his mind. It was as though the other two men in the photograph had dissolved, and this man had enlarged to occupy all their space, to move before him now alive and gently breathing.

Lawrence returned to his surroundings, sought a bar and ordered Arak. When the hour had passed he again entered the desolate room, rang the push bell screwed to the counter. Again, after a delay, the clerk appeared, sniffed and withdrew, to reappear and hand back the passport.

In the Porsche, Lawrence turned the new page. The stamp of purple ink and Arabic script covered all the space. The size and the declamation of it seemed to imply a special significance, as had the scratched arrow on Bellini's photograph. Lawrence put away the passport and pushed the key into the ignition.

CHAPTER FIVE

A NARROW lane backed the terraced houses in Belmont Park, edged by a narrow area officially described on council maps as Green Belt, although the wild grass and weeds that grew there were unbenefited by anything leafy. Behind number seventeen, a powder-blue Hillman imp was parked on the verge, a man and a boy on either side of the bonnet, in companionship with rags and polish. The child frowned in concentration, sleeves rolled on his immature arms, his fine dark hair falling over his eyes. He paused in his efforts and blew a breath. It was hot in the clear sunlight.

'Daddy,' he said, 'when will you be going away again?' He pushed back his hair and waited gravely.

'I don't know, son.'

'But you will be going away again?'

The man stood back to judge his work, dipped the rag in the polish.

'Well, now, that depends on Mr. Kemal, the man I've been working for.'

'It really is super, owning a car, isn't it?' the child said. 'When I'm more grown up, will you teach me to drive it?'

His father rubbed at an offending spot.

'That won't be for some time yet.'

'I wish I was grown up enough now. When did you learn to drive?'

'Oh, a long time ago. I drove a truck at a forestry camp.'

'Was that before you became a translator?'

'That's right.'

Nicholas looked over the bonnet. 'What's up? You falling down on the job?'

'Not really.' The child rubbed his arm. 'My elbow got tired. It feels as though it's rusty.'

'Does it now?' His father smiled at the expression, then leaned on his polishing rag, matching the rueful gravity of the face so much a diminutive of his own. 'A rusty elbow is a very serious thing. There's only one way to cure it.'

'Yes?' The child's face was keen with interest.

'You go like this.' Nicholas rubbed wildly with his cloth. 'You go like this, and this, and this. And you keep it up until the rusty elbow is oiled again.'

The child clicked his tongue.

'Oh, peanuts!' he said.

Nicholas laughed.

'Come on. Let's get the job finished.'

The dictionaries and the pad and the fountain pen were laid out on the table, the old briefcase in its accustomed position beside the chair. But he was unable to work, watching the time, as he had been unable to work at this time every morning since the messenger had first appeared, delivering the brown paper packet which Nicholas would sign for, his heart already bumping, and take from it the booked air ticket, the ten pounds in single notes, the unsigned typed instruction on a yellow page.

The blankness of the summons, beyond discussion or appeal, only Kemal's dark face to bid him from the distance, had become in some way a discomfort, a reduction of free will. Waiting like this each morning for the messenger who could appear, disturbed Nicholas with an uncertainty that disrupted the day. Even his freedom to decline or refuse another journey would be involved in complication. How would he give notice? He knew of no address for Kemal, or for the hushed, walled villa.

Cora stood in the door, her voice a little strained. 'Would you like tea now, Nicholas?'

He said he would, and thought what she means is that it's past the time, there will be no messenger today. He unscrewed his fountain pen, hearing her banging the kettle about in the kitchen. Neither admitted to the other this uneasiness which had entered their lives.

He had made two trips, each of three days, and been paid six hundred pounds. Buying the car had been a great excitement. It was less than two years old. The used car dealers sprayed their upholstery with something that smelled of new leather, he had read that in a newspaper, and wound back the mileage indicators, but the car could almost pass as new, the model had not changed.

The day after each return, at the same time in the morning, a Post Office messenger had arrived with a brown paper package, got his receipt and ridden away. Each payment had been cash, sixty five-pound notes. It appeared so much more than figures on a cheque. Cora had caught her breath at the sight of it. For a long time they had let it lay on the table, discussing how it might be spent.

Cora put the pottery mug at his elbow.

'I'm going to the shops,' she said. 'If we lunch early we can have a full afternoon in the country. It's such a beautiful day. Bobby won't disturb you. I'll take him with me.'

She had been full of these small considerations. On the priest's last visit, before she had hurried him out to see the car, she had asked, 'You don't mind, do you?' when Nicholas had to take his work upstairs.

Cora had been quite startled by the insecurity that had come upon her when Nicholas first went away, the emptiness that seemed everywhere in the house. She had never considered such a thing and felt it first as a resentment for which Nicholas was somehow to blame. In bed in the dark after the messenger had arrived for the second time, and Nicholas had gone, resentment had failed to support her. She had felt painfully, achingly alone. In all the other years of their marriage Nicholas had never been away overnight. She wondered what he might be doing in that foreign place which she had difficulty trying to picture, and felt a sudden jealousy that he might be enjoying himself. She didn't even know when to expect him back and frowned, resenting that. But she could not sleep and lay on her side of the bed, remembering.

Hilda Swan had been her schoolfriend. When Hilda had announced, taking tea with her mother in the house reordered for paying guests, that she was leaving home to attend a business college in London, Cora's mother had been thoughtful. After Hilda had left she had asked quite bluntly if Cora would like to go with her friend. She could afford a small allowance, she said.

At first it had been an adventure. They had taken a bedsitter in a basement at Notting Hill Gate. It had its own entrance off the street, through a cubby of a kitchen, and a shared bathroom behind it with an old gas heater which was for ever exploding, and a mouldering velvet chair which had once been grand.

Hilda had quickly made boyfriends and settled to enjoying herself. 'You're only young once,' she used to tell Cora. 'I'm going to have a bit of fun while I can.' But Cora had been unable to have that kind of fun, she was awkward, and her religion wouldn't let her. More and more frequently, if she had been out and let herself in with a key, Hilda and one of her boyfriends would spring up rumpled off the settee or the bed, Hilda flushed, straightening her clothes, cold and unfriendly, the boyfriend being sheepish. Cora had had to learn to knock. On other evenings her room-mate would ask if she couldn't have the place to herself, she was entertaining someone to dinner. Cora would sit in a cinema, seething.

Nicholas taught in the language school that shared premises with the business college. He often ate in the same Wimpy Bar. Hilda, of course, knew him slightly. She seemed to know all the young men in the building. 'Look,' she had said, 'I know you disapprove of me, love. What I do doesn't hurt anyone. They have their bit of fun, and I have mine. You don't ever get taken anywhere. You might as well be at home with your mum. Let's make up a foursome. And, you know, if the man fancies you, if he wants to have a bit of fun, relax, as they say, and enjoy it. For heaven's sake, you're a big girl now. It has to happen some day.'

Cora's skin had positively burned. Her thoughts had darted about in such disorder that she had scarcely been able to answer. At last, stiffly, she had said, 'It hasn't been successful on other occasions. You all made that clear enough.'

Hilda had widened her handsome eyes. 'That,' she said, with exasperation, 'is because Miss Goodie is too stuck-up to enjoy herself.'

Hilda had arranged the party. She had a boyfriend now who dealt in antiques. He owned a sports car and dressed carefully. 'He's ever so sophisticated,' Hilda had said. Nicholas had been invited for Cora. The sophisticated boyfriend brought wine and vodka, Hilda had begun drinking now. Cora did not notice how often he topped up her glass, or the signals between he and Hilda. She felt quite transported, wonderfully at ease, laughing and joking. In the kitchen, when she could, Hilda would whisper to her, 'Isn't he handsome? He fancies you, there's no doubt of that,' and later, 'Remember now, if he wants to have a bit of fun don't be stuck-up about it.'

All Cora's erotic suppressions, the long teasings of Hilda rumpled, Hilda flushed, Hilda's whispering in the kitchen, smeared lipstick and concealed touches, her own increasing tumults and yearnings, culminated in an excitement she could hardly bear. She was quite tipsy. Nothing seemed real, except the heat that beat through her. When Hilda and her boyfriend excused themselves, Hilda switched off the main light because, she said, the room looked prettier that way, Cora had heard the door bang behind them as though it were a signal. She had blinked to focus the fact she knew quite well, now looking uncertainly at her. Then she had gone to Nicholas, put herself against him. She had looked up, not seeing his shock, and said, her voice thick, 'I want to have a bit of fun . . .' For an instant she had to unjumble her thoughts, frowning. Suddenly she felt him against her. 'I want you to do it to me . . please? Nicholas? Now?'

She had counted it a judgement that she fell pregnant. That she had to marry a stranger for it. He had been tender with her, never doubting his responsibility. It was a judgement that she had to marry this man who was not even English, whose strange life, when she learned of it, had so offended and upset her that she had shut her ears against it and put it out of her mind. She had counted it a judgement that she should be ill and incapable in the small flat Nicholas had taken, giving up his teaching job to work as a translator to be at home and give her care. And it had been a judgement and a relief when that pregnancy aborted in the seventh month.

Alone in the bed which they had shared since Bobby was little, Cora missed her husband, his patience, his love and his strength and the comfort of his body beside her. All that other was so long ago that it might not have happened. She began to think of how they would use the money. There could be other business meetings abroad. Before Cora fell asleep she had forgotten everything else.

Nicholas drove home in the leavings of day, the abundant green of the forest they had rambled already darkening into sleep. Worn out by the walk and his shouted discoveries, the little boy in the back had closed his eyes.

Nicholas asked, 'Would you like me to put on the heater?'

'It has got chilly,' Cora said.

The fan buzzed importantly. The car began to fill with warm, comforting air. Nicholas had not told Cora that he had interpreted in the Russian Embassy. That would have upset her. She had asked few questions, mostly about the Arabs and the buildings, sufficiently impressed that Nicholas had been lodged in a company house, that the meetings had dealt with an international project for water conservation. The importance of that had pleased her. In the rear-view mirror he saw his son asleep, his cheek on the cushion, and smiled. Cora noticed.

'What's amusing you?'

He nodded at the mirror.

'Bobby. He's sound asleep.'

She looked over her shoulder.

'He has tired himself out.'

Nicholas said, 'Cora, there's something I've been thinking about.'

She gave him all her attention.

'You know, I might be able to get a post as an interpreter. With one of the big business houses, or perhaps something to do with government.'

Kapitsa had put the thought in his head with his talk about returning to Russia.

'Government!' Cora said. 'But Nicholas, what a wonderful idea.'

'I'll ask Wilson at the publishing house about it. He could probably advise me.'

Cora said, 'Do you know something?'

'What?'

'You've changed in some way, Nicholas. We both have.'

And then with surprising, deliberate humour, 'That's what happens when your husband gets off by himself abroad.'

The anodyne of routine which can encompass a life in obligations so minute that looking back there can seem nothing to account for its passage, a few events of tragedy or joy the only landmarks for all the years, had again begun to settle on Nicholas when the Post Office messenger rang, handing over the package and the chit to be signed.

Cora had heard the bell while making the beds, and came quickly down the wooden stairs, the uneven expression in her eyes.

'Is it . . .' she began.

Nicholas opened the envelope.

'Yes,' he said and spilled the contents on to the table.

Cora waited, unable to fix her feelings.

'When do they want you?'

'Tomorrow,' he said. 'The afternoon flight,' taking leave in his mind, already in that other country where Kemal's hot eyes would grip him, in the rooms where the fat Arab with his wheezed, foul breath now knocked before he entered.

'Tomorrow,' Cora felt full of being alone. 'Does he say for how long?'

Nicholas shook his head.

'No. Just the usual.'

Cora said, with the old resentment, 'He might at least have the consideration to say how long you'll be away. He just sends these things and expects you to jump. As though he's God or something. I never liked that man's look.'

She was distraught, her eyes stretched and strained, spots of passion on her cheeks.

'Do you want me not to go?' Nicholas asked and was prepared to accept her answer, to abide by that as the decision he half wanted to make for himself.

'I never said that. It's so good to have the money. It's just the way they do things. Making a mystery of everything as though there's something dishonest about it. I don't like that kind of foreigner.'

But she still seemed uncertain to him.

'If you don't want me to go, I won't,' he said. 'After all, I might have been away, or on an urgent job, or ill,' and thought, why should I make these excuses?

More normally, Cora said, 'Of course you must go. We can't turn down all that money. You'd have to work for months at translating to earn what you get from Kemal. It's just that, I don't know, it seems to get me worked up.'

That night, sitting on the bed to say goodnight to his son, to see him tucked in and turn out the light. Nicholas said, 'I'm going away again. Just for a few days. I got a letter this morning.'

'Oh,' the child twisted, 'must you?'

'Well, now, where do you think we got the money to buy the car? I get well paid for going away.'

The child thought about it.

'It really is super having the car. I just wish—'

'What do you wish?'

'That you could earn the money without going away.'

'Some fathers have to go away all the time.'

'You're not some father,' the child said. 'I don't care about them. You're *my* father.'

85

Nicholas tousled his head.

'That's right. We'll say goodbye in the morning.'

The child did not answer.

'Sleep tight.'

Nicholas rose and switched out the light. Later, in his own bed, Cora moved towards him, perfumed and soft.

'Nicholas?'

'Yes?'

'Would you like to have me?'

'Yes.'

'I want you to,' she whispered.

The aircraft landed in teeming rain, letting down through greasy clouds that choked the windows. Nicholas had waited at the bookstand. There had been no Kemal. The driver met him and drove dangerously to the house through an obliterated landscape, muttering at the stickings of the windscreen wipers, craning out of the window, his hair and face running with rain that whipped back until Nicholas had to move across the seat.

He did not see Kemal until the next morning, uncomfortably tense, taking from his leather envelope another collection of yellow sheets for Nicholas to translate from the Russian. Another mish-mash, pages and pages of it, like speech heard through blankets, or a record played at the wrong speed.

It was such a useless labour, a trial and irritation, pinned by Kemal, his long-fingered hands tapping the table, his thin shoulders hunched high to his savage face, wheedling and insisting that some lines among so many must make sense. It was absurd to be brought so far and paid so much to be presented with a childish conundrum. 'Arabs ... Green ... Area Red ... America ...' always the same words, made offensive by repetition, emerging like flashes of coherence in a delirium. It was intolerable that Kemal should press him so, jaw muscles clenched into cords, his eyes burning, about this mish-mash which he would not explain.

'It is in the Russian language, Brother. Try to make something of it.'

And again Nicholas tried, that day until evening, searching in the piled pages to make a collection of words unconnected in meaning, like the gleanings of an idiot's pockets. He rang the bell to order coffee and took satisfaction in the fat Arab's knock, wondering again where the man waited, behind which door across the passage, to answer these biddings so promptly.

In the rain which continued to fall, only broken by short periods in which spilling from a pipe was loudly heard, Nicholas paced the rooms made glum and ugly by the cheerless grey light.

He had not permitted himself introspection about his strange employment, or the way it had come to him. He had been too absorbed in adapting to the events, to the foreignness of every-thing, to this house, Kemal, the shock of the Russian Embassy, the silent manifestations of the fat Arab. He had not only had the present to contend with but the awakened ghosts of his past to lay, the nightmare he had strenuously put behind him. Now, in the gloom of the rain-blocked windows, the offence of the yellow pages had become intolerable. Because he could make no sense of it, not only of the words but of these exercises, there must be a meaning to it. Kemal's refusal to explain, his anxiety and frustration, must conceal another meaning. Nicholas felt it as an apprehension, as one can feel startled from sleep by foot-steps. Even the money cautioned him now. It was too much, for too little. He thought back to his first uneasiness, Kemal pos-sessed of his name and address which he did not use on the box-numbered advertisements. And the instruction that for business reasons these journeys must not be discussed.

After his first walk in the Souk he had not seen the cheerful Bashir Masoud again. He had been guided, or guarded, by an older, silent man, refusing conversation, sitting at another table in the Italian restaurant to drink coffee and smoke the cigarettes which had stained his teeth and fingers yellow, always seeming to watch him without once meeting his eyes.

The fat Arab's heavy knock, two thumps, interrupted Nicholas in his pacing. The door opened, Kemal entered. The formal greetings were exchanged.

'Well, Brother? The work, did it go well?'

'It did not go well,' Nicholas said. 'I do not like this work, Brother.'

He took the sheets on which he had listed the words in columns and handed them to Kemal.

Sitting at the table, Kemal brooded over the pages, went through them a second time and cursed. His eyes considered Nicholas with a distance almost hostile.

'Is this the best you could do, Brother?'

'It is all that I could do. It is a waste of time. A stupid puzzle without meaning.'

87

Kemal began to jig his leg, squeaking the chair, staring at the rain-shrouded window.

Nicholas said, 'I would like the car this evening, Brother, to take my food in the city.'

'It is the time of the rains. You would be more comfortable in your own house.'

Nicholas felt a hot flare light in him, for this day, his thoughts, the weariness of Kemal's unrelenting pressure which scraped his nerves.

'Nevertheless, that is my wish. I am much shut up in this house of mine, Brother.'

Kemal breathed loudly, straining as though he were leashed.

'Shut up? Why say that, Brother? What thoughts have entered your mind?'

Something violent and dangerous had intruded between them, something irrational, as so much now appeared irrational. Kemal's eyes were clamped on him.

'What has entered your mind? Something there, perhaps, in the Russian language?'

The flare that had lit in Nicholas had hardened into purpose, as in one accepting challenge. It withered now on this absurdity. He turned away in negation.

'In that nonsense? What could there be in that nonsense to enter anyone's mind?'

Kemal began to loosen. Slowly, he arranged the yellow pages, tapping them on the table.

'I will send the car, Brother.'

Alone again, waiting, Nicholas washed and changed. He had bought a lightweight suit and considered ruefully that he would get little pleasure from it now. And suddenly he did not want ever again to see these rooms, to be subjected to Kemal or to the idiotic translating exercises. He did not want to enter again the grim, guarded gates of the Embassy which was not, and could not be, his soil. Or suffer the tolerance of the Comrade Chairman and Kapitsa's suggestions about returning home. He had a home. He was happier in it than he had ever been. He wanted to get back to it, and stay there. He had enjoyed his luck and it had truly changed many things. But he would not return here where too much was unexplained. He would spend no more mornings in an uneasy house waiting for the summonses of the Post Office messenger. He had reached his decision and felt boyishly light and hopeful. From now on he would make his own luck, for his wife and his son and all the years yet to be lived.

There had been little to do, one short meeting in the Embassy which he had interpreted without interest, transposing the words as one might exchange inanimate objects, only wanting to be done with it all and away, where neither the past nor this present could claim him. On the third day he departed, as he had arrived, in drumming torrents that extinguished all land-marks, hardly anything visible except the pitted neck of the driver and the khaki shoulders of his uniform. He had not told Kemal that he would not come to Tripoli again. He just wanted to go without bother, in a riddance which he had made final. The rain ceased. The car turned into the dingy airport.

Nicholas sat in a grubby upholstered chair in the hangar which had been smartened into a reception hall and then al-lowed to grow shabby again. He was fearful that his flight might be cancelled, that he would have to return to that house and those rooms which he had rejected for ever. He waited, mindless to all about him except this need to will the weather, to fix the lifted clouds long enough to escape.

The crackling, spluttering system announced the flight, in Arabic and then in English. The sun shafted theatrical beams through the clouds. Nicholas stood up and looked about him for the last time.

The ground hostess checked her seating plan, took a number from its slot and stuck it to his boarding card. The passengers queued at the door then walked towards the brown and gold Caravelle, avoiding the water that pooled in depressions. Nicholas climbed the gangway, found his seat, buckled the safety belt and turned his head to the window. The sun broke more clearly through the clouds, beating on the metal of the fuselage, thickening the air in the cabin. Water lay everywhere on the perimeters of the airfield, glistening among the palm trees and farm houses. It had been water and the need to conserve it that had first brought him here. Nicholas smiled a little at the thought and wished Kemal well. In Area Red . . . in Area Green . . . There is much to be reclaimed, Brother.

The aircraft taxied out and pointed into the wind. A brown and gold vehicle hauling a trailer scurried across the grass, water squirting from its wheels. The aircraft settled and shook, the engines roaring and whining with the fury that would pitch it into the sky. The palm trees and houses and minarets raced, blurred and fell away. Cloud darkened the window. Then all became blue and brilliant.

'Can I get you anything, sir?'

The hostess picked her way along the aisle, neat, attractive, her professional smile practised and convincing. Nicholas nodded at the young man seated next to him and excused himself to lean across.

'Have you any English newspapers?'

'We have the *Daily Express*, sir. Would you care to order from the bar?'

'No, thank you.' Nicholas sat back.

'Would you care to order from the bar, sir?' she asked the other passenger.

'I'd like a scotch whisky,' David Lawrence said. He readjusted his seat and closed his eyes.

He needed to close his eyes, for concealment. There was too much pelting in his mind – the first law, Character, is take nothing for granted – they had not conceived of this possibility. It was outside the frame of reference, unacceptable to the hypothesis Morrow had schemed. The man was neither Russian nor Arab. He was English, flying direct to London. The hostess delivered the newspaper, he heard the man's voice thank her. Lawrence had not had time to observe him at the airport, rushing to confirm his booking after the first certain recognition, rushing again to the departure lounge, pushing to be near him. Could Bellini have made a mistake? Identified the wrong man? Lawrence dismissed the doubt. The second photograph eliminated the chance of error.

'Whisky, sir?'

Lawrence sat up.

'Thank you.'

'Ice and water?'

'Just the ice.'

He unbuttoned the tray, pulled it down over his knees. The steward put two lumps of ice in the plastic glass, took a whisky miniature from the trolley. Lawrence broke the seal and half filled the glass. He glanced covertly at this man who had so occupied his thoughts. The sharply-cut profile, the warm skin of his face, even the hands holding the open newspaper startled Lawrence with familiarity, an unreasonable sympathy and attraction. His fine, dark hair fell over his temples exactly as it had done in the photograph. Lawrence opened his cigarette-case and turned in his seat, smiling.

'Would you care to join me?'

Nicholas shook his head.

'I don't smoke. But thank you.'

He had not turned away. Lawrence said quickly, 'We were lucky to get off. Does it often rain like that?'

The young man seemed eager to talk, his smile frank and friendly. Constraint still impressed itself on Nicholas, even now that he was free. He lowered the newspaper, to chat and forget that other.

'I really don't know. This is my first experience of the rains.'

Lawrence said, 'I wish the travel agency had advised me about it. I stopped off to see Leptis Magna, and didn't get past the hotel.'

'Leptis Magna?'

'The Roman ruins. It was a great city at the time of Septimus Severus. I know all about it.' He made a wry face. 'From the tourist brochures, that is.'

'I see.' Nicholas smiled agreeably. 'You must have been disappointed.'

'I was rather. The hotel was another disappointment. Only coffee and cake in the bar. The night club turned into a TV room. How they have the nerve to call it The Mansions, I don't know. Have you ever stayed there?'

'No.' Nicholas shook his head. 'I was lodging privately,' and thought how little he had seen or known, a walk in the Souk, a drive through the streets, the Italian restaurant which had once been gay.

The hostess and steward smiled their way past, being attentive. The aircraft was two thirds empty, the dotted heads settled to reading or rest, voices occasionally heard, raised to laugh or report from a window.

'If you were lodged privately, you can consider yourself lucky. The only decent meal I had was in an Italian restaurant off the Souk.'

'The one on the corner?'

'Yes. Bellini's. Do you use it?'

'I don't know it by that name, but I sometimes have dinner there. Before the revolution it was a great meeting place.'

'You knew it then?'

'No, I was told about it.'

91

'You must know the city well.'

'Not at all. You seem to know more about it than I do. I'd not heard of Leptis Magna, or seen the Mansion Hotel.'

Lawrence marked the information. It would interest Morrow. He sought for a direct question, one natural to the conversation.

'Pressure of business, I suppose?' and topped up his glass, draining the miniature to make it unimportant.

Nicholas felt a reluctance to answer.

'Yes,' he said, and then, 'I suppose that would be it.'

Lawrence gathered all his charm, to indicate understanding, to share the resignation that business pressures imply. He lifted his glass and said confidentially, 'I know how it is. I'm in business myself. What's your line, may I ask?'

The question was simple, frankly put, a young American exchanging information to reduce the tedium of travel, something to share in these random intimacies, lofted high above the earth, or at a ship's dining table, or seated in a train on long journeys. Life stories, family affairs, surgical operations, that would never be discussed elsewhere between strangers, offered as though by compulsion between travellers who never meet again. But Nicholas did not want to answer this question that could evoke too much.

He said, 'I do language translations,' and shuffled the newspaper.

'That's clever of you. I'm a bit of a dud at languages.' And then, boyish and impulsive, putting out his hand, 'Let me introduce myself. David Lawrence.'

Withdrawn, Nicholas met the clear blue eyes, the handsome face and charming smile, and had to answer this warmth, the optimism and innocence of it.

'Nicholas Arden. Pleased to meet you,' and gently returned to the protection of the *Daily Express*.

Lawrence fumbled the airline magazine from the carrier net under the tray, opened it and propped it up. Dimly, he registered the pages, but too much turmoiled in him. When Nicholas had accepted his hand in his own, to grip it in introduction, it had seemed to Lawrence to squeeze at everything in him. He could still feel that other hand on his, the way it had raced his heart. He swallowed at the desolation filling his throat, the loneliness he had known as a child and afterwards, that still had the power to unexpectedly possess him.

92

'The same again, sir?'

Lawrence looked up and nodded. The steward dropped ice cubes into the glass, put the small bottle beside it, trundled the trolley away.

It had not happened like this since Princeton, and now he understood why he had been drawn to the photograph of this man, the resemblance clear now in the flesh. He had made a fool and an exhibition of himself then, a ruin which he could only escape by escaping everything and everyone, to forget it, or forgive himself for the wild shocking minutes in which he had lost all discretion. Lawrence turned his head and shut his eyes. He felt a great peace and comfort now, so close that he could hear the other's breathing, the intimate movements of his body in the seat, glimpsing the face so like and unlike the room-mate he had loved.

Nicholas Arden. He did language translations. The excitement which should have been all his concern now brushed him, pushing farther away the treacherous rush of feeling. If a conspiracy was being raised in the oil states, Nicholas Arden could be playing a part. But how could an Englishman fit that theory? Take nothing for granted.

Lawrence, startled with premonition, turned quickly to the other man as though he might find in his face some confirmation. Could Nicholas Arden be a Russian, one who spoke Arabic and English?

'Would you care for the newspaper?'

Lawrence accepted, moved again by this face, the dark eyes and gentle gravity, avoiding any touch, hardening to the purpose that had brought him there.

'Thank you.'

There, on the front page, a photograph across the middle columns answered his needs like a gift. He had learned to be cunning, to dissemble and confuse. He made his voice innocent and helpless.

'The Russian leaders are touring again. What names! I never know how to pronounce them.'

He ran a finger slowly over the caption, pointing attention to the words. Nicholas pronounced them for him, unthinking, his voice suddenly changed. Lawrence said, 'Stalin. That was simple enough. Although it wasn't his real name was it?'

'No.' Nicholas said. 'His real name was Joseph Vissarionovich Dzhugashvili. It is Georgian.'

93

'Have you been to Russia?'

'I was born there.'

The question had been so unexpected that Nicholas heard himself answer with shock. It had been like a game that Bobby brought back from school – Daddy, I will say a word and you answer with the first word that comes into your head. You mustn't think. He had not thought, and now there was nothing to retrieve, only to wait on this young man's interest, the further questions and his need to refuse them.

Lawrence turned the folded newspaper, the chill of discovery paling his skin. He had to fill this ominous silence, feeling almost guilty, like a man who puts one coin in a poker machine and wins the jackpot prize.

'The Common Market,' he said, as though he had not heard Nicholas's answer, his own question having been asked absently and over other demanding thoughts, 'that seems to be the one problem we Americans don't have these days.'

'Would you care for tea or coffee, sir?'

'Coffee, thank you,' Lawrence said, smiling and turning the page.

'Would you care for tea or coffee, sir?' the little hostess asked Nicholas.

'Tea.'

'Milk and sugar, sir?'

'Yes, please.'

'Black or white, sir?' she asked Lawrence.

'Black.'

They waited, oddly concentrated, while she prepared the cups on the trolley, as people do during service, waiting in temporary suspension until other things can be resumed. Lawrence tried to still on his face any evidence there of the triumph running in him. Max Morrow had said it would be up to him. He had brought it off. He had to congratulate himself for it. But he felt disturbed at this discovery and the implications of it. It could make a competitor or an enemy of this man towards whom he felt so differently. It was as though he had betrayed a friend. What would Max make of it? He played his hands to win. Anyone who got in the way of his winning had to be disarmed or destroyed. Lawrence hardly touched the coffee. Again he closed his eyes, pretending sleep, and wishing that things could be otherwise.

'This is the captain speaking. We're now over—'

94

Nicholas sipped the tasteless tea, already growing cold, and watched for the landmark from his window. He estimated on his wrist watch the time that still had to be passed until all of this was over. He had not sent a cable. Kemal never announced until the day of his departure which flight he would be booked on. His homecomings had all been surprises. Bobby would be in bed, emptied of everything except his innocence, as even the most corrupt seem to be in the abnegation of sleep. It would not be too late to wake him, a few minutes to say that he was home. Nicholas moved his cup to still its chattering on the saucer, so as not to disturb the young man beside him who looked so very young now in his own sleep. He made himself comfortable, the buzzing and tremor of the aircraft's flight an inducement to doze time away.

They walked out of the terminal together, the doors leading to the taxi rank magically hissing open on approach. The evening was hazed and cool, the lights of the cars burning yellow.

Lawrence said, 'Perhaps I could drop you off.'

'I doubt if we're going in the same direction.' Nicholas was amused again at this friendliness, so anxious to offer itself. 'I live in the suburbs.'

'Oh,' Lawrence sounded disappointed. He put out his hand. 'It's been a pleasure to travel with you.'

'Goodbye, and good luck.'

The rank attendant asked, 'Where to, sir?' Nicholas waited.

'Go ahead,' Lawrence offered, 'I'm in no hurry.'

'Are you sure?'

'Yes. Do go ahead.'

'Belmont Park,' Nicholas said, '—off the Heath.'

The attendant led the way to a cab.

'One for the northwest,' he told the driver. Lawrence watched the cab pull out, as though he were losing something, moved again by the clasp of hands.

'Where to for you, sir?'

'Sorry?'

'Where are you going?'

'To town. I have to find an hotel.'

The attendant put his head in a cab window, lowered his voice, 'Got a Yank for yer. He wants ter book an hotel.'

'Book one? I'll sell him one,' the driver said, starting the engine.

The call came through in the early morning, bolting Lawrence upright from sleep. He did not know where he was and struggled to remember, quite lost, until the telephone rang again and then ceased, waiting on his attention. Fumbling, he found the switch of the bedside lamp, reached for the receiver.

'We have your call to Beirut, sir.'

Lawrence thanked the voice and held on, hearing the exchanges completing the link, pushing back the covers to sit on the bed.

'Hello?'

'Max?'

'Is that you, Character?'

'Yes.'

'Where are you?'

'London. The Mayfair Hotel.'

'Uh – huh. What do you know?'

No surprise that he should be in London. No confusion from Morrow's own sleep, his voice clear and certain.

'I met our man. He's English, Max. Or at least he lives in London.'

'He's English?'

'He carries an English passport. But I've got something else for you.'

Lawrence wanted to make an effect.

'He was born in Russia.'

He could almost hear Morrow thinking, rearranging his mind to this information as he would at a surprising move made in a chess game.

'You're sure he carries a British passport? Did you see it?'

'Yes. I saw it at Immigration.'

'You're sure he was born in Russia?'

'Yes. I questioned him.'

'What else have you got?'

'He does translating work. I've got his name. It's Nicholas Arden. He lives in a suburb called Belmont Park, which is off some Heath or other.'

'Anything on what he was doing out there?'

'I think he said he was on business.'

The silence became so extended that Lawrence thought he had lost connection.

'Hello? Are you there?'

'Yeah. I'm thinking. I can't figure what we've got here.'

After a further silence Lawrence asked, 'What do you want me to do?'

'Sit tight. What's your telephone number?'

Lawrence checked the service card on the bedside table and told him. Morrow repeated the number.

'Have I got that right?'

'That's right.'

'I'm going to book a call to you now, for 1800 hours tomorrow. Be there to take it.'

'Check,' Lawrence said.

'You did a great job, Character. You got everything but his wallet.'

'Thanks. What do you make of it, Max?'

'I don't know. But if he's an alien, carrying a British passport, I do know a way to squeeze him. You got a good room?'

'Yes. It's fine.'

'Enjoy yourself. Stand by tomorrow evening.'

'That's it?'

'That's it. Goodnight, Character.'

The line deadened. Lawrence replaced the receiver. He had taken a pill to get to sleep and was too heavy with it to think. The telephone made its discreet jingle.

'Have you completed your call, sir?'

'Yes. Thank you.'

'Goodnight, sir.'

'Goodnight,' Lawrence said, and put out the light.

CHAPTER SIX

THE warm glory of the late summer days continued to bless the city. It was almost hot, walking. Lawrence had last been in England as a boy, crossing on the *Queen Mary* with his mother, at the invitation of a great-aunt who had married into a good family. He remembered the big house in the Cotswolds and the elderly, silent gamekeeper, lumped with satchels and pockets, a gun under his arm, whom he had followed through forests full of mystery, so dense it seemed always twilight.

They had come up to London for the theatre and gatherings of distant relatives to whom he would be presented, fussed over by the women, 'My dear, he looks like a young Rupert Brooke,' or introduced to a variety of men who would say, 'So this is David. How d'you do? Enjoying your visit I hope,' and return to their drinks and conversations. They had stayed then in what his great-aunt called the Town House, a narrow, dark and musty-smelling building on a wing of St. James's Square, which Lawrence could not identify now, only the dark stones of that area familiar, office plates patched at the entrances and neon lighting seen through the windows.

He was content to be solitary, had become practised at it, and enjoyed these contrasts to his accustomed surroundings, a homesickness that suddenly stirred him with nostalgia implicit in all that he found familiar. He walked in the park, between the sprawling of young office workers eating in the sunshine. Swans and ducks paddled in the pond, upending themselves to forage. It was all so languid and tranquil, so distant from the concerns of political conspiracies, the calculations of Max Morrow, the power manipulations of old men like Sam Hodges, lumbering the world with his thugs.

Lawrence found a deck chair and watched the other strollers in the park, prams being wheeled and dogs walked, young couples in jeans carrying their sandals, or lying face to face. All that other seemed outrageously unreal. Bellini's photographs, the manoeuvrings and bribings of influence, the couriers with their commercial espionage. It had seemed an unusual excitement, clandestine and clever, even romantic, appealing to the elitist in him. But now he was wearied of it, as another abnormality in his life, a further separation that further confirmed his isolation.

He feared for Nicholas Arden, unable now to be pleased at his own cleverness, and he feared that evening's telephone call in which he could learn from Morrow how he would squeeze this man. Lawrence got up and began to walk again, forgetting to eat, seeing and not seeing, in glimpses from a personal limbo.

In the terraced house at Belmont Park, sun entered the sitting room from the garden behind the house. Cora cleared away the dishes and brought tea in pottery mugs.

'Don't forget to answer Wilson's telephone call.'

'I won't. It's too early yet. He takes a long lunch.'

'And Nicholas, do ask him about that other matter.'

He had slept late and was still drowsy with peace.

'What other matter?'

'You know, about trying for a post as an interpreter. Perhaps with government.'

'I won't do that on the telephone. I'll do it when I see Wilson.'

Cora said, 'I suppose it's silly, but I'm glad that you've finished with that other thing. It has been, I don't know, upsetting. It all gave me a queer feeling, as though there was something wrong.'

She put back her hair with a gesture like a girl. 'I don't mean that I'm not proud that you could earn all that money. It's just, I don't know, perhaps I'm no good at being by myself.' She made a puzzled face. 'Everything seemed to get so disorganized. I had to remind myself to do the shopping.'

She had always been dependent. She had never had a reason of her own. Nicholas drank his tea, touched with sadness for all he understood, and all that she would never understand.

'Would you like me to drive you to the shops this afternoon?'

'That would be a help. I'm out of almost everything. Did I tell you that Bobby cleaned out the car while you were away? He was out there for ages with a brush and pan.'

'I know,' Nicholas smiled. 'He told me last night.'

'I'll wash up and then we can go. The supermarket has specials today.'

Nicholas unfolded his newspaper, hearing Cora clattering in the kitchen. He was content. In some way everything had changed for the better.

Lawrence had turned up the room heat and lay on the bed in a robe, the radio playing softly. He had read for a while and then napped after his walk, waiting on Max Morrow's telephone call. It had already darkened when it came, the grey that had pressed on the windows deepening as he watched, like a succession of lights being extinguished or the peaceful departure of a life.

'Mr. Lawrence?'

'Speaking.'

'Are you expecting a call from Beirut, sir?'

'I am.'

'The operator has left a message for you, sir. Your party will call again at the same time tomorrow.'

All the day had been time passed for this. The inevitable disappointment of a failed long-distance call began to fill him.

'Is there trouble with the line?'

'No, sir. The line was clear. Your party will call again tomorrow.'

It was useless to hang on like this as though it might alter something.

'I see,' Lawrence said, 'the same time tomorrow. Thank you.'

He replaced the receiver, got up and poured himself a whisky from the bottle ordered from room service. The ice in the bucket had begun to melt. He took out the larger pieces with his fingers. What was Max Morrow doing? The postponement of the call seemed ominous. The signal of some preparation too weighty to be easily arranged. Arden's face returned to haunt him, he shivered again at the thought of his hand clasp. What were they planning to do to him? He did not want that man hurt.

'There's only one law in life, Character, whatever a man is about. You win or you lose. There's no percentage in losing.'

He had accepted so many instructions, storing them away like treasures, trying to model himself on them. Morrow would destroy Nicholas Arden without an instant's compunction, or a succession of Nicholas Ardens, if they stood between him and the winning of anything he had undertaken. There's no percentage in losing. Morrow had never lost in his life. That was his pride and his reputation. He had fashoned himself like a shining blade. Men like Sam Hodges opened their purses to him, to have him on their side.

Lawrence stopped at this realization, knuckles tight on the glass. Max Morrow, his mentor, was a mercenary. Had he become a mercenary, too? Must that now be added to all the other?

Another day of Indian summer spread its balm, populating the pavements, seeming to slow the great city's traffic with lingering enjoyment. Tourists emerged to wander, feeding the pigeons in Trafalgar Square, swelling the numbers outside Buckingham Palace. Cab drivers drowsed at their ranks and forgot to count their losses.

There was no reason for Nicholas to notice the Mini parked near the house, returning with the morning papers, opening the door with the key because Cora had gone to the hairdresser. He had almost let himself in when a man hurried from the car, coughing to draw attention.

'Mr. Arden? Mr. Nicholas Arden?'

Nicholas turned in surprise.

'Yes?'

The man was dressed neatly, a dark felt hat with a rolled brim set low on his forehead. His moustache had begun to grey. The collar of his white shirt was starched. He had the spruced, regimented air of some vague career in the services.

'I wonder if I might have a word with you, sir?'

Nicholas responded slowly. There was something about the man's use of the 'Sir' which disturbed him, making procedure of it, something authoritative in the manner of his waiting.

'Yes,' he said, 'what is it?' and felt the clumsiness of the words.

'A routine matter. It won't take much of your time.' The man smiled ingratiatingly and gestured at the half-open door. 'If we could step inside for a few minutes . . .'

In the sitting-room he took off his hat and laid it on a chair. The band had made a purple indent on his forehead, cocked over the right eye like a practical joke.

'Allow me to introduce myself. Sub-Inspector Cooper, Department of Immigration.' He looked about. 'Alone in the house, sir?'

The insecurity of every displaced person, however long forgotten, knocked at Nicholas.

'Yes. My wife is out,' he said, and strengthened his voice. 'What can I do for you, Inspector?'

'Oh, it's nothing to be alarmed about. You're a naturalized citizen, Mr. Arden. All rights and privileges, what? A department of the Ministry has made an inquiry. Probably some botch up in records. One of the chiefs would like to have a chat with you. Outside my division, can't help you there. However, if you could pop in tomorrow morning,' he snapped a small envelope from his pocket and half withdrew a card, 'and hand in this ... you will find the necessary particulars noted there ...' he was almost singing the words, 'as near to ten thirty as possible ... do try to be punctual ... your co-operation will be much appreciated.' He finished as though concluding a recitation.

Nicholas took the small envelope. It was unaddressed, cut to fit the card on which he thought he had glimpsed a name.

'Very well, Inspector. Thank you.'

The man took his hat and settled it carefully on his forehead, pulling it on with both hands.

'Well, now. There we are. I must be off. Glad to have made your acquaintance.' At the door he paused. 'Glorious weather,' and crossed the pavement to the car.

He could will himself to forget the past, but the fear of anything that represented the power that some men could wield over others, had entered into his bones. He sat to remove the card from the envelope, telling himself to be calm, that there could be no danger here, only some bureaucratic routine, like the form fillings and quizzings and tests by which he had renewed his driving licence. The card looked reassuringly innocent, expensively printed, deckled at the edges. It said simply: Mr. J. R. Cairncross. In the bottom left corner an address, and written in small neat figures: 10.30 a.m.

Nicholas still sat in the chair holding the card when he heard Cora at the door. Quickly he returned the card to the envelope and put it in the pocket of his jacket.

She put down her purse and a string bag of small purchases. 'Not at work yet?' she asked, surprised.

'I was just about to begin.'

'Well?' She brushed at a wing of hair. 'What do you think? I went mad and had a rinse.'

'It looks very attractive.'

But he had hardly looked at her hair, his attention wandering in the room. Cora frowned.

'Are you feeling all right?'

'Of course. Why do you ask?'

She sniffed.

'You seem to be miles away.'

Nicholas had arrived early to be punctual, to ask his way and find the unfamiliar address. The buildings were old grey stone, heavy and monumental, close to the Thames Embankment. A large cobbled courtyard, with cars parked and a uniformed man in gum boots washing a Humber Pullman, fronted the porticoed entrance. Pigeons pattered about, searching the cracks of the cobbles. Again an unclouded sun shone.

An elderly man in uniform sat in a glass-fronted box inside the wide doors. Uncertainly, Nicholas took the card from its envelope.

'I have an appointment. Is this the right building?'

'Mr. Cairncross?' The attendant ran his finger down an opened book like a ledger.

'You'd be Mr. Nicholas Arden, then?'

'I am.'

The man folded his spectacles and laid them beside the book.

'If you'd be good enough to follow me, sir.'

Nicholas walked behind him down the corridor, turned into a wing. Heavy wooden doors, decorated and polished, lined the plain grey walls. In each door a small brass number was set. At 27, the attendant knocked. A distant voice bade him enter. The attendant opened the door and looked in.

'A Mr. Nicholas Arden for you, sir. Ten thirty appointment.' He stood aside. 'Will you go in, sir?'

The man who half stood behind the big table, pointed the stem of his pipe.

'Do be seated, Mr. Arden.'

There were chairs against a wall, one set near the table. A big glass-fronted cabinet held files bound in linen and tied with tape. There were hunting prints in heavy frames. Otherwise the large room was bare.

'Now then.' Cairncross scratched a heavy cheek with the pipe stem and blinked about the strewn table. 'Where are we?' He found a manila folder and drew it to him, opening it to flip through the papers. 'Here we are.' He beamed through his glasses at Nicholas and struck a match to light the pipe, drawing on it, continuing to speak in broken mumbles.

'I've asked you – puff – to come in – puff – this morning – to clear up a few – puff – details of your history, Mr. Arden.'

Now he had the pipe burning.

'According to your papers you were born in Baku, Azerbaijan, in the Union of Soviet Socialist Republics.' He looked up. 'Correct?'

'That is correct.'

'You were taken by the Germans in 1942 and put to forced labour in Nazi Germany.' Again he looked up. 'Correct?'

'Correct.'

'And very unpleasant too, I'm sure. You came to Britain from a Displaced Persons' Camp near Colmar in September 1945, and were given work in a forestry camp in Scotland. In February 1947, Rehabilitation found you a job as a language teacher and issued you temporary residence papers. You applied for and were granted . . .' he searched further in the file, 'the privileges of a naturalized British citizen in . . . in . . . March 1951, changing your name by Deed Poll into the nearest Anglicized equivalent of your patronymic. Since when you have been self-employed as a translator in Arabic, Russian and English and . . .' he found the reference and finished in a gallop, 'now residing at Belmont Park, N.W.18, married with one child, male, mostly commissioned to translate by Empire Publishing Limited, Furnival Street, Holborn.' He snapped the file shut and sat back.

'Do smoke if you wish. There's an ash tray there, near you.'

'Thank you. I don't smoke.'

Nicholas sat tensely on the hard chair, his hands held in his lap, unable to still his nerves, unable to guess at the meaning of his being here.

'Very sensible, too. As you can see, I'm addicted to the pipe.' He put his hands on the table and leaned over them. His scalp was ridged under the balding grey hair. He did not raise his head to ask the question.

'Have you kept in contact with your fellow countrymen, in Britain?'

Warning, cold and menacing, hovered in the room. Nicholas swallowed.

'I have not. Before I was married I went a few times to the Russian Club. The secretary had given me help. I was trying to learn if my mother was still alive.'

'What did you learn?'

'Nothing. The inquiry was not answered. None of our inquiries were answered. Stalin's government regarded us ex-prisoners as traitors.'

'I see.' Still the bent head, the ridged scalp shining. 'And what have you been doing recently?'

There was something wrong. Nicholas knew it now. There was something wrong in the work he had done for Kemal. Something that could put him at risk.

'In the last few months I have acted as interpreter at business discussions in Tripoli.'

Cairncross looked up, over his glasses, and drew on the pipe.

'Mr. Arden, I take it you're not reluctant to answer these questions?'

'I am not.'

'Good. Good. Now let us begin at the beginning. How did you secure this employment?'

'I sometimes advertise in the Personal Columns of *The Times*. A Mr. Kemal, an Arab, a director of Trans-Arabia Projects, called on me and offered the employment.'

'Trans-Arabia Projects,' Cairncross said, musing. 'And what was being projected across Arabia?'

'Do you mean what were the talks about?'

'That is what I mean.'

'The talks were about water conservation.'

'Ah.' Cairncross sat back. 'You're sure of that, are you?'

He was not sure now. He was not sure of anything.

'That is what I believed.'

Cairncross stretched his arms and grunted loudly. He clasped his hands and put them on his forehead.

'Mr. Arden, I want you to know that I have the authority to ask these questions. If you have any reservations about going further, you do have rights in the matter.'

More certainly and strongly, Nicholas said, 'Mr. Cairncross, I have nothing to hide. I was doing a job. And that is a matter in which I also have some rights.'

Cairncross lowered his arms and turned to be comfortable.

'True. True. I want you to understand that you are not being, er, interrogated. You're being asked to assist in inquiries which interest Her Majesty's Government.' He popped his eyes over his glasses. 'You see, we have reason to believe that you might have unwittingly involved yourself in something somewhat more sinister than the conversation of the element, water.' He sighed. 'Would you care for tea, before we go on?'

Nicholas shook his head.

'Very well,' Cairncross took a pen from the stand and arranged a writing block. 'Now, let us learn all we can. Where were these discussions held?'

Nicholas heard his voice sink on the answer.

'In the Russian Embassy.'

He waited on Cairncross, who made a note, but did not otherwise react.

'Now,' he said. 'Let us try to remember every detail of these talks, everything that happened from the first moment you entered the Russian Embassy. Who was with you, who you met, who was present at the talks. Anything you might have seen or heard. Omit nothing, however trivial, that you can call to mind.'

It was absolutely quiet in the room, Cairncross waiting, making a small pattern on the pad with the desk-set pen, seemingly absorbed in some private consideration which had struck him. Nicholas made himself relax. He could see it all and hear it all and feel it all, and wanted to rid himself of it, as of a sin to be confessed. Kemal's dark, savage face filled his vision.

'Kemal met me. The air ticket had been brought by a Post Office messenger. It came in a brown, addressed envelope, with ten pounds in single notes and a typed instruction on yellow paper that on arrival I should go to the airport bookstall . . .'

He had told it all. He was finished. His throat was dry with the long recitation. The room asserted itself again. Not once had Cairncross interrupted, turning over page after page until they were heaped on the table. He studied Nicholas who was silent now, rubbing at his eyes, and pushed his chair back. He had seemed tall behind the table, but walking to the glass cabinet, Nicholas saw that he was short in the legs with a little stomach that pushed at his waistcoat. Cairncross opened a narrow door on the cabinet.

He said, 'Water or soda, old boy?' his back turned.

'Water,' Nicholas said.

Cairncross made his preparations and walked to Nicholas with a glass.

'I'm afraid there's no ice,' he said, and sat on the table, swinging his leg.

The whisky was strong and reviving, going down like something solid and burning. Nicholas felt the blood come to his face. Cairncross emptied his glass at a swallow and gave a small belch.

'Sorry about that,' he said and dabbed a handkerchief on his mouth. 'Care for the other half?'

'Thank you.'

Cairncross took the glasses and refilled them, shutting the cabinet door with a snap. He returned to his perch on the table. 'This ... gibberish. These translations you could not understand. They would have been taken from a tape, old boy. Your friend Kemal must have had the Russians bugged. Someone, with a limited knowledge of Russian, would have made transcriptions from the tape.' He peered sideways at Nicholas. 'You see that, don't you? All clear now?'

And now it was clear to him, the inexplicable mish-mash which he had likened in his mind to voices heard through blankets, or a record played at the wrong speed.

'But why—'

'Obvious,' Cairncross said, swinging his leg. 'The mysterious Kemal doesn't trust his Russian partners. Ask yourself this question: Would he go to the trouble to eavesdrop on their private consultations if the issue at stake was one of hydroelectric schemes and water conservation? We can answer that in the negative.'

He put back his head and half emptied the glass.

'Now let us turn our minds to these references to a timing schedule. "To meet the timing schedule in Area Green, etcetera. The complexities of meeting the timing schedule in Area Blue, etcetera, etcetera." We ask ourselves: Is it conceivable, that subterranean water deposits, or surface deposits, area by area, are to be conserved simultaneously, according to a master schedule?' He tapped his nose with his pipe stem. 'Reason, my dear Arden, shouts from the rooftops, no!'

Cairncross began to fill his pipe from a rubber pouch. Piece after puzzling piece began to fit together in Nicholas's mind. So much was already explained. His isolation in the villa. The scene that first day in the Embassy. Kemal's pressure over the

107

translations. Kapitsa's arrival in the restaurant. But he was without a key to the pattern, still lost to understand what he had got mixed up in.

'What is the explanation? What have I been interpreting?' Another thought struck him, slowing his voice. He had been led on simply answering questions to begin with, believing this to be some issue of his naturalization. It wasn't that. It had not been that from the beginning. Nicholas felt his body stiffen.

'You knew that I'd been out there, didn't you? How did you know?' He stood up abruptly, spilling whisky from his glass. 'This isn't immigration. Where am I? Who do you represent?'

Cairncross cocked an eye at him, over the pipe bowl, drawing at the match cupped in his hand.

'Steady, now,' he said. 'Nothing to get upset about.'

'I demand to know.'

Cairncross was concentrated on getting his tobacco burning.

'And so you shall.' When he was ready he put a hand on Nicholas's shoulder. 'Do sit down, old boy.' He walked around the desk and let himself down into the chair.

'First of all, this is a department of the Foreign Office. I won't confuse you further on that score. Secondly, we heard of your work for Kemal in a roundabout way and interested ourselves. Putting first things last, I think the explanation you asked for is something to do with oil. The Arabs, backed by the Russians, are plotting something sinister in the oil states.' He struck another match. 'There. Does that satisfy you?'

It did and it didn't.

'Why does that matter so much? What could they be plotting?'

Cairncross jabbed the pipe stem at Nicholas.

'Why does that matter so much? There isn't a government in the West that could go to bed and sleep knowing that trouble could be brewing in the oil states. Britain, I feel free to tell you, could hold out for only sixty-four days if her oil supplies were interrupted. After sixty-four days – blackout, close-down, anarchy. Back to the Middle Ages.'

He observed Nicholas critically and made a sketch in the air with his pipe stem.

'I see by your face that you begin to understand. All the world knows about atomic bombs and hydrogen bombs and this-and-that bombs and small wars here and small wars there and revolutions elsewhere. But the day-to-day danger, my dear Arden, is not the shadow of the apocalypse but the sword of Damocles, as they say. And that sword, which could drop on our necks at any time and behead us like a chicken, was laid down a few million years ago when a myriad of alive things disappeared under the crust of the earth and turned into fossils.'

Cairncross coughed and looked self-conscious.

'Somewhat mixed as to metaphor perhaps, but I believe you take my meaning. Now, when do you next expect a brown paper package from Kemal?'

Nicholas said, 'I'm not going back, Mr. Cairncross.'

'Oh?' He popped his eyes again. 'Does Kemal know that?'

'No. I didn't discuss it with him.'

'Good. So it is conceivable that he might need you again?'

Nicholas said quietly, 'I'm not going back.'

Cairncross lifted his blunt face. Light glinted abruptly on the steel rims of his spectacles. In a voice also quietened, he said, 'That won't do, Arden. That won't do at all. We want you to go back. I have been very frank with you, exactly for that reason. Knowing what you now know, you will know what to look out for. A few words perhaps, a hint here or there, which might previously have meant nothing to you, now might speak volumes. We need you, Arden.'

Their gazes were fixed on each other. Nicholas did not reply, but the resolution in his face was clear.

Cairncross spoke very gently.

'Would you say that this country, this country which gave you refuge, this country of your adoption, has treated you kindly, Arden?'

The gentle voice was loaded with meaning. And still Nicholas did not reply. Cairncross continued.

'I would say that the answer must be in the affirmative. All you are being asked to do is evidence your appreciation. To co-operate in a matter that might be critical to us all. You understand that, I'm sure. You are a man of considerable intelligence.' He waited.

Nicholas could feel the trap closing about him. The other man's blunt, homely features had suddenly set, the pale eyes as remorseless as pebbles.

Cairncross said, 'Assuming something sinister is going on, your own part in it, as a naturalized citizen, could be read as being murky. There are those who might take a dim view.'

Now Nicholas was full of a danger of his own. He said, 'I will not be blackmailed, Mr. Cairncross,' and thought of his home and his family, the precious humdrum security.

Cairncross took no offence at the word. Some of the hardness melted from his face, but he remained intent.

'I am sure you will not,' he said soothingly. 'You are a man of great courage and endurance. Your record proves that. It is one for which I have the highest respect. I – you might say Her Majesty's Government – am simply asking the help and assistance, in what might prove a delicate matter, of a good and loyal British citizen.'

There was no help for it. In what Cairncross had left unspoken were risks that he could not run. He did not believe in the blackmail but he could not afford to put that to the test. All his new hopes and intentions, the good changes which had altered his marriage, seemed to him to recede and become abolished. The helplessness of his past rose and gripped him, and he struggled to resist it. It wasn't like that. He would only need to be careful. Act, if Kemal called him again, as he had on his other visits. He tried to make himself accept.

'Very well. I will do as you ask.'

Cairncross beamed. 'Excellent. Excellent.' He tapped out his pipe, stretched, and clasped his hands on his forehead. He peered at Nicholas like that, reminding him of some large, friendly animal. Then he said, in an altered, darting voice, 'There is much to be reclaimed, Brother.' He lowered his hands. 'Mmm? What?'

He had sounded almost like Kemal. It startled Nicholas. 'Why do you say that?'

'The question is why did the mysterious Kemal use that expression so often.' Cairncross took out a pocket watch. 'How very late it is. I've kept you all morning. Time well spent, however. I'm sure you agree. Now, as to the future. When Kemal calls you again – I have a conviction that he will – if he presents you with more Russian gibberish, you must contrive to take a copy. What else? Ah, yes . . .'

It seemed strange to Nicholas that the sun still shone, that pigeons still waddled and pecked at the cobbles of the big courtyard, that the elderly doorman in his box should have looked up from his newspaper to say, 'Goodbye, Mr. Arden.' Everything real had become unfamiliar, distorted by the upheavals in his mind.

It was after seven o'clock when the telephone rang in David Lawrence's room. Again he waited, while anonymous voices completed the connection. 'London, this is Beirut,' and 'I've got your party.' Distant clickings and mufflings and fadings and strengthenings until Morrow's voice filled his ear.

'Hello? Are you there, Character?'

'Max? What happened last night?'

'I wasn't ready for you. How's the holiday going?'

'Well enough. London is having an Indian summer.'

'My favourite city,' Morrow said. 'Have a meal at Kettner's for me. Order the steak and kidney. If you see a big man eating there with a flaming beard like a corsair, introduce yourself. He's a friend of mine. Buy him a vintage port.'

Lawrence tried to restrain his urgency. He didn't want to chat.

'What's happening?'

'That guy in the second photograph, the Arab holding the car door. He's been identified.'

Lawrence felt a cold qualm, a further threat to Nicholas Arden.

'Who is he?'

'Not in front of the children. I'll fill you in when you get back. But the plot thickens. I've got a number I want you to call tomorrow morning. You got a pencil and paper?'

Lawrence was ready.

'Yes. Go ahead.'

Morrow gave him the number.

'Got it? Read it back.'

Lawrence checked the number.

'Right,' Morrow said, 'that's a direct line. It will connect you with an Official Person. I will spell his name for you.'

Lawrence made the note.

'What do you want me to do?'

'You will be given an appointment. When you've been briefed, get yourself back here. Telex me your ETA.'

'Is that all you can tell me?'

'What do you want to know?'

There was so much more that he wanted to know. What had happened, or what would happen, to the man he could not forget?

'Nothing, really.'

'That's it then. Goodnight, Character.'

'Goodnight,' Lawrence said.

After a time he did not want to think any more. Lawrence dialled Information and asked for the address of Kettner's restaurant. He would order the steak and kidney. If he saw a big man with a flaming beard like a corsair he would introduce himself and buy him a vintage port. In the bathroom he pushed the plug on the wash bowl and leaned to examine his face in the mirror.

'To hell with it,' he told himself, 'to burning hell with everything.'

The doorman had been writing in a large book. He smiled and nodded. 'Goodbye, Mr. Lawrence.' The pigeons moved reluctantly. Lawrence walked over the cobbled courtyard towards the streaming traffic, seeing nothing. Nicholas Arden was alive for him now in a way that wrenched at his being. All that tormented history had somehow been in his face. A memory which Lawrence did not know he had slammed and jolted into his mind. In the steaming Tripoli terminal Arden had carried his jacket. The shirt he wore was short-sleeved. Jostling to be near him Lawrence had seen the long, wide, white-puckered scar on the inside of his right forearm. Once, there would have been a number there. A tattooed, indelible number.

'Watch where you're going, can't you?' The man's face was pinched with anger. He caught at the packages he carried.

'I'm sorry,' Lawrence said, only now feeling the impact of this man he had bumped blindly into, who stood to watch him go, muttering his disarrangement and outrage.

Nicholas Arden was innocent, and now they were sending him back. He had a wife and a son. They were sending him back into dangers he would not even understand. Wars had been fought over oil. Conspiracies and plots and counter-plots, assassinations and judicious murders clotted on the history of oil like barnacles on a hulk. Who would care about Nicholas Arden, the innocent, save the man who had cleverly betrayed him?

CHAPTER SEVEN

LAWRENCE cleared Customs, he had nothing to declare, and looked about in Reception against the likelihood that Max Morrow might have decided to meet him. The airport was very busy, but more concerned with leave-takings than meetings. There would be no difficulty in finding a taxi. He pushed through the glass doors and was struck by the sultry heat, as he had been when descending from the aircraft, and regretted the cleanliness and order and civilized peace of the warm days and cool nights he had left. He pushed his bag before him into the cab and instructed the driver to take him to Rue John Kennedy.

At the consultancy Freni welcomed him and took his bag. She told him that Mr. Morrow was in the private room. Lawrence paused and asked who was with him. Nobody, his visitor had just left.

Morrow sat on the settee in shirt sleeves, reading clips off the press teleprinters, bottles and glasses on the brass table. He checked his watch.

'Which airline did you fly?'

'The local team.'

'Something's wrong. They must have been bang on time.' Morrow put down the clipboard and stood. 'Welcome home, Character. You've earned a drink. What will it be?'

'I'll take a scotch.'

'Not the Arak?'

'I think I've lost my taste for it. Who have you had visiting?'

'Kramer came over from the Embassy.'

'Anything important?'

'Not really. We were shooting the breeze.'

Lawrence took off his jacket and loosened his tie, accepted the glass Morrow handed him. They asked their questions simultaneously, a collision of words. Morrow bowed. 'After you, then.'

'Well,' Lawrence said. 'Who is he?'

'The Arab at the car door? His name is Captain Abdul

113

Hamil, one of the chief architects of the revolution, an ex-chief of Libyan Army Intelligence. Our people believe that at Federation he was appointed Chief of Intelligence Police for the United Arab Republic. He's a hard man, a Muslim zealot like his Number One. After the revolution he set up the Jehad Fund in King Idris's old palace – the fund for the Holy War against Israel.'

Lawrence turned away. Captain Abdul Hamil, Chief of Intelligence Police. Nicholas Arden's Kemal. An old desolation splashed up in him. There was nothing more to be hoped for.

'What's wrong? Cat got your tongue?'

Lawrence sat, looking into his glass. Hopelessly, he made a last try.

'Does it have to be oil? Couldn't it be water conservation?'

He met Max Morrow's suddenly hardened eyes.

'Water conservation, crap! What are you talking about?'

Lawrence shook his head, took a cigarette from the table box and lit it. When he had gathered himself, he began the explanation. It took a long time, answering Morrow's probes and interruptions. Morrow was on his feet, prowling the room, when he finished, on his toes like a boxer.

'That is it.' His voice had sharpened with excitement. 'The balloon's about to go up, Character. We've busted into the big one.'

Lawrence saw this man he had so admired as though a searchlight had lit him in the dark, a searchlight that also illuminated himself, by an accident of refraction.

'You like this, Max, don't you?'

The observation, the tone of it, conveyed no significance to Morrow, continuing to prowl.

'Sure I like it. We're into the action.'

'This Nicholas Arden. The man you squeezed. Doesn't his history mean anything to you?'

'He got unlucky,' Morrow said. 'It could have happened to any of us.' He buttoned his cuffs and put on his jacket. 'I'm going to the Embassy.' He paused. 'You look like a case of jet fatigue. Get yourself home and rest up. You did a great job.'

Lawrence sat in the darkening room and poured another drink. Freni knocked at the door.

'I'll lock up,' Lawrence said. 'You go home, Freni.'

He was still there when only the brass table and the bottle and

114

the crystal glasses reflected the last light. They had busted into the big one. Lawrence had done a great job.

The next morning, early, Lawrence telephoned Max Morrow in his suite. He confessed to feeling a bit done-in, and was told to rest-up for the day. After breakfast he drove to the village and collected the manservant he had inherited with the lodge. Even on the heights the winds that blew at this season deposited the dust carried across the sea. As pervasive as powder, it had contrived entry to his shuttered house and lay on the tiles and mosaics and the antique brass in a grey film. Lawrence set old Abdul to work and went to walk in the garden. The late rains had started new growth on the pomegranates and limes, shoots of tingling green that glinted like lacquer in the sunlight. The bougainvillaea was in blossom on the wall it shared with the climbing geranium which the hottest driest weather seemed never to discourage. Lawrence carried a mug of coffee to a stone bench under the figs, crunching the falling leaves that had clenched their points like fingers as they dried and died. Wasps buzzed loudly, hovering and passing before him. In this walled seclusion he surrendered to all that had re-positioned in him, the alterations for which he must account.

He had never really stood for anything. His entire life had been flight or self-indulgence. The fear or defiance of scandals. He had persuaded himself that he was liberated, living his private life on his private terms, rejecting the codes and the notional morals behind which the abject hide for security. Lawrence quirked his lips, remembering another instruction of Max Morrow's. 'If you don't stand for something, you fall for anything.' It was true. He had even fallen for that.

Robins flitted in a carab tree. 'Bang!' Lawrence said in his mind, and wondered if they would complete their migration. The Lebanese shot everything that flew, stalking the trees and fields in cartridge belts, a few pitiful bodies in their hands. He had seen a dove flying a tree line, through a cannonade of hidden hunters, swerving at the bursts, beating on until it crumpled and crashed. The image swapped in his mind for another and he made an effort to reject it. It could be like that for Nicholas Arden, the man Lawrence had helped to hunt.

He left the untasted coffee on the bench and walked again among the fallen fig leaves to ease his confusion in the comfort of growing things. Succulents ran in a shaded corner, climbing the stems of wild grass, spiked with discs of yellow flowers that

115

would fold as the sunlight faded. Lawrence thought of the girl he had met with Barbara Barse at the Casino du Liban, she had worn yellow and he tried to remember her name. She had been coarse and stupid and arrogant, he did not forgive her that. But he could have turned her out, or telephoned for a car. He could have left her to sleep on the sofa as humiliation enough. He had not needed to shock and degrade her. Lawrence shivered in the sunlight and returned to the bench.

He had come to no true terms with himself. All his bravado was sham, the facing down of a grieving he would not admit. He had buried himself for two years, taking his satisfaction with Arab boys, and thought bitterly that their corruption did not touch them, their bodies were unconnected to their minds, smoking cigarettes, sipping his drinks, impatient to return to the back streets to swagger and exhibit his money. Loneliness and hopelessness filled him like ashes.

When David Lawrence entered the house much later he had made two decisions. Soon, he would return home. Not for a visit, to stay. He would truly face himself this time and see what could be built. Already he felt lightened, full of the first purpose he had ever set himself. But not yet. Not until he had tried to deliver Nicholas Arden from the hands of those who could harm him. He owed him that. Somewhere, in what had passed from that man into him, in what he had learned of his life, in the premonition which had moved him when he first saw his face in the photograph, their lives had been joined in a fate. He would be a friend to that man, whatever the cost. If he had to fight Max Morrow for it, that was a price he would pay.

For the next week Lawrence had little time to consider his resolution. The preoccupations of that were shattered by another event. Max Morrow was already in the office when Lawrence arrived next morning, tie loosened, sleeves rolled, tearing messages off the agency teleprinters, adding them to the file on his clipboard. There had been a pro-Communist coup in the Sudan.

All that day and the next, Max Morrow rushed in and out, telexing code to his Washington headquarters, snapping orders, calling for reference, hurrying to meetings at the American Embassy. The press bar at the Hotel St. Georges was noisy with speculations. Lawrence forgot himself, his self-concern overwhelmed by Morrow's mobilized force and demands.

A civil aircraft flying from London, carrying the President and Prime Minister of the new revolutionary government, was forced down over Libya, en route to Khartoum. The two men were removed by soldiers. Speculation among the Middle East watchers passed from reason into other realms. In the next days there were further upheavals. A counter coup was successfully mounted. The leaders taken from the pirated aircraft were executed in Khartoum. The resurrected government announced that the pro-Communist plotters had been arrested.

Morrow opened the door to the private room and put out a bottle and glasses. He poured two drinks and sat on the sofa.

'Here's to tranquillity,' he toasted.

Lawrence asked, 'Do you think it's over?'

'All bar the shouting – and the shootings. The Middle East is getting to be a lousy investment risk. What was it your journalist friend Quale said? The Russians are riding a tiger out here?'

Lawrence nodded.

'They just fell off. They just fell flat on their red asses.' Morrow shook his head in enjoyment. 'Fancy the Russians jumping in like that the first day, to recognize the coup. The thieves are falling out, Character. It's going to be a long time before they patch up this one. The hot and burning Arabs won't believe a Russian now if he gives them the time of day.' Morrow finished his drink. 'We're clean on this one. Nobody could have called it. I'm going back to the hotel to take a sauna. Tomorrow we should start in on a political analysis.'

He left David Lawrence to his thoughts.

London's Indian summer ended in rain, wind and cold. The city slipped into winter, late dark in the mornings, early dark in the afternoon.

The terraced houses in Belmont Park were centrally heated on the ground floors by gas-fired units that blew a stale hot breath through the ventilators, condensing on the windows. Nicholas rubbed a patch clean and looked out. A few over-coated figures went by, collars up, heads bent. On several mornings he had seen a green Mini Minor parked in a side street, a dim figure inside. It could have been watching the house. It was the same colour as the car from which Sub-Inspector Cooper had hailed him. He told himself they had no need to watch him. If the messenger rang with his brown paper envelope he could not refuse to accept it. If he signed for it and did nothing, it

117

would be easy for Cairncross to know. The boards of the ceiling creaked. Cora was cleaning upstairs. Nicholas looked towards the village, in the direction from which the messenger could come.

There was nothing he could do. His fate was a boy on a bike. Again his mind returned to Room 27 in the block of grey stone. At night, in his sleep, Cairncross watched him, popping his eyes and beaming, suddenly changing into threat, the blunt, friendly features growing stony, the steel-rimmed spectacles gleaming with an evil light that startled Nicholas into waking. Twice he had carefully left the bed, feeling for his slippers and dressing-gown, to go down next to the wall and not squeak the stairs, compelled to recall everything yet again like a record he was unable to stop. Once Cora had followed him, clutching her nightdress and shivering, her eyes dark with sleep, her lips soft and puffed with it, her voice faintly alarmed and incredulous.

'Nicholas? What in the world are you doing?'

He had pleaded a touch of indigestion, which she said she was unable to understand, there had been nothing indigestible in the food.

He had done nothing to prepare Cora for what might happen. In the first days he had swung on a pendulum, the decision to defy the man in Room 27 sometimes bringing him to his feet as though a hand had plucked him up. Once, on the way to the Publishing House it had changed his direction, back to the Embankment and the old stone building behind the cobbled court-yard. But it never lasted, fragmenting away to leave him barren.

Again, Nicholas rubbed at the window, looked out. The street was deserted, wind bowling trash along the gutter. A sudden anger at himself, at the entrapment, shook him. The uncertainty and confusion departed. The pendulum he had swung on steadied and was still. Kemal, whoever he was, could threaten nothing he had not already known. Cairncross had told him what to look for. He would go back and make the means to find it. This time, he would use Kemal.

He heard Cora coming down the stairs and turned to meet her. She stopped, her arms full of soiled linen, his position at the window touching her with intuition. Nicholas took the bundle and led her to a chair, making a lie for her comfort, a reason she would understand.

'Cora, there's going to be a slow-down at the Press. Wilson

118

told me about it yesterday. There's not going to be much money for Christmas.'

She said nothing, her eyes uneven, tensed into resistance as though she guessed. He waited, finding it difficult to go on without having something to answer.

'I've thought about it. If Kemal calls me, I want to make one more trip.'

'Oh, no, Nicholas.' Her voice was almost beseeching. 'We've still got money from your last trip.'

She wanted him here more than she wanted the money. He made himself sternly responsible.

'That money is for the new washing machine. And the other things. You've been going through pamphlets for weeks. We don't want to spend it on living.'

'But we can manage,' she said. 'I couldn't rest if you went again. All those countries are dangerous. Look what they did last week, forcing down a British aeroplane with British passengers abroad. They're no better than pirates. I can't think why the government didn't do something.'

'That concerned another country. And besides, the trouble is settled now. We must be practical, Cora.'

Her voice shook.

'But we agreed. You said yourself that you didn't want to go again. You know how upset Bobby gets. You've been away such a lot.'

'And just look what we've got to show for it. You enjoy the car, don't you?'

But she didn't answer that question, alarm and upset in her eyes.

'Nicholas, is there anything you haven't told me? Is there anything I don't know?'

He said staunchly, 'Of course not.'

'You've made up your mind, haven't you?'

'I'm trying to do what is best and sensible.'

Cora got up, looking away.

'Very well, Nicholas. I won't argue about it. You know how I feel. I won't pretend that I understand it, after all that we agreed.' Suddenly her lip shook. 'Obviously, there's something pulling you back to that miserable place. Something more important than us. I suppose you met somebody.'

He didn't understand at first, and then took her into his arms.

'Oh, Cora,' he said, and shook his head. 'Cora, how can you be so silly?'

Muffled on his chest, she said, 'Things like that happen. How do I know it's silly?'

He rocked her like a child.

'Let's try and forget about it. It might not happen.'

But it did happen. Insidiously, on a morning he had truly forgotten it, preparing to drive Cora to the shops.

While she put on her lipstick, Nicholas had gone to clean the windscreen and warm the engine. The cold had increased overnight. Frost whitened the plot behind the house. He had opened the door on the messenger, absurdly poised, an arm out to press the bell, the surprise arresting them both for an instant. Nicholas signed the chit and shut the door, laid the familiar envelope on the table, carrying it there like a weight.

Cora came down the steps, announcing to the boy's room that they were leaving now and would not be long. He heard her in the entrance, putting on the leather coat that crackled with newness. Because he had told her he would wait in the car he had to call her name. She looked in, tying the belt, a string bag hooked over one elbow.

'I'm ready.'

He was standing at the table. She did not see the envelope. He pushed the package towards her and waited.

'Oh, no!' Her shoulders slumped.

'It just came.'

She moved slowly towards him, her eyes fixed on the package as though it were that drawing her steps.

'What does it say?'

'I haven't opened it.'

He saw the struggle in her face, lifted the envelope and tore the flap. He looked inside and withdrew the folded yellow sheet, read the typescript and pushed it back. She needed to delay the reality, however hopeless or ridiculous.

'Is it Kemal?'

'Yes.'

'When does he want you?'

'On Wednesday.' He made his voice bright and cheerful, brisk with all he did not feel. 'We've got all weekend to enjoy ourselves. Come on now, cheer up. How smart you look in that coat.'

She crackled the leather with her hand, voice absent.

'It's the smartest coat I've ever had.'

'After this trip I'll buy you another. I'll buy us all smart leather coats. We'd better go, or you'll miss your specials.'

She nodded and tried to smile. At the car he unlocked the door and let her in, took a cloth from the glove box to clear the frosted windscreen. On Cora's side, a face appeared suddenly in the small patch of cleared glass, stopping his arm before he collected himself. Her eyes had glistened with tears. Going down the hill to the village he put a hand on her knee. Her own quickly closed over it. They drove like that, until he had to change gear.

Outside the terminal's main doors the Mini-cab found an empty space and nipped in. Nicholas got out and paid the driver from the ten pounds in single notes, new and unfolded as he always found them inside the covers of the air ticket. He carried his bag across the pavement, through the electronic doors, going directly to the Libyan–Arab Airlines desk. The procedure had become routine, no longer requiring effort, managed automatically without occupying his mind. He put the checked air ticket into his passport and went up the stairs to the coffee lounge, stopping to buy the afternoon editions. Nicholas gave his order and took up a newspaper, restlessly scanning the pages. His eyes passed over the columns, finding nothing to hold his attention, nothing that could establish itself against the tide of his thoughts.

He had called Cairncross that morning as instructed, from a pay telephone in the village.

'Who are you calling?' And again, after the coins had dropped, in the same flat tones, 'Who are you calling?'

'I'm calling Mr. Cairncross.'

'Who is it?'

'Nicholas Arden.'

In the pause Nicholas could almost see Cairncross lighting his pipe.

'Thought I recognized the voice,' he said, his tones changed and familiar. 'I take it you're off again?'

'Yes. This afternoon.'

'Good man. The regular message I presume? No noticeable changes?'

'None.'

'You will call as soon as you return, won't you? I'll be here, God willing.'

'I will.'

'Good luck, old man. Take care.'

The waiter brought the coffee. Nicholas hardly saw him. Take care, Cairncross had said. The terminal echoed and droned. The announcement system cut in with flights and gate numbers, signalling attention with a preliminary whine. Cairncross dwindled, popping his eyes and beaming. Kemal appeared on Nicholas's fixed stare, lines running on his ravaged face like slashes, dark eyes unreadable and burning. In Area Red . . . the timing schedule in Area Green . . . there is much to be reclaimed, Brother.

He wanted to be there, had already entered the annexe of the time machine that would transport him. He would wait at the bookstall for the driver. They would take the remembered road through square white houses and minarets and palm trees, and the camels and donkeys in the fields. The gates would open on the walled villa, in which feet that had no bodies that he had seen would be heard shuffling along the darkened passages. The fat Arab would bring his food, in the rooms he had once left for ever.

The moment his sleep left him, Nicholas was aware of everything. The lumped mattress, the next room, the green outside the windows, the passage behind the closed door. Every cell in his body was vividly alive. Somewhere voices called, water gurgled in a pipe. He got up, groaning the bed springs, registering every sound with a separate clarity.

In the sitting-room he rang the brass bell and drew the curtains. A warm, soft autumn light washed in, touching everything like a blessing. Two heavy thumps knocked the door. He told the fat Arab to enter. The pitted pores of his face were greased with a sweat that owed nothing to the cool, sunlit morning.

'Have you eggs?'

'There are eggs.'

'Have you potatoes?'

The fat Arab inclined his head.

'I will eat two fried eggs. With these eggs you will fry potatoes. With the eggs and potatoes, toast. The coffee will be served with milk.'

The fat Arab fidgeted and mumbled.

'What did you say?'

'There is no milk.'

'Then you must find milk, Brother.'

Nicholas waited while the fat Arab looked vacantly about as though he might conjure up milk in the room. Then he nodded in resignation, and went out. In the bathroom Nicholas packed the plug with the cloth that was never washed and sat to adjust the taps. He was hungry. He had not wanted to eat last night, walking again in these rooms. He had ordered coffee and then on an impulse opened the untouched whisky that had been a concession from Kemal. He had drunk two large measures with the coffee, gone to bed and slept his first untroubled sleep in weeks.

Nicholas had bathed and dressed when the fat Arab knocked with breakfast. The milk was in a tin, punctured with something that had lifted the metal in jagged points, but it served to bridle the bitterness that sugar could not absolve. Nicholas ate hungrily and waited on Kemal.

He heard his knock from the bedroom, hanging up the tropical suit he had hardly worn, and took his time, steadying the hot spurt in his stomach.

'*Neharkum sa'id.*'

'*Neharkum sa'id we mubarak.*'

Kemal wore a tan safari suit, so like a uniform that the authority of his manner seemed enlarged and confirmed by it.

'I am grateful that you could come, Brother. Have you been comfortable in your house?'

'It was my pleasure to come. I am comfortable, Brother.'

Behind the cover of the formalities, Nicholas stalked this man in his mind, who was, and who was not, Kemal. Whose business card and elaborate pretences concealed another man and purpose. He had sought Nicholas out to use him. He had fixed a price that he knew could not fail. Whatever it was that Kemal conspired lurked in darkness and hid in shadows and Nicholas knew with an icy certainty that he would be expendable to this man. Kemal was alien, not by his birth or tongue, but in the convolutions of his brain and his spirit, as those others in the past had been alien. Nicholas felt calm with preparation, seeking Kemal's forbidding face with a recognition almost detached.

'Did you find somebody to provide company on your flight, Brother?'

'I sat alone, Brother.'

123

Something had changed. Kemal's tension had altered into nerves. A fine tremor quivered his eyelids.

'Do we go again to talk with the Russian comrades?'

'No, Brother. That business is finished.'

A warning to be wary touched Nicholas.

'And why have you brought me here, Brother, if that business is completed?'

'There is translation to be made. From the Russian language.'

Nicholas said, 'It is a long and costly way to bring a man, to make a translation from the Russian. Particularly if no sense can be found in it. I do not understand this, Brother.'

Kemal's thin shoulders hunched about his face. His eyes burned at Nicholas.

'Is it important that you must understand?'

Nicholas met the challenge and rejected it. There had been a tremor in Kemal's voice, as fine as the tremor on his eyelids. In revelation he saw that Kemal was at the edge of nervous exhaustion, all his body a silent protest.

'It is important to me that my time should not be wasted, Brother. Even for such generous pay.'

And now Kemal's command left him, voice hoarse, the words pushing out in disorder.

'In this country . . . in this people . . . the Imperialists and the Godless who everywhere wear two faces . . . in this country, we do things our own way. That is all you need understand. Soon everyone, everywhere, will understand. You are a guest in this country . . . and in this people . . .' He stopped, controlling himself. Gradually, he loosened. 'I have had fever. Pay no attention, Brother.' The statement gave him strength. He looked up, insisting. 'I have had fever.'

Nicholas said, 'You should take rest, Brother.'

But there was no fever in Kemal's eyes, or on his skin. Nicholas had seen fever enough. Whatever burned in Kemal was beyond the cancellation of medicines. He looked for the leather envelope in which Kemal carried the yellow pages. 'Do you want me to work now, Brother?'

'I will bring the work,' Kemal said, 'my visit was to see that you were prepared. Take your ease, Brother.'

Because he had made his decision and armed himself, picturing that room in the Embassy where he would watch for the clues that Cairncross had furnished, Nicholas felt robbed.

There would be no more reports. No more guarded questions in which he might now have read a meaning. The business had been completed. In the Areas designated by colours the needs of the timing schedule were prepared. It must be this that accounted for the disorder in Kemal. He was like a man strung for some imminent fatal action, committed irreversibly to a course that shrieked his nerves.

Nicholas went to the desk in the bedroom and opened a pad, making notes to fix the words in his memory. Kemal had said that everywhere the Imperialists and the Godless wore two faces. Godless could be a reference to the Russians. Soon everyone, everywhere, would understand. Cairncross might make something out of that. It had been an indiscretion, forced out by all that Kemal contained.

There was no more doubt. No more wonder at the alarm he had caused in the Embassy. Something of menace and turmoil waited its ordained time. Something too great in importance for the secret partners to trust each other. But somewhere the scheme had been breached. In some way, Cairncross and his unseen colleagues had reached out for Nicholas Arden.

When he heard the fat Arab's thumps, Nicholas came quickly from the bedroom. Quickly enough to see in the passage that direct light never reached, figures whom he thought wore uniforms, something bulky that was passed to the fat Arab whom Kemal pushed inside the shut door.

Kemal said, 'Put it on the table, and go.'

It looked like an upright typewriter, zipped in a case of synthetic leather. But Nicholas remembered Cairncross, sitting on the corner of the table and felt himself squeezed. 'Is this the work, Brother?'

Kemal said bleakly, 'This is the work. This time, it is well done.'

The cased instrument was like a lodestone, claiming all their attention, a magic box, or something malevolent which could be dangerous to touch. Kemal went stiffly to the table, unzipped the cover and pushed it back. The tape on the recording spool had been connected for play-back. He gestured Nicholas towards him.

'The batteries are new. The machine has been tested. There can be no question of failure, Brother.' His eyes said quite clearly: Remember that. He touched each button lightly, enumerating its function. 'Have you used such a machine, Brother?'

Nicholas shook his head.

'It is a machine of German making.' And then again, head bent, 'There can be no question of failure.'

He pushed a wheel at one end of the panel. A round eye of light blinked on. A soft, shushing noise, very faint, came from somewhere behind the instrument.

Kemal tapped another wheel. 'This is the volume control, Brother.' The shushing loudened and coarsened, suddenly broke into voices and a confusion of background sounds. Kemal moved the wheel, lessening the impact. 'Can you hear that clearly, Brother?'

'Yes. Well enough.'

'It is in the Russian language. What is being said, Brother?'

All that mish-mash, that gibberish, had been taken from tapes like this. Cairncross had guessed it. Somewhere inside the Embassy compounds, someone like Kemal, perhaps a servant, had hidden the listening instrument whose intelligence another had sought to record on the botched yellow pages. Nicholas heard a girl's voice complaining and a further confusion of voices discussing domestic matters. He made an effort to determine his will, and heard Cairncross mumbling over his pipe stem, 'Remember, Arden, forewarned is forearmed. You have the advantage, as we say in the trade, of knowing that something could be rotten in Denmark. The mysterious Kemal has no reason to harbour suspicions of you. You've nothing to worry about, really. Just use your wits, old boy.'

It was sufficient to believe in. For the present it could be true. Nicholas reached out and pressed the stop button.

'Why did you do that, Brother?'

'It is difficult to catch the words. There is much noise and confusion. I will need to play the words many times and write them down.'

'What was being said, Brother?'

'There was a little girl. It appeared to be a family talking.'

Kemal pushed viciously at the Start button and then at the button to speed the tape, holding it down while the reel thickened. He stopped the tape and reversed it. Nicholas heard the male voices and caught with recognition. Kemal waited, then stopped the machine.

'Was that matters of family, Brother?'

He had to face Kemal who had come so close that Nicholas

could feel his breath on his cheek, the tension in the lean, hunched body stifling in this proximity.

'No. That was some talk of engineering.' He needed time, and took the risk. 'Everyone works in his own way, Brother. I have to be alone. I will take much time to do this work. If you come back this evening, all will be ready.'

Kemal's long calculation of Nicholas was naked of any pretence, bearing down with a weight he could feel in his throat. Nicholas thought, he's telling himself that he can afford this. He's telling himself that I cannot cheat him now. We have come to the end of something. If there is nothing on this tape, there will be others. Slowly, Kemal relented and turned to the window.

'Very well, Brother. I will do as you wish.' He pressed the Start button. The Russian voices crackled in the room. A chair scraped. Music was faintly heard. 'It is well done,' Kemal said, 'there can be no question of failure. I will leave you to your work, Brother.' He nodded and went without looking back. When the door had closed, Nicholas stopped the machine and listened. He waited, and heard a car start.

As Kemal had done, Nicholas turned to the window and rested himself in the soft autumn sunlight, which seemed as though it had withdrawn and had only re-entered at Kemal's leaving. The green things in the garden and against the white wall tried to erase the conflicts in his mind, to reassert order and security as do familiar recognitions after dreaming.

Kemal was under some compulsion, ready to risk what might be found on the tapes. Quietly, Nicholas went to the door, laid his ear on the panelling to listen. A muffling of sound came to him, meaningless and muted, like the sound of the sea that children listen for in shells. He turned the knob and pushed the door open. Against the opposite wall, the man who squatted, smoking, started and pushed himself up. He said nothing, eyes wide, a trickle of smoke extending from his nostrils.

'I would like coffee,' Nicholas ordered, as though it were natural the man should be there, and shut the door on him. He needed no more confirmation. Kemal had made him prisoner.

When the fat Arab thumped, Nicholas took the unwanted tray. He could see nobody else in the passage.

'I will take no food today,' he said, 'I have much work. It is my wish that I should not be interrupted. Do you understand that, Brother?'

The fat Arab wheezed and nodded, backed into the passage and pulled the door shut.

It could not be denied or avoided, but his hand had stiffened with reluctance. Nicholas pressed the Rewind button. It hummed and stopped with a clack. He pressed the button to start the machine, loudened the volume control. The coarse shush-shush of the lead filled the speaker. Shakily, he went to the sofa and waited on the thin voice of the child, the household noises and the other voices.

Nicholas sat with his head in his hands, going away from this room, leaving himself and the sensed danger as he filled with the old familiar tongue. He had not heard a woman's voice speak Russian, or a child's, since he himself was a boy. The little girl's voice seemed to be speaking to a doll, singing it to sleep with a nursery rhyme that tormented him with faint remembrance. The woman's voice scolded, shooing at something that could have been an animal and faded under a drowning roar like the passing of a jet aircraft. Somewhere, somebody laughed. The little girl's voice piped very clearly, filling Nicholas with sadness and the reminder of other places and rooms. More distinctly a woman's voice called, 'Natasha!' and then again, 'Natasha!' A dog barked. The voices faded. The machine began its shush-shushing. Nicholas remained with his head in his hands, hearing it again, matched into memories forgotten.

And now it was women's voices, sailing gaily in, a clatter of cups and the observances of lemon and sugar. Someone named Maria said that she was hot and sticky from basketball and how much she and Nicolai looked forward to their leave. Another said she thought Nicolai looked very tired. The leave would do him good. It was such a hot country. So trying for them all.

Nicholas felt a pang to hear his Russian name spoken, and wondered about Maria, the wife of Nicolai, where she came from, how she had lived and what might be her appearance. The voices chattered on, then stopped. The machine shushed sleepily, as though to soothe him. On the far edge of consciousness he heard the male voices cut in.

There are remembrances that can grip with the possession of a dream, so that while awake consciousness is severed from reality, returned to a past become present. In the beginning of his freedom it had happened often to Nicholas. A bombed site, tumbled in ruin, could halt his mind, and flame and smoke, while aircraft dived and bombs burst and earth, stone and bodies gushed upwards. Sometimes it would be a glimpsed face, masked by illness or suffering, which would change into all those other faces, and walk the street, or hang on straps in the Tube. He could pause at a window filled with food and see only starvation's stumbling misery, skeletal heads and skeletal arms picking through garbage for scraps.

He heard the words grow louder in his mind from a stupor of mixed recall, while the blood drained and his body blanched with the force of electric shock. Relentlessly the lowered, communing voices drove the words into his brain like nails.

'—Everything will be pre-empted. Nothing can stop it now.'

He wanted to cry, no! To claw himself out of the pit of this outrageous dream.

'—They are readied from every side. It will be early in the New Year. When it is over, it will be better politically for all the world.'

Nicholas tried to push himself up, transfixed by the shining metal machine washed in the warm sunshine, one baleful eye turned towards him. The lowered voices ran like fire in his brain. One of them was Kapitsa's.

'—America will be able to do nothing. The fields can be put out like candles.'

Nicholas sank back, his eyes clenched. The voices went on and on.

Twice he reran the long section of tape, his hands almost useless, his mind shaking as all his body shook. Then the machine clacked and was silent. It seemed to blank him out, as though too much struggled there and a circuit breaker had switched off the load. In blankness he poured a whisky, slopping it so that it splashed on the cabinet shelf, ran and fell in drops to the tiles. He forced the spirit down, while it shocked him back to awareness, slopped more into the glass and drank that until all the reeling stopped.

And now the past, which had lived in him unnoticed for years, the way the organs in a body are unnoticed until they ache or ail, became a comfort and refuge. Nicholas drew deliberately on it, reviving it without mercy, to match this monstrosity and steel himself with calm. Kemal had been unable to trust the others in the ingenious madness of the plot. He had been compelled, as a paranoiac is compelled, to search for evidence of treachery, or weakness in resolution. The line between

129

fanaticism and insanity is drawn unbearably thin. Again images of violence erupted in Nicholas's mind. In Area Red ... the timing schedule in Area Green ... there is much to be reclaimed, Brother.

Cairncross had looked over his glasses and suddenly said that, his voice ruminative and odd ... there is much to be reclaimed, Brother. Surely, Cairncross could not have had an intimation of this. A loathing for his own involvement crept over Nicholas, heaping his stomach with nausea. And a hatred for the man who had involved him, and the forces of evil everywhere.

He had no fear for himself. That was overwhelmed in the fear for what he knew. He was selfless in his need to get away and stop it. To run through the cobbled courtyard and the grey-walled passages and hammer at Room 27.

That evening, perhaps earlier, Kemal would return. Before then, he would have to escape. He turned to the windows, the citrus, the blossomed bushes and the white stone wall patched with patterns of damp. The guard would be squatted again outside the door. The fat Arab and others were somewhere in the house. He remembered that today was Thursday and weakened with relief. There would be an outgoing flight in the afternoon. Again the wall drew him and he estimated it against his height. He would need such a small and precious fragment of time. A few minutes to pass between the trees. A few minutes to leap and find a grip. He had the language, had passed for an Arab in the Souk. There were few who could mark or identify him.

A frightened mind can be made impotent by options, hypnotized by the danger of choices past the possibility of action. Nicholas had no option or choices. He put on the jacket in the bedroom, wearing no tie in the Arab fashion, checked his air ticket and passport and wallet. He put his ear to the door and heard nothing. In the sitting-room he slipped the catch on the window, peeped out, searching the garden and the corner of the house and saw and heard nothing there. For an instant he thought to take the recorder, so inert and unknowing a thing for all the awful words it could speak. But he could not be encumbered at the wall, and switched it on with sudden cunning, for a cover. Nicholas almost wondered at the calm clarity working his mind and took up the straight, hard chair. Holding it, he stepped through the window.

The ground was damp, as hushed as carpet. Not a leaf moved

on the trees or bushes and vines, all that green seeming to exist only in a painting. Nicholas was at the wall, one foot on the chair, as though it had not needed locomotion, as though the wall had rushed towards him while he stood like that. He heard the cough, and felt himself paralyse. Slowly, painfully he turned his head, and saw the guard's back, at the corner of the house, his face tilted upwards, his left hand at his crotch in the absorption of urination.

Nicholas reached up and felt the sharp edge of coping, reached farther and closed his grip. The chair toppled as he sprang, scrambled over the wall and dropped into a lane littered with rubbish. He pushed himself up and pressed against the stone, his breath sobbed by the hammering of his heart. It was very still and quiet in the lane, sunlit and peaceful. He waited on the outcry. Nothing disturbed the stillness, save the distant sounds of the city. Nicholas began to walk, trying not to hurry.

Twice in the lanes he lost himself, getting back to the Souk, to the only streets he knew. Trying not to look over his shoulder, to all the exposure and vulnerability he could feel between his shoulder blades. Sparks of panic lit while he straggled to put them out. And then flared, remembering that he had no dinars, only Kemal's pound notes, which a taxi-driver could not accept.

His legs began to jolt. And then he had turned a corner, into a street that he recognized, beckoning him towards the Italian restaurant and the old man in the white apron. He saw that the door on the corner was open, and swallowed with gratitude.

The restaurant was empty. The Italian was setting cutlery, moving very slowly, almost mesmerized by this automatic task which he had performed so many thousands of times. He looked up, and stopped, one hand full of knives and forks and spoons.

'*Neharkum sa'id.*'

'*Neharkum sa'id we mubarak.*'

The Italian's face was musty with perspiration, and it showed under the thinning hair so carefully drawn across his scalp. He looked past Nicholas as though someone stood behind him.

'I wonder if you could help. You know me, don't you? I sometimes eat here.'

'I know you,' the Italian said.

'I need to change some money. Some sterling.'

The old man nodded.

131

'The banks are open. You will have no difficulty.'

They were both foreigners, strangers among the Arabs. Nicholas had to trust him.

'I would rather not go to the banks. It's personal, a private reason.'

Again the Italian looked past him.

'It's very important. I have to get to the airport. I'm catching the flight to London. The money is for a taxi.'

The old Italian began stolidly laying the table.

'Have you a booking on this flight?'

'No. Not yet.'

Nicholas felt his eye twitch. His thoughts rushed to Kemal.

'It's very hot,' the Italian said, frowning. 'The temperature is above one hundred.'

The banality made Nicholas's nerves scream.

'If you wish,' the Italian said, without looking up, 'I could send my boy to do your booking. He would make a small charge for the service. You could wait here.'

Nicholas tried to make his voice firm.

'That would be very kind. It is hot. I've been walking. I don't feel very well.'

'It is hot,' the old man agreed, and wiped his hands on the apron. 'If you'd like to sit over there, in the corner, I will bring you coffee. When customers come you should order something to eat.'

In the corner, Nicholas closed his eyes again, a sudden weakness in his muscles. 'Bless him,' he thought, 'bless him.' And then, 'I'm going to get away. I'm going to get away.'

Across the wide boulevard that fronts the Castle, cars double park at an angle. Date palms rear abruptly out of the concrete on the short walk to the waterfront. The sides of the Castle are tall and sheer, designed to be unscalable. A few square windows can be seen, high up under the flat roof, and a close row of small arches at one end.

Comrade Kapitsa of the KGB entered the Castle that afternoon with the listening device in a briefcase, uncovered during a renovation by the Ambassador's chauffeur, who was also the Embassy carpenter. Kapitsa's instructions from his Ambassador were to be brief and formal. Other representations were being made in Egypt and at the Headquarters of the United Arab Republic.

When the flagged Embassy car had gone from the palmed court behind the building in the latening afternoon, Captain Abdul Hamil, Chief of the Republic's Intelligence Police, the man known to Nicholas Arden as Kemal, hurried to the old Chevrolet. He clutched the front seat on his short journey to the walled villa in Garden City, one eyelid quivering in spasm, his dark face slashed with lines that had deepened. Comrade Kapitsa had told him what might be on the tapes. In the mind of the Chief of the Republic's Intelligence Police, Nicholas Arden was dead.

CHAPTER EIGHT

WHEN one no longer wants a thing, reasons are found
to no longer like it. Its errors and deformities present themselves suddenly, or are sought out by the rationalizing mind.
The change which had come over David Lawrence both up-
lifted and depressed him. He was full of his new purpose, wondering at it, as a child might at something precious found in a
pocket. But the wonder of it only served to disgust him with
everything else. He kept off the back streets driving home, pre-
ferring the aggravation of the traffic to the squalor of tenements,
drains and refuse. He was depressed by the sewage that drained
into St. George's Bay, the dingy shade of the mountain snow,
the vulgarity of the rich and the touting venality of the poor.
Even the old mosaics in the lodge, the stained-glass panels and
the brass, offended him with their finicky, intricate extravagance. Only the garden pleased him, and he spent his time there
when he could, in the sun with a book or a drink.

Lawrence had uncovered a stranger within, or his true self let
become strange. He needed time and privacy to become accustomed to this new person, the new ways he saw through him.
Morrow had observed this withdrawal and had been briefly
irritated by it. He was accustomed to having all the young
man's attention.

Lawrence kept the photograph of 'the man in the middle' in
the top drawer of his desk. He often took it out, studying the
face, furnishing the once unknown image with everything he
now knew, feeling that man alive and near him. He did not
know how he could help, or of what help he might be in need.
He waited, unable to declare himself to Max Morrow, unable
to pack up and leave, until something was over, until he knew
all was well.

Lawrence understood that his guilt for the betrayal of
Nicholas Arden was symptomatic of other guilts. He understood
that there could be no going forward for him if this was left
behind. He had an act of expiation to make, no matter how
symbolic. It could be easy or hard, and either way it did not
matter.

In the absorbing, new-found clarity that seemed to dazzle everything with light, Lawrence also knew that part of his motive was selfish. He wanted the thing to be hard, as a masochist wants to be punished.

Morrow had fashioned himself like a shining blade, and that was his virtue, to cut. He could feel for himself and perhaps a little for those who were closest to him. But he had none of the imagination which is the condition of charity for others. Max Morrow would be nobody's Samaritan. And Lawrence knew that if it came to a challenge between them, he could not expect an ounce or quarter from the man he had so admired.

Relaxing after the counter-coup in the Sudan, the bottle out in the private room, Lawrence had probed for what he needed to know.

'If Arden does go back and picks up something that matters, how will we know?'

'He will make his report to Cairncross. Cairncross will report to his chiefs. If they dope it out and are sure they have something, the chiefs will pass it to State.'

Lawrence lit a cigarette, training his voice to be casual.

'If Arden does get on to something, and this Captain Abdul Hamil knows it, would he be in danger?'

'If Arden gets on to something, and lets Hamil know it, the man is a bloody fool. He's holding the cards. Cairncross dealt him the hand.'

Lawrence asked softly, 'But supposing Arden doesn't know how to play a hand like that?'

Morrow looked hard at him.

'It doesn't seem to get through to you, Character, that this game is being played for the biggest pot in the world. Pick up any newspaper. Someone, somewhere, has killed a gas station attendant for the fifty bucks in the till. Or mugged an old-age pensioner for what he's got in his pockets. The game out here isn't for millions. It's for billions. If Nicholas Arden makes only mistake enough to give Hamil a painful thought, he's as dead as Mohammed, and faster.'

Against the constriction in his mind Lawrence said, 'And that's what we squeezed him back to?'

Morrow finished his drink.

'No. We didn't squeeze him to get him dead. We want him out of there alive and well, with whatever he might be able to tell us.'

135

Again Lawrence stayed on after Morrow had left, drinking too much, going to the window to look across the city to the hard, clean line the sea drew on the sky. White ran on the blue-green of the water, dissolved, disappeared to rise and run again. The caps were like a continuing thought on the water, little white truths which even when spent, rose again to insist somewhere else. The truth that Lawrence had to hold to was that no man is the sacrifice of another. Someone, somewhere, and always, must stand up and be counted for that. What had Nicholas Arden to do with the profits of the oil conglomerates? Or the political intentions of the dark men who had needed his Russian tongue, the accident of his birth to a Muslim mother, the death rides into slavery and survival at last in another country?

In the bathroom Lawrence ran the hot and cold water, cupping his hands at the taps, to bathe the weariness that stiffened his face. He decided to have a drink at the Press Bar, find somebody to eat with. He didn't want to be alone tonight.

The next morning, putting together the political analysis, Lawrence was surprised to hear Morrow in the outer office. He had said he had appointments for the day. Lawrence put down his pen and waited. Morrow came in, carrying his briefcase and a light raincoat.

'I'm off, Character.'

Lawrence pushed back his chair and stood up.

'Off where?'

'Home.'

He had not intended to leave until the weekend. Lawrence said, carefully, 'Has something come up?'

'I don't know. State wants me.'

There had been no signal for Morrow on the Washington telex.

'How were you contacted?'

'Through the Embassy. Early this morning. Kramer booked me a flight, V.I.P.'

Something had happened. Something on which there could be no waiting. It was there in the hard, satisfied set of Morrow's face, the combative waking in his eye. If the professionals had made a break-through there might be no need for Nicholas Arden.

'Is it anything to do with this other business, do you think?'

136

'I don't know. But it's likely, Character.'

Morrow indicated the papers on the desk. 'How's that coming on?'

'It should be ready to Xerox tomorrow.'

'Don't Xerox it. Type me up a fair copy and send it in the Diplomatic Bag. The Washington Office can put it on Beirut paper. Kramer tells me that a lot of outgoing mail is being sampled. Everybody has the jumps.'

'What time is your flight?'

'In an hour.'

'Do you want me to drive you out?'

'No. Kramer has an Embassy car downstairs.'

'You'll keep in touch?'

'I'll telex you after I've been with State. Keep your nose clean.'

Lawrence nodded.

Morrow said, 'Any message for your mother? I could call her.'

'No. I'll write her.'

'That's it, then.'

He left. Lawrence stood at the desk, looking after him. In all the time he had known Max Morrow they had never shaken hands.

Two days after Morrow had left, Lawence completed the Sudan compilation and drove the material to the outer suburb where Freni's father, the consultancy's confidential typist, lived in a small apartment. The visit involved hospitality and repeated reassurance that Freni's manners, competency, and punctuality continued to give satisfaction. Leaving, Lawrence decided on impulse to call on Barbara Barse. He still felt the need of company and had driven in her direction.

The gateman gave Lawrence a welcome and announced that Miss Barse was at home. Lawrence drove through the gardens and parked alongside a new Mercedes. The sky had cleared, the wind had dropped, as it often did at this season. The autumn sunlight was almost hot. Barbara Barse was in the loggia, reading on a long cane chair. She closed her book and sat up.

'What a pleasant surprise, David.'

He leaned and kissed her forehead. Barbara rang a table bell.

'What would you like? Coffee, tea, a drink?'

'How's that special brandy of yours?'

'Dwindling, I'm afraid. However, special drinks for special friends. Sit down and tell me about yourself. Max said you'd been away.'

Lawrence nodded.

'A short trip, Barbara.'

'Where have you been?'

She excused herself to speak to the servant.

'Tripoli, for a few days. And a few more days in London.'

'Business?'

'Business.'

Barbara leaned back and carefully crossed her legs.

'Don't tell me about it. I've never quite understood what it is that you and Max do. That man is for ever coming and going. Poor Helen. It gives me a headache to think about it.'

'Who owns the new limousine? Have you house guests?'

'Just got rid of some. A couple I met in Paris, and a painter friend of theirs. Very disappointing. They didn't entertain me at all. The limousine, as you describe it, is temporarily mine.'

'Another car? Really, Barbara.'

She said, in a miffed voice, 'Don't be so puritan. It bores me. Why shouldn't I have another car, if I want one? Actually, it's on hire. I'm having work done on the Bentley.'

Lawrence drank some of the coffee and filled the cup from the brandy bottle.

'What's up with the Bentley?'

'I'm having the glass replaced.'

'A different colour of tint? Something to match a new outfit?'

She wagged a finger at him.

'You don't really approve of me, do you? You think me entirely frivolous. I will have you know that I have a very good brain when it's needed.' She leaned back. 'Actually, I'm having the Bentley bullet-proofed.'

He laughed and felt better for it.

'Bullet-proofed? Whatever for?'

She frowned and looked a little discomforted.

'Well, not exactly bullet-proofed. Just the glass. I've a horror of being cut by flying glass.'

Lawrence was still amused.

'And why do you expect glass to go flying?'

'Don't be so superior,' Barbara said. 'The young never believe that anything nasty can happen. It is a very tedious quality in them. How about all that shooting in the streets last year? One could be hit quite easily. With all those Palestinian refugees raving in their camps, the city is becoming unsafe. Every time Sadat says something that pleases them, they bang off their beastly guns.'

'You can solve that problem by not driving near the camps.'

'I'm taking a very sensible precaution, and you know it. I've no intention of spending the rest of my life in a mask, or having to hide away like the Phantom of the Opera. If you must know, Max suggested it.'

'Max?' Lawrence was incredulous. 'Max suggested bulletproofing?'

'Well, not actually. But he's been suggesting that I should go home. He keeps saying that he's got something up his nose, a most inelegant expression, that trouble of some kind is coming.'

'Did he specify the trouble?'

'Trouble is trouble. I am entirely uninterested in its brand name.'

Lawrence took a cigarette from a box.

'You're getting jumpy, Barbara. Max suggested that you should go home, because he thinks you're wasting yourself. If you want the quote, he said you should go home and breed horses, or take up good works. He thinks you're suffering from an extreme case of boredom.'

'Does he now?' she said tartly. 'If Mr. Morrow wishes to alleviate boredom, he should begin at home, by spending more time with his wife. I find my condition entirely suitable. From what I read about conditions at home, one isn't safe in a bulletproof vest.' She put down her drink. 'Are you dining anywhere tonight?'

'No.' Lawrence shook his head.

'Then you may escort me to the Café du Liban. After dinner you can watch me play the tables. There is something very gloomy about you. If I didn't know you to be heartless, I could suppose that you were in love. Now come inside. I would like your opinion on the new decorations. Tiki has the most wonderful taste. I might even marry him. He would make the most obedient husband.'

There was little to occupy Lawrence after the dispatch of the

139

Sudan material. He set himself without interest to extracting captions for the monthly newsletter. Morrow had written a good deal of it himself, in the green ink he customarily used.

Each time Lawrence checked the agency reports on the tele-printers he dawdled in the room, hoping that the direct line with the Washington office would signal itself on circuit. After the third day, with no message from Morrow, he found it hard to concentrate on routine. There could have been other reasons for Morrow's recall. Lawrence had only limited knowledge of the consultancy's Washington operation. But it was hard for him to believe that it was not connected with oil. What else could have justified the urgency? The direct contact with the Embassy? The immediate V.I.P. loading?

Each day Lawrence had eaten a snack in the Press Bar at the St. Georges Hotel. The correspondents were listless again after the brief Sudan excitement. There was general opinion that Hassan was finished in Morocco. Someone was running a book on how soon the Royal House would topple. Moroccan crafts-men were said to be refurbishing the King's chateau outside Paris.

A visiting English journalist had tried to get into the closed territory inside the Lebanese border with Israel. He had been roughed up by the guards and had his cameras confiscated. He had pleaded that he had taken a drive and got lost, and was now confined to the hotel.

'It's crawling with armour up there,' he was saying. 'I got a long-distance shot of a convoy bigger than anything I saw in the 'Nam.'

The UPA man introduced Lawrence, and said that David was in public relations. The flushed journalist paused for a superior examination.

'Indeed? And what do you relate, publicly?'

He turned back to the others.

'How deep is that closed territory?'

'About fifteen miles,' someone said.

'And none of you have ever got in there?'

'You can't get in.'

'I got in. I tell you it's crawling with armour up there . . .'

Lawrence returned to the office late. The English journalist had received notice of his expulsion. A page had called him to the manager's office. Two security officers had given him the statutory twenty-four hours. On his return a party developed.

Lawrence went unsteadily to check the telex and then mixed an Alka-Seltzer, taking it to his desk. He had a great need to do something, to take some action. His room seemed unbearably quiet and still. He pulled some papers towards him, but the typescript blurred. He went to the window and watched the little white caps running to the skyline, as they had for days. He had to do something.

'Would you put me through to Mr. Kramer, please . . . David Lawrence.'

He heard the telephone buzzing, and then Kramer's mid-west tones.

'Yes?'

'Robert?'

'Yes. Who is this?'

'David Lawrence.'

'What can I do for you, David?'

There was little friendliness in the voice. Kramer had no time for amateurs.

'I'm wondering if you've heard anything from Max?'

Lawrence sobered a little on the cold silence.

'Why should I have heard from Max?'

'I just thought,' he said clumsily, 'that you might have heard from him.'

'In that case I must disappoint you.'

'Sorry to have troubled you.'

'Feel free,' Kramer said, so as not to mean it.

Again next day Lawrence went to the St. Georges for company. Freni was Xeroxing the monthly newsletter for that afternoon's mail. He had nothing further with which to distract him during the waiting. He had tidied up in the office before coming out, locked away all the papers, not intending to return. He had an appointment to play squash at the club with a new acquaintance from the American University. Lawrence had accepted a further drink and was thinking about the time, when he had the feeling that Max Morrow had telexed. The instinct troubled him until he had to go back and see.

Freni was busy putting the newsletters into covers. There had been no telex. It left Lawrence feeling slightly foolish, as he had done after his telephone call to Kramer. He waited uncertainly, Freni politely halted in her work. Resentment filled him for Morrow's silence, and then a sudden determination. In the machine room he sat on the stool and called the Washington office, lighting a cigarette while he waited an acknowledgement. The telex tapped out readiness to receive. Lawrence headed his message, picking it out with two fingers. After the brief exchange was completed and the key shut, he sat on in the room. The signals clerk had checked with the office manager. It was understood that Max Morrow was still in Beirut.

Lawrence arose late next morning, fuzzy with hangover and the leavings of a sleeping pill. In the kitchen he switched on the percolator and considered boiling an egg. The unrest in his stomach discouraged him. He tried to eat a little cereal. The unused today and tomorrow seemed like a desert to be trudged. He drank the strong coffee and refilled the cup.

After breakfast, still in pyjamas and slippers, Lawrence smoked a cigarette in the garden. Earlier in the month, Abdul had planted seeds of marigolds and zinnias. Already their leaves were as long as a hand. It occurred to him that he would not see them flower in the spring, and felt a touch of sadness. He had been happy for a time in this house, or had thought himself to be happy. It was strange that it all seemed so strange now, empty and unwanted.

Nettles had sprouted in a tub of geraniums. It would have been easy to pull them out. But any physical effort seemed beyond him. Grasp the nettle, he thought aimlessly, and wondered why. It was because he didn't know what he was going back to, and was afraid. Lawrence thought of that other man and felt himself ashamed. The sun went in behind cloud, leaving a sudden chill, darkening the garden. Lawrence went inside to bathe and dress. He thought a walk might be good for his liver.

When Middle East Research had ceased operation due to loss of influence and connection, caused by arrests, flight, sackings, one assassination and two changes of government, the consultancy had welcomed MER's offer of its Tripoli agent and the Alitalia steward. The profitable enterprise of smuggling had become hazardous for the crews. Lawrence paid the courier in cash when he made a delivery. Bellini's retainer continued to be lodged at a bank address in Rome.

Lawrence had not heard the postman's noisy Lambretta or his ring at the door, soaping himself in the shower closet. He was leaving for his walk when he saw the envelope on the tiles, under the mail drop. The handwriting was unfamiliar. He knew nobody who might write to him at this address, special delivery

142

from Rome, and took the letter to the sofas. A smaller, sealed envelope was inside, unaddressed and stained. Lawrence opened the single, folded sheet of Alitalia notepaper.

'Dear Sir: I am changed to another run for two weeks ending 1st next month. I am posting this for hurry.' The note was signed, 'Your Servant.'

A surge of emotion rose in Lawrence. He stared at the small, dirty envelope, unable for a minute to open it, afraid of what might be inside, of what it could mean to him. He stilled his hands to tear off a corner, took out the sheets of ruled paper. It was hard to read the scratched Arabic. Lawrence composed the translation in his head.

'I think your man in trouble – he came to exchange money on the day of the 12th – he wanted to go to the airport – he had no bag – he waited for car and sat in corner – he would not take coffee – he said if any men come and ask things he had not come to my place – he left in car two minutes from mid-day – no men did come – I think your man in trouble.'

Lawrence let the pages slide from his fingers. Nicholas Arden had gone back. Something had happened. Something he had needed to run from. He heard Max Morrow again: 'If Nicholas Arden makes only mistake enough to give Hamil a painful thought, he's as dead as Mohammed, and faster.' Lawrence blundered to his feet in a misery of guilt.

He had no bag. He had asked Bellini not to report his visit if he should be questioned. Lawrence picked up the pages again, moving his lips on the words. The headache which had threatened him all morning began to beat behind his eyes.

'—No. We didn't squeeze him to get him dead. We want him out of there alive and well, with whatever he might be able to tell us.'

Something had happened. Something which Arden had needed to run from. Lawrence had waited on this and now he didn't know what it meant. What had Nicholas Arden discovered? Why had he not been able to play the hand Cairncross had dealt?

Another thought jolted Lawrence with a force that made him wince. Max Morrow seemed to be there in the room, speaking aloud his reminders.

'—It doesn't seem to get through to you, Character, that the game is being played for the biggest pot in the world . . .'

If Nicholas Arden had escaped did that mean he would be

safe? Lawrence read yet again through the scratched, mesmerizing words. He could see in his mind dark men like hounds, running on that other man's trail.

'—He came to exchange money on the day of the 12th—'

Lawrence checked the calendar on his watch. The fourteenth. Arden had left Bellini's two minutes before mid-day. If he had got away, Arden would have reported to Cairncross. A tide of relief rushed through him. Almost running, he went to the bedroom to fetch the telephone number. Shakily he dialled for an overseas call, tormented by the slow procedure. He heard the operators exchange a joke and almost shouted into the mouthpiece.

An hour later the telephone rang. Lawrence sat slowly down and lifted the receiver.

'I have your London connection ringing, sir. You are lucky to get it so quickly. There's not much traffic on Saturdays.'

Lawrence struggled for a remark. Saturday. He had forgotten that today was Saturday. Miserably, he thanked the girl. A man at last answered the buzzing.

' 'ullo?'

Lawrence said, his voice sagging, 'Could I speak to Mr. Cairncross?'

'There's nobody 'ere, sir, of that name. Everything 'ere is closed up.'

Trying, he said, 'Is there any way I could get Mr. Cairncross's home number?'

He heard the man suck a breath through his teeth, imagined him shaking his head.

'I wouldn't know about that, sir. I'm only the watchman.'

Desperately, Lawrence asked, 'Is there anybody else in the building?'

'There was the cleaners in, but they've gone now.' As though to compensate for that, the voice added, 'If you know where the gentleman lives, Enquiries might be able to 'elp you.'

Lawrence said, 'No, I don't know the address.'

'What was the name, again?'

'Cairncross. Mr. Cairncross.'

Again he heard the man suck his breath.

'There'd be any number in the book of that name, sir. You'll have to wait until after the weekend, I'm afraid.'

'Yes,' Lawrence said. 'Thank you.'

Sunlight glowed again through the stained-glass panels, intensified to fill the air with splashing colours. Lawrence lay back on the cushions, his hand limp on the replaced receiver.

Much later, he had tried to eat, picking at a sandwich. Old Abdul had arrived to do something in the garden. Lawrence had sent him away. He felt too raw to endure company, his nerves unable to support the old man's rambling interruptions. He had continued to drink, not noticing, out of the reflex need to use his hands. The whisky had compounded his early morning hangover. It weighted the flesh beneath his eyes, touching the fair skin of his face with tiny wrinkling lines. When the doorbell chimed he heard it as though from a distance, feeling himself too dulled and weary to answer. Again, the chimes climbed the scale. Lawrence rubbed his face and went to the door.

For an instant he thought that the sunlight in his eyes had tricked him. Everything jumped out of recognition, flickered and then steadied.

'Well, Character?'

'What . . .'

'I called you,' Morrow said, 'the line was engaged.'

Lawrence backed inside, too surprised to think.

'What . . .' he began again. And then, rushing, 'I tried to get you on the telex. Nobody knew where you were. When did you get in? Why didn't you signal?'

Morrow appraised the almost empty bottle, the dishevelled hair and face.

'It's a long story. You'd better sit down.'

'When did you get in?' Lawrence repeated.

'Late last night. You look as though you've been on a party.'

Morrow opened the cabinet and chose a glass. Lawrence tried to clear his eyes, brushed a hand hurriedly over his hair. When Morrow had prepared a drink he sat down and crossed his legs. The perfect polish on the antique leather of his shoes deepened in a shaft of coloured light. The tight tanned skin on his keen face seemed to brighten. Lawrence felt his spirit fall back under the cold, almost distant scrutiny.

Morrow said, 'We've got a problem, Character.'

Lawrence fumbled for a cigarette. He waited for Morrow to continue.

'I'm not sure where to begin,' Morrow said.

'What were you wanted for?'

Morrow seemed undecided how to answer.

'State swore me in.'

'State swore you in? Why?'

'We were wrong about the oil.'

'Wrong?'

'It isn't nationalization.'

'What is it?'

Morrow turned, his face set.

'State wants you sworn in, Character. The Embassy, first thing Monday morning.'

The pain behind Lawrence's eyes stabbed him fiercely.

'What the hell is this, Max?'

'I can't tell you until you've been sworn.'

Lawrence felt the room fill with warning. His head began to clear.

'No,' he said. 'I'm not going to be sworn for something I don't understand.'

'You're my employee,' Morrow said, 'I've been told to have you sworn.'

Morrow's will was bent on him. Lawrence looked up. Slowly he rose to cancel the advantage.

'I won't be sworn.'

'You could be making trouble for yourself.'

'I won't be sworn.'

Morrow sighed. A ripple of fatigue passed over his features. There was ash on the sleeve of his coat. He picked it off and leaned back.

'Last word?'

'Yes.'

'You've got to know?'

'Yes.'

Morrow turned and studied the cathedral lights on the glass.

'They've got us beat.'

'Who have us beat, how?'

Morrow said tiredly, 'Captain Hamil, the others. The whole goddamn scheming pack.' He shook his head. 'I've got to hand it to them.'

Lawrence had not seen Morrow like this. His own resolution strengthened.

'Hadn't you better tell me?'

'We were almost right. The Russians in the oil states are technicians.'

'Are they going to take over the fields?'

'They're going to close them down,' Morrow said. 'They're going to choke the wells, disable the plants. The Arabs are going to slice up the pipelines, wreck the port installations. If the United Nations puts armies in, risks a third world war, it could take a year to get the oil back. In a year, in six months, perhaps three months, Japan and Western Europe would be wrecked for another decade.'

A vice clamped around Lawrence's head. Spots interrupted his vision.

'But why?' he asked wildly. 'It doesn't make any sense.'

'Sense means different things to different people. The Final Solution made sense to the Nazis. The Assassination of the Kennedys and Luther King made sense to the men who pulled the triggers.' Morrow emptied his glass. 'This makes that kind of sense.'

'For Christ's sake, what do you mean?'

'War, Character. The Holy War against Israel. The Arabs have planned a pre-emptive strike. They're going to hit from everywhere at once. Egypt, Libya, Syria, the Lebanon. This other thing, putting out the fields, only exists at present as a threat. If Israel goes down, and the West tries to help, they put out the fields and slit our jugulars.'

When he could, Lawrence said, 'How do you know? How do you know about this?'

'Every government in the West had it leaked to them weeks ago. Our own little operation confirmed it. That's why State swore me in. That's why you have to be sworn. We've got to destroy all the paper we've got on this.'

And still Lawrence could not understand.

'Israel must be told. Has Israel been told?'

Morrow said, very gently, 'Israel can't be told.'

'Can't be told? What for Christ's sake are you talking about? The President ...'

Morrow filled both glasses. White patches dirtied the tan on his cheeks.

'I want you to listen carefully.' He took his eyes off the young man's strained face and began to walk, head bent.

'Why can't Israel be told?' He ruminated on that. Then straightened. 'Israel can't be told because it would put us all on a hook. It could commit us to an action which would be suicide to take. Even a Declaration of Intent would cause the Arabs to

147

put out the fields. We can't live without the oil, any more than a body can without blood.'

In a sudden vehemence that appealed for comprehension, he swung round on Lawrence. 'Do you understand that? That's the bullet we have to bite on. That's where technology has got us. Everything, the power that works our cities, all the chemical and industrial by-products, the fuel in our cars and ships and locomotives and aircraft, every goddamn thing we live by . . .'

He stopped, breathing hard. Then began again.

'If Israel was told, knowing the West would have to stand still for what might happen, they'd put up an outcry heard around the world. We've got three million Jews in New York alone. We'd have a civil war on our hands.'

Lawrence began to speak. Morrow put up a hand. 'It's no use. These are the facts of life.' He jerked his head, as though to dislodge something.

'You've seen the Tap Line. Two thousand miles of pipes broader than a four-lane highway, laid across the desert sands all the way to Sidon on the Eastern Mediterranean. The exposed artery of our civilization. They could cut it in a thousand places. Saudi, Jordan, Syria, anywhere at all. The pipes out of the Sirir oil fields to the Hariga terminal deliver one hundred and fifty thousand barrels a day. One Palestinian guerilla with satchel charges could blow it in a dozen places in a night.'

Lawrence heard his voice crack in protest.

'But America has oil. We could get oil to Europe.'

Morrow shook his head.

'No. America is a net importer itself. All the tonnage we could spare or buy or steal would have to go to the NATO forces.' He turned. 'Do you see how they've got us? NATO could be immobilized. From West Germany to the Channel, the armour could rust on the ground, the air forces rot in their hangars, the ships of the navies rot at their moorings.'

Again Lawrence said, like a cry, 'Israel must be told.'

And again, softly, Morrow said, 'Israel can't be told.'

Lawrence stood up. Every secure and familiar thing he saw now mocked him, flickering into other images as though they too shared this hallucination.

Morrow said, to help him, 'They've planned it well. This is what was meant by those coloured areas. The needs of the timing schedules . . .'

A tremor ran through Lawrence.

'Nicholas Arden!'

Morrow walked towards him.

'What about Nicholas Arden?'

'He went back.'

'How do you know?'

'There. It's there.' Lawrence pointed to the envelopes and papers on the table, strewn as he had left them. He tried to make himself realize that it had only been this morning. Morrow gave him a glance, sat and put on his glasses.

He made the papers neat, weighted them with a table lighter, returned the glasses to his pocket. Then he pinched his nose and poured another drink.

'When did you get it?'

'This morning.'

'It's been a big day,' Morrow said, in partial recognition.

Lawrence swallowed.

'He must have found out. He must know.'

'It doesn't have to be that.'

'It is that. I know it.' Lawrence wanted to shout: I betrayed him. You betrayed him. Why did everyone force him back?

Morrow had his own thoughts, rising to pace again.

Lawrence said, 'Cairncross! Where does he live? Have you got his home number?'

Morrow stopped.

'No. Why?'

'I tried to telephone him. The watchman answered.'

Morrow studied Lawrence long and carefully before he spoke.

'You shouldn't have done that.'

'If he got away, Cairncross must know.'

Morrow did not answer.

'What will happen to Nicholas Arden?'

Morrow leaned back and shut his eyes.

'Your friend,' he said, his voice bleak, 'will tell Cairncross what he knows.'

'And then?'

'Cairncross will tell his chief.' He waited. 'His chief will tell it to someone else. This someone else will inform the Prime Minister.'

'Yes. And then?'

'I imagine,' Morrow said, 'the Prime Minister will have a bad moment. Eventually, Cairncross will tell Arden that he is mistaken. He will apologize for ever having called him in. He will shake his hand and send him home.'

'Because they know.'

'I told you,' Morrow said wearily, 'every government in the West knows.'

'And none of them will do anything?'

'I told you,' Morrow repeated, 'there is nothing anyone can do. If Israel goes down the West won't be able to lift a finger to help.'

Lawrence looked for a long time into the distance.

'If Nicholas Arden got out, can Hamil let him live?'

'I don't know. It's out of our hands.'

'It's out of our hands,' Lawrence said, with helpless bitterness. 'Everything is out of our hands. We can't warn Israel – that's the politics of oil. We can't help Nicholas Arden – that is out of our hands.'

Morrow asked, 'Where will you be this weekend?'

'Here.'

'You'd better take a grip on yourself.' Morrow made the warning clear. 'This is bigger than one young man's sensitive emotions.' He indicated the bottle. 'I'd put that away. It will give you bad thoughts. If you want to talk I'll be at the Phoenicia. If not, I will meet you at the Embassy, opening time Monday morning. You be there, Character.'

He stood threateningly over Lawrence, began something else and stopped.

'That's it, then.'

For a long time after Morrow had gone, Lawrence lay on the sofa, his face in a silk cushion. His thoughts moved without verbal definition, like a sky of shifting black and grey clouds. Several times he mumbled into the silk, until it dampened with saliva. The sun splashed no more colour through the panels when at last Lawrence pushed himself up. He lifted the bottle and drank until his stomach revolted.

In the bathroom, running hot water into the bowl, he leaned and studied his face, in an old narcissistic habit. A shaft of pure excitement so trembled his legs that he needed the bowl's support. Gradually it steadied, collected in his chest. David Lawrence leaned farther into the light from the flourescent tube above the mirror. He tried to see into the uttermost depths of the pupils staring him back.

150

Then he asked his image, seeing the measured movement of his lips, 'Are you *man* enough?' And once more, 'Are you *man* enough?'

Morrow had worried at it all the way back to town. He was inclined to trust his intuition. Driving fast in the hired car he tried to reason it away. Too fast on a corner, the car almost ran off the road. It was enough. If he was driving like that he had the jumps.

In his suite he went immediately to the telephone and called Kramer at home. 'Robert? Max ... I've got a job for you. I've got something up my nose ...'

That night, in his bed, reading after dining in the suite, Morrow answered the bedside telephone. 'Yes, Robert ...'

Slowly he swung his feet to the floor.

'You're sure? When was this?'

Hunched in concentration he removed the glasses and pinched his eyes.

'What did he do? Yes ... Yes, yes ... no trouble? No, I'm sorry. I can't brief you ... Yes, something like that. I want that airport locked tight. He might try again. If there's any charter out there, I want a man at charter. You can get that done? Sure, now?'

Morrow hung up, put on his dressing gown and slippers and lit a cigarette. He had been right to trust his instinct. The fool. The dangerous sentimental fool. Nothing had got through to him. Nothing. Morrow swung fiercely about the shadowed room. He wouldn't wait to have him sworn. He would have him sworn in the morning. Morrow checked his diary and dialled the Ambassador's home number. When he had had him sworn, Morrow would fly him home in a straitjacket.

The wrist-watch alarm awoke him at 7 a.m. Morrow ordered breakfast and the newspapers, shaved, showered and dressed. He had decided to make no mention of last night to Lawrence. It would be easier between them if that reckless folly was ignored.

Morrow telephoned the Heights and waited. The instrument buzzed and buzzed. He hung up, beginning to frown, dialled the number again. Exasperation deepened the lines on his forehead. He laid the receiver on the table, got a cigarette and lit it, began to pace, stopping to lean at the instrument and listen. Minutes passed. Lawrence couldn't be sleeping through that. He had either not gone home last night, or he was refusing to take the call. Morrow's exasperation changed into chilly anger. If Lawrence was trying to avoid him, where would he go?

This time there was no waiting.

'Put me on to Miss Barse ... then wake her, please. This is Max Morrow.'

He heard the connection being made, faint voices.

'Max? What on earth do you want? It's barely daylight.' And then less sleepily, 'My God, you've just gone away. I don't know how Helen puts up with you.'

'I've no time to chat, Barbara. Is David with you?'

'David? No. Should he be?'

'When did you last hear from him?'

'He visited last night.'

'At what time?'

'Time? I don't know. Eleven, perhaps. I was having a party. Is anything the matter? You sound like a KGB officer.'

Morrow said, 'He has an appointment this morning. At the Embassy. I couldn't raise him at home. How was he last night? Was he sober?'

'Just a minute.' Something clinked. 'That's better, I was parched. Now, what is this dawn interrogation?'

'David got tight yesterday, that's all. He's been a bit upset. I am sorry about your beauty sleep.'

'So you should be. What has upset David? I could make no sense of him at all. He fairly barged in, wouldn't stay for a drink, borrowed my car and was gone. Had I not been a little high I would certainly have refused him. My God! If he's going about being drunk in my Bentley, I'll be furious. I've just spent a fortune on it, having the glass bullet-proofed.'

Morrow felt the muscles in his face begin to draw. Very deliberately, he evened his voice.

'Barbara, did he come out in a cab, or in his own car?'

'In his own car. I saw it, farewelling my guests, and was rather surprised. I'd assumed he'd had some kind of breakdown.'

'Barbara, did David know that you'd had your glass bullet-proofed?'

'Yes. I told him when he last visited. He was most derisory about it. Max, I insist you explain these dramatics ... Max, are you there?'

'Sorry, Barbara. Go back to sleep.'

'Max! Max! Oh, really!'

Morrow had hung up.

It couldn't be believed. It was too fantastic. Morrow shakily lit a new cigarette. He wouldn't dare. Morrow could see it in his head. You would approach in the dark, at the closest point to the border. You would use the moon for light. You would keep off the made-up surfaces, find a dirt road to follow. You would steer by the stars where you had to. It was the kind of thing Morrow could do. Where you had to slam through, you would slam through. You could do it in a car like that. A car with bullet-proofed glass.

Morrow jerked to his feet. It couldn't be believed. Aloud, he said, 'He hasn't got the balls.' And then louder, 'He hasn't got the balls.'

Then he picked up his jacket, arming it on as he ran for the stairs.

CHAPTER NINE

NICHOLAS stopped the driver outside the house. He was too weakened by feeling to leave the car. The yellow plastic garbage can had not been taken in. Curtains were drawn across the living-room windows. A crack of bright light shone the glass. It seemed unreasonable that everything should be so unaltered. Children in duffle coats went noisily by, hoods up, hands in pockets, dark little humps in the dark.

A gust of wind buffeted the car, howled somewhere and departed. Nicholas drew on everything familiar, filling himself with it like a man who had stifled for breath. His mind almost creaked on this adjustment, as though it were the security and sanity and the plain face of his own street and home which might have become outrageous. For an instant he closed his eyes in gratitude. The driver coughed and fidgeted. Nicholas roused himself and got out, feeling the cold cut through his thin clothing. He paid the driver with the last of Kemal's notes and stiffly crossed to the terrace.

It seemed too much to let himself in, out of the cold and dark without warning. He felt that he had been gone many years, like an amnesiac who had come home at last and stood now at his own door fearful of what he might find. Nicholas pressed the bell and waited, huddling his shoulders against the wind.

He heard her steps rattle on the staircase. The tiny carriage lamp above the entrance lighted.

'Nicholas!' She stood partly dismembered by the cautiously unadmitting door, her eyes stretched in surprise. Then remembered and flung the door open. 'Oh, my dear. What a wonderful surprise.'

'Cora.' He had a fierce need to hold her, to smell her skin, to feel her hair on his face, hear her voice.

'Nicholas, my dear,' she gave a tiny, difficult laugh. 'You're squashing me.'

Gently, she disengaged herself. Her eyes jumped with dislocation as she looked at him.

'You're freezing. Why aren't you wearing your overcoat?'

She looked behind him, to the door he had shut. 'Where is

154

your bag, Nicholas?' And then, in the alarm that so easily moved her, 'Where is your tie? Why aren't you wearing your tie?'

'I left in a hurry,' he said.

She backed away into the sitting-room, blinking at the disorder in her vision.

'You left your bag ... and your overcoat? Your good new coat?'

'I had a quarrel with Kemal,' Nicholas said. 'There was an aircraft and I left.'

'You had a quarrel?'

'Yes.'

'What did you quarrel about?'

'He wanted me to stay on.' Wildly, he said, 'He wanted me to stay on ... for weeks. I said I couldn't do that. Kemal got angry. We had a quarrel ... You didn't want me to stay on, did you?'

Staunchly, Cora said, 'I should think not. I didn't want you to go. I told you about that man. I disliked him from the first sight of his face. Oh, my dear, how unpleasant for you. And now you've lost your things ...' She stood quietly bemoaning the loss.

Nicholas said, 'It would have been difficult to go back to the house and pack. I was afraid I would miss the flight.'

'Wretched little man,' Cora said with a dart of spite, 'they're all the same, those people. You can't trust them an inch. It must have been freezing without your coat. You've not caught cold, have you?'

'No. I'm just tired. How warm it is in here.'

'Sit down and rest. I'll make you a hot cup of tea.' She pecked his cheek and hurried to the kitchen. Nicholas heard the familiar clatter. 'Wretched little man,' Cora told herself, and called to Nicholas. 'I thought Bobby might be starting a cold. I've put him to bed with an aspirin. He will be so pleased to see you.'

Nicholas went to the sideboard and poured a sherry. There was only a little in the bottle. He remembered that it had been the priest's day to visit. He was home. For a little while he could perhaps rest his thoughts.

They had soon gone to bed, after Nicholas had talked to his son and eaten. He had gone to bed for the comfort she had to give him, signalling it by brushing against him, going to bathe and returning perfumed in her quilted blue gown, her short hair brushed and shining. She always enlarged a little like this, conscious of her importance, as one conferring a gift of value.

Nicholas had welcomed the dark, not expecting sleep, as something in which he could hide. But he had slept. Only in the early morning had his torment turned into dreams that awoke him, jerking and clammy with sweat. He pushed himself up as the kaleidescope faded. Kemal's slashed face, the voices on the tape, the eruptions of bombs and artillery. Very carefully, he lay back on the pillows. Cora must have turned her head towards him. He could feel her deep, even breathing on his cheek.

He wondered at what time Kemal had found him gone and imagined the alarmed ransacking of the house and garden. They would have found the chair against the wall. Exhaustion overcame Nicholas again. Had he mistaken what he had heard? What would Kemal do now? He began to drift, waking in violent starts.

'Who are you calling?'

Nicholas pushed the button and dropped the coins. He had to prepare himself to speak. It seemed that everything had been directed to this moment.

'It's Nicholas Arden.'

'Back already?'

'I have to see you.'

'So you shall. Are you all right, old boy?'

The normality of the words almost caused Nicholas to break. He wanted to shout the truth down the telephone, to rid himself in one cry.

'You don't understand. I have to see you – now.'

Cairncross seemed amused.

'Like that, is it? Then you had better come in. When shall I expect you?'

'I'll come now. As soon as I can get a taxi.'

He seemed to have been travelling for ever. Waiting and moving. Moving and waiting. The traffic crawled along, stopped at lights and policemen. 'Gettin' impossible, guv, isn't it?' the driver said to the rear-view mirror. Nicholas pushed against the seat and clenched his hands. Soon it would be over. Soon there would be an end of moving and waiting. A light rain began to drizzle the windows.

The courtyard was grey and wet now. A few pigeons squatted on the cobbles, their feathers ruffed.

'Mr. Arden? I'm to take you straight in, sir.'

The grey walls swam past him. The brass number on the heavy, polished door glinted. Nicholas sucked in a shaken breath. The long journey and everything behind him began at last to fade. Now he could lay down the burden. Cairncross opened the door and drew him in.

Nicholas hardly heard the amiable greetings, did not see the quick probes of the magnified eyes behind the spectacles. He was looking about the room, remembering it, to assure himself it was real.

'Sit down, won't you? Would you care for tea, or coffee?'

Nicholas shook his head, and almost laughed, his face screwed into conflict.

'Something amusing you, old boy?'

'It seems so absurd. Tea or coffee.' He shook his head, rubbed his face with a shaking hand.

Cairncross went to the desk and sat down, without shifting his eyes. He picked up a pipe and began to fill it. In his hairy winter tweeds, the blunt, peering face seemed more than ever like a friendly animal.

Nicholas looked up.

'I am tired,' he said.

Cairncross nodded wisely.

'I can see that. I find air travel very tiring myself.'

It was hard to go on. Everything in Nicholas seemed to have broken, like a jigsaw puzzle scattered into pieces.

Without volition, he heard himself say, 'I escaped.'

Cairncross fiddled with his matches.

'You escaped? Escaped from Kemal, I presume.'

'You were right about the translations. They had been taken from a tape.' Nicholas watched in a kind of fascination, as Cairncross slowly lit his pipe. 'This time he brought me the tape. There was a Russian family on it. A little girl, who sang nursery rhymes to her doll ... Kapitsa was on it. And another man whose voice I didn't recognize.'

'I see. I expected something of the kind might happen. The mish-mash, as you called it, must have greatly frustrated Kemal.' Cairncross gently blew out the match and laid it in an ash tray. He popped his eyes at Nicholas. 'And on this tape, you heard something ... sinister?'

'Yes.' Nicholas could hardly believe that this flat, dull voice was his. 'They are going to invade Israel. There's going to be a pre-emptive strike from all sides. They've got missiles set up everywhere. That's what the talks were about. They're going to wreck the oil supplies so that the West can't interfere, or deliver arms. One of the Russians said that after it is over, it will be better politically for all the world. They're going to invade Israel.'

Cairncross said, very severely, 'I beg your pardon?' He fairly bulged his eyes at Nicholas, and waited, as though for apology.

Nicholas pushed himself up and leaned on the desk. The torment now broke in his voice.

'Don't you see? Don't you understand what I'm saying? There's going to be war. Kapitsa said . . .' He struggled to remember the words. 'That the fields will be snuffed out like candles. Everywhere, in all the coloured areas, the plants will be wrecked and the oil lines cut. It's going to be a . . . blitzkrieg—' The old and terrifying word from the past came to him. 'The needs of the timing schedule have been prepared. The Jews are to be exterminated in a Holy War.' He stopped, his chest heaving.

The pipe had drooped absurdly in Cairncross's slackened mouth. Their faces remained close across the heavy desk. Cairncross almost croaked when he spoke.

'There is much to be reclaimed, Brother.' He swung in the chair and stared at the hunting prints on the wall. Then, more normally, 'Good Lord, this *is* serious.' He swung back. 'You're sure of this? The Arabs are in a position to put out the fields?'

Nicholas slowly sat back.

'They said they would bury the oil in the sands.'

'Good Lord,' Cairncross said in outrage, as though a waiter had spilled something on him. 'Good Lord, this *is* serious.' Quickly he leaned to his desk and opened a drawer, bobbed and came up with a telephone receiver. He stared past Nicholas, eyes expanded, light glinting on the rims of his spectacles.

'Cairncross. Inform Omega immediately that I have a Red Alert.' He banged the receiver back, banged shut the drawer.

'How did you . . . escape? Where were you? In the house?'

Nicholas told him.

'Kemal was to return that evening?'

'Yes.'

158

Cairncross shot up and began to trot about the room, thumbs in the pockets of his waistcoat. He stopped.

'Have you told your wife any of this?'

'She knows nothing.'

'Good. Has she any relatives she could go to?'

Nicholas answered slowly, 'She has her mother in Leeds.'

'Good. You have a son, haven't you?'

'Yes.' An awful fear lurched in Nicholas.

'We shall have to get them away. Now, this morning. Use any excuse you can think of.' He cocked his head. 'Kemal could send someone after you. You appreciate that, don't you?'

He had tried to forbid the thought. Now it swept him like panic. He had been brought to this. Bitterness filled him.

'Are you satisfied now? Have you got what you wanted?'

Cairncross bent before him, face close.

'Steady, now. I know exactly how you feel. It's sensible to take precautions. There's nothing to worry about, really.' He hurried back to the desk and dialled a number. 'Room twenty-seven – have you Hardy there? Good. Ask him to take a car immediately and bring it to the entrance.' He flicked his eyes at Nicholas and spoke a few more words, too low to be distinguished. He put his pipe in his pocket and searched for matches.

'When you go out, ask for Hardy. He shouldn't keep you more than a few minutes. Hardy will help you get your family to the station. You will be quite secure in his hands.' Cairncross propelled Nicholas into the passage. 'When you've made your arrangements, I would like to see you again. Shall we say four? At four this afternoon? Good. And Arden – don't worry.'

Cairncross trotted away. Nicholas turned towards the entrance.

The pottery mugs had been prepared with milk and sugar. Nicholas stood at the stove, watching the steam puff from the whistling kettle. Cora's sobs were loud in the silence. The central heating blew its stale, dry breath, itching the skin on his neck. The kettle began to cheep, then shrilled into a long, rising note as though in alarm at the bubbling in its innards. He measured tea into the pot, lifted the kettle.

'Here, dear,' he extended the mug.

She did not answer, sitting sideways on the soft chair, her face pressed into the flowered upholstery.

159

'Cora?'

She opened her eyes and saw the steaming mug, shook her head.

'I don't want it.'

'Come, now. It will do you good. Cora?'

Obediently she shifted, took the mug in both hands.

'It will only be for a few days.'

'But I don't understand,' she wailed.

'I had to take advice,' Nicholas said. 'I should have listened to you. Something was wrong from the beginning.'

'But the police. Why did you have to bring the police in? Why can't you come with us?'

'I told you. They want me here. I will have to identify Kemal if he tries to cause trouble.'

Again she wailed. 'I don't understand. Why didn't you say something last night?'

'I didn't want to worry you. Kemal was very angry when I left. The work was unfinished. I just had a feeling this morning that he might make trouble. The police agreed with me.'

'But this is England.' Her voice heightened in protest. 'How can that awful man make trouble for us here?'

Nicholas sat on the chair arm and fondled her head.

'I don't know, dear. It's just a feeling. They are strange people. You said so yourself. We don't want Bobby frightened, do we?'

'Oh, why did it ever happen? Why did we ever get mixed up with people like that? They can't be trusted. I told you they can't be trusted. They're not civilized like us.'

'I know,' Nicholas soothed. 'I should have listened to you. You were right from the beginning.'

'I knew there was something dishonest about it. All that secrecy. Messengers coming to the door.'

'Drink your tea,' Nicholas said. 'Shall I get you an Aspro?'

She shook her head, sniffing. The sobs began to pass.

'What are you going to tell Bobby?'

'We will just say that Gran has invited you both for the weekend. He hasn't seen her in a long time. I will make an excuse to the headmaster.'

'What am I going to say to Mum? You know how difficult she is. I can't tell her you've got into trouble. That you had to go to the police. I'd never hear the end of it. Never.'

How easily one deceit produces another, Nicholas thought sadly. How easily I find excuses.

'She knows I've been away a lot. You've written several times about that. You can tell her I've gone away again. That you got lonely and made a visit.'

'What will you do? I'll be worried out of my mind.'

'Now that's being silly,' he said sternly. 'Mr. Hardy is going to keep an eye on the house. If Kemal tries to cause trouble he will be taught a lesson. I will be all right if I don't have to worry about you and Bobby.'

'Oh, Nicholas.' She flung her arms around him, slopping tea from the mug. 'Oh, my dear.' She buried her head in his chest. 'I couldn't bear it if anyone hurt you. I know I've not always been a good wife. I've been selfish and bad-tempered sometimes. I promise I'll never be like that again.'

He felt it in his heart like a pain, comforting the childishly thin shoulders, so unlike the volume in the hips swelling against him. She was in many ways like a child. Part of her had never grown up. A fierce sense of possession charged itself in him.

'Don't worry,' Nicholas whispered. And then with belief, 'Nothing can hurt us now.'

He had made the excuse to the headmaster, fetched Bobby from the school. The child had been excited by the importance of being got from class, the other children curious and envious. He had been further excited by the unexpected treat of a trip in a train. Driving home in the little car the boy wondered if it was disloyal, and shifted uncomfortably.

Nicholas said, 'You've not seen your gran for a long time, have you? Don't make too much noise in the house. Gran isn't used to children.'

'She's all right,' Bobby said. 'She doesn't like noise when she's playing cards. She buys me sweets, though. I wish you were coming. Will you be all right on your own,' He considered further and said bravely, 'Would you like me to stay with you, Daddy?'

Nicholas patted his knee.

'No, son. You look after your mother.'

'You won't be lonely?'

His father looked at him and smiled.

'I've got things to do.'

The child frowned.

'We're getting to do a lot of travelling in this family.'

Nicholas nodded gravely.

'We men,' he said, 'always travelling somewhere. We live out of suitcases, you and I.'

'Oh, Daddy!' The child laughed, and squirmed on the seat. 'It will be super to ride on the train, though.'

When the carriage doors were at last banged shut and the small head in the window drawing away, Nicholas stood in the clutter and clatter of the platform and watched until the track emptied. He felt that his vitals had been drawn from him. All his efforts had been for Cora, a concentrated pretence almost believed, that this was ordinary. A gay-sad leavetaking like the others, a routine family affair.

'Don't worry,' he had told her. 'There's nothing to worry about.' And, 'Yes. I will telephone every night. Enjoy yourself. Don't worry.'

Nicholas walked the platform towards what must happen next.

'Enter.'

The attendant stood with his ear bent to the door, to hear through the heavy, muffling timber.

'There you are, sir.'

Nicholas felt a small concussion of air on the back of his head as the door shut.

'Ah!' Cairncross took out his pocket watch. 'Punctual, I see. Do sit down.' He put both hands flat on the big, leather-edged blotter. Briefly, he considered Nicholas and then studied his hands.

'I have an apology to make.'

A voice was raised faintly in the passage. It accentuated the silence, the bent head, the continued scrutiny of hands. Nicholas waited, a vague prickling on his skin.

'The fact is ... er ... Arden, a mistake has been made.'

The bent head, the deliberation, irritated Nicholas like an offence.

'A mistake?'

'Yes ... er ... our mistake, of course. In this trade, you see, one must look into everything. The fact is, we've had further information. We were mistaken about Kemal. The talks you interpreted were, in fact, concerned with water conservation.'

Only then did Cairncross look up, briefly pop his eyes. 'What do you think of that?' he asked, like someone displaying a curious object.

It was difficult for Nicholas, this violent lifting of everything again to be replaced in the opposite direction. He strained to put it into order.

'But it can't be . . .' he began.

'I assure you it can,' Cairncross said briskly. 'We have our sources. I won't go into that. I'm afraid, Arden, that we've caused you all this trouble for nothing.'

Nicholas tried to accept, but could not.

'No. The tape. It was on the tape.'

'The tape.' Cairncross scratched his blunt nose with a thumb. 'Some confusion there . . . yes. Of course that could have been anything. A joke, idle speculation. You were under a strain. Might have made a mistake yourself, what?'

It was hard to think. Everything was distorted, like the images in Fun Park Mirrors. Could he have been mistaken?

'I recognized Kapitsa's voice.'

'Possibly. But one can be easily misled by a tape. You'd not heard much Russian in a long time, had you?'

More surely, Nicholas said, 'I was not mistaken. Kapitsa is a Georgian. So was my father.'

Cairncross tapped his fingers, grunted and sat back. Then he leaned forward, making his voice final.

'I can only assure you, Arden, and this you might say, is official, that a mistake has been made. I recommend that you put it entirely out of your mind. Once again, I apologize for all your inconvenience.'

A bitter mix rose in Nicholas. He stood at the wall, a foot on the chair, and heard the guard cough. The scabbed door of the airport lavatory stared at him, while the long minutes passed in sweated apprehension: Cora sobbed into her chair. His son's face dwindled down the platform.

'Inconvenience,' he said. 'Yes. I have been inconvenienced.' He stood. 'I sent my family away. It's a comfort to have your apology.'

Cairncross tapped his fingers, musing, eyes lowered.

'Know how you feel, old man. A most regrettable mistake. I understand your feelings entirely. However . . .'

He popped his eyes and tried to beam. 'All's well that ends well, as they say. What?' He got up. 'I won't waste any more of your time. You'll think I've done that enough, no doubt. And rightly, too. Please accept my hand. And my thanks.' With the solicitude for one ill or infirm, he escorted Nicholas to the door.

'Let me add that it has been a privilege to meet you. Hardy will drive you home.'

The door closed. Cairncross blew a short breath, flapping his lips. Then he trotted quickly back to his desk, sat, opened the drawer and bobbed for the telephone.

'Cairncross for Omega . . .'

Nicholas walked between the grey walls towards the entrance, hot with confusion and the remainder of his anger. Something else nagged at him, like a familiar face one can't put the name to. It was the pipe. In all that time Cairncross had not touched his pipe.

Hardy stopped the car and turned in his seat. 'There we are, sir.'

He seemed less shadowy now, as though Nicholas had not had time before to properly register his presence. He had a thin face for a big man, an oblique way of avoiding encounter. Nicholas thanked him for his trouble and got out. Hardy nodded. The big Vauxhall reversed and turned. It had gone before Nicholas found his key. Crossing the road he had seen a movement at the curtained windows next door. His neighbours had interested themselves in this traffic of persons and cars. Nicholas put the key to the lock and let himself into the cheerless silence.

He tried to think, eyes closed, slumped in a flowered chair, the radio playing for company. He felt immensely tired, too tired to rise and draw the curtains. Too tired to make tea for that ritual comfort. The edges of his mind began to blacken. He watched the black deepen inwards until consciousness expired.

Voices woke him, close in the room. A start of alarm splashed upwards. He held his breath. A door creaked.

Someone said, 'It's gone.' Another, deeper, voice: 'Don't you think you'd better explain?' Nicholas opened his eyes. The first voice said, 'But I tell you it was here . . .' Shakily Nicholas got up and turned off the radio.

He looked at his watch. He had been asleep for almost two hours. It still hung heavily on him. His mouth was dry and sour, eyes hot and gritty. Nicholas drew the curtains on the window and went upstairs to wash. He was hungry now, but did not have the heart to cook for himself or face the cold comfort of a tin. He would telephone Cora to put her at rest and eat something in the village. The stairs sounded unusually loud in the empty house, as though hurt by his weight.

Leaving, he remembered the loss of his good new raincoat and found the old duffle in the laundry. Inconsequentially, it worried him again that Cairncross had not smoked his pipe. That he had required to lay his hands on the desk and study them like something foreign.

Nicholas made an effort to cancel the monologue that circled so monotonously in his brain. He went from the house by the back door, pulling it locked behind him. The sky had cleared, a half moon hung in the cold. He crossed the plot in which so little grew. The picket gate had come off its top hinge, he had intended for weeks to repair it.

A car, which he did not recognize, had parked farther down on the verge. As he reversed to turn, the headlights made out figures, dim behind the misted glass. Lovers sometimes parked there. It was a cold, cheerless night for that. Nicholas turned quickly, so as not to disturb them, and switched on the heater.

Despite the cold it was gay in the village. Friday night was late shopping. The Christmas decorations were out. Carols sounded from the radio- and record-boutiques. Couples consulted at windows dressed with tinsel, cotton-wool snow and rubicund Santa Clauses with sacks and reindeers. Children pulled at their parents, blowing excited, frosted breaths.

At the toy shop a big red scooter with pump-up tyres, a chromium luggage rack and kick-stand, was spotlighted in the window. Nicholas stood in his old duffle, as suddenly excited as the children. Handbrakes gleamed on the handlebars, a little tool kit hung on the carrier.

He imagined his son waking to that on Christmas morning. What would Cora say? She was strict about extravagance. A salesman picked his way to the window, checked the price ticket and returned inside. In alarm, Nicholas plunged for the door.

The railway station was almost opposite the toy shop, a low and ugly entrance gaping like a mouth. Nicholas crossed the road to telephone. He was triumphant at having secured the scooter. If he told Cora now she would have time to get used to it. He was in the box, arranging his coins, when he remembered that he was supposed to be away. He hesitated as his pleasure soured. Nicholas jabbed angrily at the dial. Cairncross had apologized for the inconvenience.

If Cora's mother answered he would have to say he had just got back. The trunks operator took the number. He had just got back and had found Cora's note.

A year ago a small Chinese restaurant had opened in the village, signifying the aspirations of the new developments around the Heath. Nicholas and Cora had several times treated themselves there on Kemal's money. He felt relaxed after talking to his wife. It had helped settle her fears that he had been Christmas shopping. Nicholas turned inside. He would order wine. Have a good meal. Get all that other out of his head.

The restaurant was furnished with banquettes along either wall. In one a family ate gaily. A few young couples huddled in others. It was quiet at this early hour. Nicholas sat down. A candle in a Chinese ginger jar smoked on the table, attempting atmosphere. The room was dim, the light suffused from strips battened to the ceiling. Nicholas decided to eat the set meal. Ordering was simpler and more varied that way. Appetite woke in him, kindled by the kitchen smells. It had been good to talk to Cora, to reassure her truly not to worry. He thought of the scooter again, removed from the window now, and smiled. Nicholas closed the menu and sat back. Two men occupied the banquette next to him, their heads above the partition.

A knife rang on a glass to call attention. The man on the outside lifted his head. 'Waiter!' he called, and turned to the kitchen.

Nicholas started with surprise. It was as though he were back in the car, seated behind Hardy.

The waiter came from the kitchen.

'Bill, please,' the policeman said, and settled his hat.

Nicholas puzzled, about to speak. Hardy had not said he lived in this area. He heard coins being dropped in a saucer.

'You'd better get up there,' Hardy said to his companion. 'You can join Tims, at the front of the house.'

A disgruntled voice answered, 'There goes my weekend.'

'You haven't got that on your own.'

'It's a funny one,' the other said. 'I don't like these jobs where you draw your issue.'

'It might be rough. He had to send his family away.'

'You haven't a clue what's on?'

'You know as much as I do, chum. You've got your issue and you're signed out to use it.'

166

'I don't like it.'

'We're not paid to like it. See you in the morning.'

Hardy stood up, nodded and left, putting on an overcoat at the rack near the entrance.

Nicholas pressed against the hard partition and felt sick. The other man tipped his head to empty a glass, pushed himself up the seat and went heavily to the coat rack. Nicholas hardly saw him.

'Yes, please?'

The Chinese waiter smiled, poising his pad and pencil. Nicholas struggled to come back.

'You order now?'

Nicholas shook his head.

'No. No, thank you. I've changed my mind. I've forgotten something. I'm sorry.'

At the door he fumbled into his duffle. The waiter watched him until he was gone. He had to get home. He had to get home and think. Almost mindlessly. Nicholas drove up the hill, turned on to the verge and stopped. There was now no other car on the space.

Inside, he leaned on the door, purposeless for a moment. He closed his eyes, feeling nausea again, then crossed the lit room, hurried up the stairs to Bobby's window. He pulled the curtain, looking over his bare lot to the lane. He saw the beamed head-lights approach before he saw the car. Farther on they dimmed. The car reversed neatly and darkened on the spot where he had thought to have disturbed lovers.

Again he tried to reject it, creaking the stairs, darkening the sitting-room to search the front street. Beyond the light on the corner, another car pointed at the house. Nicholas closed the curtains and blundered towards his chair, sagged there in the heavy duffle. When he could think, he would, there was no-thing he could will at present.

He opened his lids, cold and deliberate with anger. For a time he sat on, a darker hump in the dark, then crossed again to the window. The sky had lightened. Wind bent the trees near the corner. Something flared briefly behind the car's windscreen, floated across it and was extinguished. The watchers were light-ing cigarettes. It would be cold inside that metal, cold in the other car behind the house.

Nicholas had sweated in his coat, and threw it off. He pressed the switch on the table lamp, glowing colour into the room.

Everybody had used him. In subtle blackmail Cairncross had sent him back. He had been expendable to Kemal. How suavely Cairncross had lied.

'—Know how you feel, old man. A most regrettable mistake. You were under a strain. Might have made a mistake yourself, what?'

And Hardy: '—It might be rough. He had to send his family away. You've got your issue, and you're signed out to use it.'

He had not been mistaken. He had tried to believe that he had been because too much had happened. Because he had quailed from the responsibility of knowing.

Why had Cairncross lied, acting his beams and eye-poppings, plump pink hands laid on the desk, unable to use his pipe?

Nicholas lifted the priest's bottle and sighted the level against the light. Cairncross had lied. The Arabs were poised to bury their oil in the sands. Why had he lied? Why must Nicholas Arden believe that he had misheard the evidence on the tape?

He had endured and survived that ultimate insanity for the single keeping of himself. Now two others dwelt in his life, and a red scooter for Christmas morning.

There could be no appeal to Cairncross. Whoever, or whatever, Omega might be had given Cairncross instruction. They would try to keep him alive, but they had to keep the knowledge of that from him. What did it mean? Why must Nicholas Arden believe that he was mistaken?

For a long time, he walked the room. A drizzle darkened the street lamps. At the window he could see only dimly the car pointed at the house.

Kemal would not have delayed. When and how would they come for him? What faces would they wear? Would it be some of those he had heard moving in the walled villa. Or the ugly silent man who had watched over him in the Souk? Would it be Kemal himself whose slashed face he would see for the last time?

There was sherry left in the bottle. Nicholas poured some and drank. Again he was compelled to go to the window, rubbing at the condensation. Rain distorted the glass, whipping there in bursts. In this blurred vision, the street and the trees seemed to buckle. The car on the corner appeared to expand and contract. For an instant it was all touched with nightmare. He was waiting there for a Post Office messenger riding a bicycle. He would hand over a brown paper envelope. He would give Nicholas a chit to sign . . .

In the hours of early morning Nicholas dozed unevenly in the flowered chair. Images of violence rose like monsters in his dreaming. He grieved for the Jews who had suffered so cruelly in the madness he had survived. He had always since felt somehow bonded to them. They had been made brothers in that torment. Nicholas started awake in revelation.

When Kemal got his war, Nicholas Arden would be safe. In that wreckage of other bodies, his body would be made secure. They would strike from all sides, bury the oil in the sands. Until then, because he had the secret of that, Kemal must kill him unless he spoke it. It had been spoken. He had told it to Cairncross. Cairncross had needed to lie. Omega had ordered Nicholas Arden's voice to be stopped. The very knowledge of it had to be stopped in his mind.

Why?

Because they were going to let it happen. It was the oil. 'The Sword of Damocles' Cairncross had called it. 'The sword that can drop on our necks at any moment and behead us like a chicken.'

In the shadows Nicholas stumbled to his feet.

In that other night no rain blew.

In the darkly folded mountains, furred with cypress, a silvered moon touched the slopes with a soft, pale illumination. Clouds that would vent tomorrow's rain moved in from the sea.

Lawrence spread the map on his knees, cupped the lens of the torch in his hand. He tried to estimate which small settlement he had passed, lurching the Bentley carefully along the dried and littered water course, checking the compass taped to the steering column.

The water course had turned on itself, swinging the compass needle like a shout. He had been trapped there, sweating, the wheel slippery in his palms, before finding a break in the cracked-earth shoulders, an old crossing or subsidence on which the Bentley had spun, roaring the heavy motor in a betrayal that knocked at Lawrence's heart.

He had kept away from the area in which the English journalist had made his entrance. The area crawling with armour. Here in the south-east corner, where the borders of Lebanon, Jordan and Israel came together, Lawrence had plotted a more open course. The Palestinian guerillas were said to garrison this pocket. They would be lightly armed and equipped.

The clouds put the moon out. Lawrence scrambled the maps aside, slowly turning the car in the dark until the compass pointed direction. He held the small torch, cupped and shaded in his hand, pressing the button to check the bearing. For a long time he bumped on like this, hunched to the windscreen, straining to see. Occasionally an image flashed like lightning. Illusions leapt at his eyes, making him wrench the wheel in panic. It was like walking a minefield, blindfolded.

The thought shot ice through his veins. Here, the open country could be mined. Almost irresistibly, Lawrence was moved to throw his arms across his face. The big Bentley bumped slowly onward, butting into the black.

He had stopped on a climb, feeling the tilt of the seat, fearful of what lay beyond, the likely topple downwards. Lawrence knew his senses to be deranged by the long blind groping. He felt giddied by it, disoriented, as though spun on a swivel chair. Nothing shone or moved or sounded. Only his mind and the trip metre assure him that he moved towards his objective.

He drank shortly from the bottle beside him, opened the door and lifted his head to the glimmering sky until he felt steadied again. He would have to wait until the moon bared to calculate the obstacles ahead. Lawrence got in and shut the door. He checked his watch. In another hour, a little more, it would be light.

He had to be close to the border. It was miraculous that he had not been challenged. Luck, Max Morrow had said, about his wartime exploits. You work it out and you take your chance. If the luck is with you, you win. Lawrence had worked it out, taken his chance, now he prayed for his luck to hold. If he got through, one day, he would meet Max Morrow again. He would meet him as he had never done, one man to another.

Lawrence thought briefly about Nicholas Arden, seeing his face and feeling his touch. But he was committed now beyond that. He had arrived at this instant out of all his life.

Lawrence waited on the moon, strung on the excitement of resolution. Morrow had thought to have stopped him at the airport. He would never have reckoned on this. Lawrence nipped at the whisky and wound it in his mouth.

Around him, the earth began to lighten. Lawrence ground the

cigarette with his heel. Quickly, he checked that the windows were tight in their seals. Barbara's bullet-proof glass.

On the last dash he would punch on the interior lights. He would race for the border lit like a show-case. They would shoot for the man inside. He didn't want them shooting for the tyres.

The Bentley crawled up the steep slope. The white moon popped through cloud. He was on a ridge, above a wheeled track skirting it. A track that pointed directly towards the border. Lawrence closed his eyes, shuddered on one long deep breath. 'Here goes,' he said aloud. The big Bentley began to roll.

He was in and among the bivouac of tents without warning. The moon had sailed into clear sky. It seemed that the tents had popped out of the ground. The Bentley slewed to miss them. Lawrence hit at the lights, flicked the twin headlights to high beam. The Bentley skidded, almost stopped, as he searched for the track between the tents. The wheels spun as he pushed the throttle to the boards. Faintly, briefly, he seemed to hear shouts, a sudden popping of small-arms fire. The Bentley began to roar, racing through the automatic gears, a collecting velocity that thrust Lawrence hard against the seat. He was clear, rushing down a river of light.

The moon outlined the camp ahead, a dark scattering of shapes. Lawrence was too fixed on that to see the deep washout. The Bentley hit it with a terrible jarring shock. The steering wheel slammed into his chest, pitched him choking across the seat. For an instant there was no more feeling, as the Bentley floated upwards.

Lawrence had grasped for the steering wheel and pulled himself up when the wheels crashed again to the ground. The car seemed to crouch and wallow, tipped slowly to one side, then the other. It had righted itself before he regained control. The tents and huts rushed towards him. Other headlights sliced through the dark. Lawrence stiffened his arms. The heavy steel shell sped its course as fixed as a projectile.

He seemed outside himself, as removed as a spectator. Jeeps or scout cars were racing at him, a dazzle of lights which the tinted windscreen almost refuted. Bullets exploded on the glass. Lawrence clearly saw the vehicle angled towards him, and the stuttered flashes of orange and red from the mounted weapon behind the driver. An instant before impact he tipped the wheel towards the hurtling shape.

The scout car hit the Bentley forward of the off-side front wheel. The door bulged inwards. Glass shattered. Ludicrously, for a second, the scout car hung tipped there, crawling the Bentley's off-side like a great grey beetle. Then it fell off the screaming metal.

Crushed, pushed to one side, whistling the wind in its wound, the big Bentley raced across emptiness.

Nicholas opened his eyes on sunlight. The bedroom curtains were back, as Cora had left them. A cologne had spilled in her disordered packing. The dry, sweet bouquet of it was like a presence in the room. Nicholas closed his eyes. His hands were cold outside the covers. He had slept in his clothes, sweated in the bed, the neck-band of his shirt was damp and choking. He unbuttoned the collar, pulled it back and lay there. The reality of last night crept slowly over his body. For a little longer he clenched his eyes against it, listening to street sounds. A milk truck rattled empty bottles. A child called out near by. The telephone next door rang unanswered, barely muffled behind the thin wall.

The small, inoffensive lives enclosed by the street mocked at Nicholas with their peace and order. He opened his eyes on the small room in which drawers stuck and a thin line cracked the ceiling. A room perfumed by his wife's cologne. He had not known how precious it all was to him.

Nicholas went to the window. There were other cars parked at the corner. A man carried a crate, balancing the load on a knee while he opened the luggage boot.

In Bobby's room, Nicholas looked over the back lot. His own car was alone now in the lane. He hesitated, among his son's books and small treasures. The bed was tumbled as the child had left it, the small indent of his head on the pillow. Nicholas released himself from the room's grasp. Every cell in his body expanded with purpose.

Purposefully, he shaved and changed, got money from a drawer. Standing in his duffle coat he drank a mug of coffee. Nicholas left the house by the back door, crossed the soggy lot to the broken gate and the little car.

He was on the incline to the village when he checked the rear-view mirror and saw the following car. In the traffic of the main

172

street it seemed to keep an even distance. Opposite the railway station, Nicholas drew in to the kerb. He watched the taxi rank and waited. The village bustled about its Saturday morning shopping.

A cab entered the rank. Before it stopped Nicholas was already in the road, running the crossing. A motorist hooted at him. On the pavement a woman in furs, wheeling a shopping trolley, halted in disgust as Nicholas grasped at the cab's door. The driver shrugged. One hire was as good as another. 'Where to, then?'

Nicholas steadied himself.

'The Israeli Embassy. Can you hurry?'

Nicholas leaned into the corner. Quickly he scanned about him.

'Number Two, Palace Green,' the driver said.

Nicholas watched in the rear window for the sudden appearance of another car. A black car like the one that had stood in the lane, or a Vauxhall such as Hardy had driven. A florist's truck followed closely behind. Near Maidavale it turned away. He had lost Hardy's men. They would be searching among the Saturday shoppers, looking for men with dark faces.

In the bright cold of streets and houses, Nicholas put his mind forward. Would he be believed at the Embassy? Would they credit his story of a walled villa, a burning-eyed Arab who was, and was not, Kemal? In Area Red ... in Area Green ... the needs of the timing schedule?

Would they believe his story about a snub-nosed man trotting in Room 27, laying pink hands before him, popping his eyes through steel-rimmed spectacles?

'—This is Cairncross. Get me Omega. I have a Red Alert.'

Nicholas touched his pocket. He had the stamps in his passport for proof. He had the number of the unlisted line into Room 27. He had kept the sheets of yellow paper, typed with Kemal's instructions.

The taxi stopped. The driver ran a finger down the index of the street guide.

'Palace Green,' he said, and deliberated. 'You can come on it from two directions. There's an entrance from Millionaire's Row – that's what they call Kensington Palace Gardens. Or ...' He looked again at the map. 'You can come at it out of the High Street.' He snapped the book shut. 'If you're in a hurry, guv, that's the quickest.'

173

'Go that way,' Nicholas said.

The driver nodded, pulled out again into the graceful old street, streaming with cars and buses. He found the turning.

A traffic policeman signalled the cab to the kerb, then bent to the window.

'Where to, driver?'

'Got a fare for the Israelis.'

'No double parking. I'm afraid,' the man said. And to Nicholas, 'You'll have to walk from here, sir. It's only a step.' He nodded and went off under the plane trees.

Up ahead, set back from the street, behind a circular drive, a white flag with two horizontal blue stripes, the Shield of David in its centre, hung from a staff above the entrance. It was very quiet, very still, at this end of the close. The winter sunshine seemed to drip in the foliage of the plane trees, splashing patterns on the pavement. The cab driver was very slow arranging his change, bending to dip into a canvas bag, running coins for inspection, as though the decimal currency caused him confusion still. Nicholas wanted to abandon the change.

The traffic policeman had gone almost from sight, hands clasped behind him. Nothing else in the close moved. It was as though life had been suspended, or held its breath.

'There we are, guv.'

Slowly, carefully, the driver counted the coins into his palm, made an error, shook his head and again began. Nicholas straightened. The cab reversed in a loudening whine. The note changed as it turned. Nicholas stood a moment, looking to the Israeli flag across the road. It hung above the unmoving plane trees as still and stiff as drying washing. Between the cars he saw the heavy, panelled door, a bell, a plaque over the porch.

For an instant Nicholas stood. The flag and the door and the plaque seemed to fill and beat with resonance. His entire life seemed to rise up under his tightening heart. A strange joy for what he was about to do almost clouded his eyes.

He was in the road when a hurried movement snatched at the corner of his vision.

They came quickly, almost running, behind the cover of parked cars. Two dark-faced men, bareheaded. Heavy men in tan raincoats, slowing now, their faces turned flatly at him, like the palms of halting hands.

Lumped in the old blue duffle, Nicholas moved a few more steps, as though his legs had misunderstood the message shouting in his mind. The dark faces that stared so flatly at him together wagged a warning, an agreement that might have been rehearsed.

Nicholas sought about him for aid, his neck seeming to creak on his stiffened body. Watchfully, the dark faces quested with him. A car was entered farther up the close and went noisily off. Nicholas stumbled backwards.

He had to get to the High Street. He had to hide among people. On the other side Kemal's men began to follow. Nicholas began a hesitant, stooped run. He heard their shoes slap behind him.

Pedestrians bunched on the corner. Nicholas pushed among them. He tried to look back, saw only the critical faces surrounding him. The lights changed. He was carried in the quick surge of bodies over the crossing, bumping in his disordered progress on those hurrying from the opposite kerb.

A bus shook and idled, nose against the crossing. The shock of the confrontation hung in Nicholas's mind like webs. The bus rumbled louder, as though it must signal for attention. As his hand grasped the rail Nicholas saw the two men running through the stationary traffic, gain the pavement, brace in recognition. The bus began to move. The dark-faced men in raincoats sprinted along the pavement.

Nicholas hung a moment, swaying against the lurch of the gear change, then pulled himself up the steps. On the upper deck he turned, labouring to breathe. He saw the swirl of tan raincoats on the platform, heard the bang and scrabble of feet.

The few passengers turned their newspapers, balanced shopping on their knees, dreamily watched the passing of department stores, boutiques and restaurants. Nicholas slumped into the empty rear seat.

He was safe for the moment. They wouldn't come for him here. Nicholas struggled for some memory of their faces. Where had they marked him? Had they followed him in the Souk? Watched him from the walled villa?

The conductor climbed the steps, went down the aisle, blank-eyed and introspective.

'Fez. Fez, pliss.'

Blankly he returned, sucked at something in his teeth. Nicholas choked the words that crowded in his throat. 'There are men trying to kill me. Downstairs. Dark men in raincoats.'

'Fez,' the conductor said.

Where was he being carried? Nicholas swallowed to clear himself. 'Where are we going?'

The conductor lifted his long face, eyes dull and tired.

'Where do you want to go?'

'I don't know . . . that is . . . what route are we on?'

Nicholas fought against the imbecility of the words.

The conductor looked briefly away, protesting this additional burden.

'If you don't know where you want to go, I can't help you, can I? We're going to Shaftesbury Avenue.'

The conductor gave Nicholas a ticket and went gratefully away. The bus made its stops, began to fill with louder, younger passengers. Nicholas eased out of the blue duffle. They would look for that. He emptied the pockets, put the coat on the floor. If he pressed out with the others . . . they wouldn't be looking for a man in a grey suit.

Sunlight struck through the windows. For an instant Nicholas saw those other faces. Kemal, Cairncross, the fat Arab, Hardy. The dark men below, for whom he could furnish no lineaments. He thought of his family, and his hands clenched.

'Fez,' the conductor said. 'Fez, pliss.' And on the steps, 'Piccadilly Cir—ciss.'

The aisle began to fill, a shuffle of bodies between the seats. As they reached the stairs, Nicholas pushed among them, head turned away, hunched into his shoulders. The bus began to slow. Downstairs others balanced their way to the platform.

He tried not to run. Commanded himself against the awful need to look back, which could bare his face and betray him. It was as it had been on the pedestrian crossing, images without dimension, pictures flashing on a screen. Figures without the distinction of faces. A clutter of advertising signs. Pigeons lifting under his feet.

Narrow streets appeared, blinked into others. Cars loomed and vanished. The hot smell of salt beef intruded from a sandwich shop. The men gazing in the window turned away. Their dark faces screamed at Nicholas, jolting him like an assault. Then they had passed, laughing softly, chattering in their own tongue.

Nicholas slowed and steadied. In a corner doorway he leaned to calm. The narrow street was filled with men, slowly moving, seemingly alone. The thin light had a brittle clarity. In it, the absorbed flux about him seemed to move in a collective trance.

He saw that the little shops, inspected with such desolate attention, were hung with posters of exposed female flesh, posed, arched, contorted into images of unrealized sexual fantasies.

There were no tan raincoats or slapping feet in the alley which had brought him there. It was quite empty, dark with damp on the edgings. Perhaps Kemal's men still rode the bus. Perhaps they had sought him, found the blue duffle, the empty leaving of their quarry.

A taxi pushed slowly past. Nicholas jumped from his corner, an arm flagging, compelled without thinking into action. The passengers inside glanced briefly at him, smug in the security of possession.

Across the road, Nicholas stood uncertainly for a moment. A thin, fair young man, as pale as an albino, smoked a cigarette and repeated, 'Here it is, sports. The greatest striptease show in the world. Tanya from Russia, Fifi from France, Sabra the Cat Lady . . .'

Nicholas skirted the men staring at the posters. A recording of *Hello, Dolly* scratched thinly from another club.

He did not jolt and stop as he had at the Embassy, or leaning, move a few more steps, like the last wind-up in a clockwork toy. The image had been recycled, a treacherous trick in his mind. It was the way he had seen those other faces on the bus. They had spun for a moment, then vanished. Sickly, Nicholas waited on the image to disappear.

The dark face in the tan raincoat seemed as remote and absorbed as those others, who looked inwards at what they saw. His eyes almost passed over Nicholas, then visibly widened and started. He seemed to stretch in his drape of coat, the head lengthen on its neck. His mouth opened, pulled into a grimace. He stood like that, not moving, screened in flashes by other bodies.

Nicholas felt himself drain, become opaque, as though the blood had left his body. The dark face struck him into inertia, as small animals are said to be made helpless by a snake. And like an animal, cornered, he twisted his head for escape.

A voice said behind him, as though in a private confidence, 'Continuous showing. The hottest revue in town. New act starting now.'

A decorated car with ladders on the roof probed carefully through the idlers, blocking from sight like a mercy the fixed face across the road.

The man in the doorway said softly. 'Downstairs, sir. On the left. New act starting now.'

A gloomy light lit the stairs from below. A small, bare table was set at a curtained doorway. A man sat there and smoked, a cash box and an open book before him. He did not look up as he took the money, pushed the book and pencil at Nicholas. Canned music muffled on the curtain.

The small cellar seemed full of stirring, thick with inhaling and exhaling, like a packed dormitory entered in the dark. Spotlights threw colours at the blonde girl prancing on the little apron stage, slipping out of her garments with ridiculously exaggerated gestures. 'I'm singin' in the rain' the music said, as she bent and writhed. 'Just singin' in the ... rain.'

Nicholas pressed back among the shapes standing behind the few rows of wooden seats. The alteration of light had blinded him. Someone bumped his arm, moved away. He sought about him for an exit, a chink of light or a door.

The blonde stepped out of black panties, held them up daintily in two fingers, dropped them wisping to the floor. A voice called loudly, 'You're not a natural blonde, duckie, are you?' Laughter sounded in appreciation. The girl seated herself astride a bentwood chair, pushed back her long hair, fondled her rouged breasts, anguishing in little sighs and moans.

Dimly, Nicholas made out figures and faces about him. There seemed to be no way in or out, other than through the heavy curtain. If only he had a weapon. A stick or a stone, anything. He strained his ears to hear feet on the stairs.

The blonde twisted and writhed on the chair, sucked the tip of a feather boa, groaned, and drew it slowly between her legs.

Nicholas backed against the wall, close to the curtain. Blood hammered in his head. The lights on the stage blinked off. In the darkness a few in the audience called and clapped. Something rasped heavily across the boards. The cellar filled with scuffling feet and shifting bodies, suppressed coughs and flame of matches. Two frosted lamps lit on the walls. The blonde girl came quickly off the stage. Wrapped in a fluffy kimono, she tripped down the passage, smiling and throwing kisses. The stage lit again as she passed Nicholas. The frosted lights snuffed out. A fragile girl in a scrap of leopard skin hung chained inside a small cage. A whip cracked.

Nicholas backed away from the curtain, found the wall with

178

his hand, edged there until the door the blonde girl had taken yielded. In the crack of light he saw an empty landing, a flight of steep stone steps. He stepped through into musty damp.

The sprung door had closed into a rubber seal. There was not the tiniest sound from the cellar. Somewhere a tap dripped. Nicholas looked up the greased stone steps, their edges worn into hollows. The dripping water seemed to grow louder as though counting to the end of something. The walls and the smell of rotting damp pressed their corruption upon him. He had to move, before the girl in the cage completed her act.

The right-angled turn at the top of the steps pitched Nicholas into the short passage, presenting itself so abruptly that surprise stopped him short. He saw a narrow runner of red linoleum, a naked bulb on a cord, a bare wall and a single door.

Ahead there were voices, clinking glass. A girl passed quickly across the frame of light, brushing at her hair. Laughter went on and on, then spluttered. 'I like it,' someone said and the laughter rose again.

The smell of damp had changed into musky sweetness. There seemed no way out, other than ahead, through the rampant laughter, the light and clinking glass. Nicholas could not bear the pressure of the narrow walls, inescapably aimed at the light. Behind and below him, a few bars of music abruptly rose up. High heels went click-click on the stone. The one door clamoured at him. He reached towards it, wrenched at the knob.

In the deliberately ostentatious room, schemed for colour and furniture, the three men sat silent under a relief of the American eagle. The Ambassador was heavy, thick under the chin. He wore a waistcoat with his tropical suit, a stratagem that concealed the shirt that would otherwise bulge from his waistband. Morrow sat bent, elbows on his knees. Robert Kramer lit a cigarette, stiff in his chair, dribbling the smoke cautiously as though it might be an intrusion.

The Ambassador shook his head and sighed, grimaced and rubbed his face. He shifted his bulk and frowned at Max Morrow.

'I'm going to get hell about this. It's going to be hell on wheels.'

'Not your fault, Ernest,' Morrow said, sitting up. 'Nobody could have called it.'

'You called it,' the Ambassador said. 'You had Robert here

shut down the airport.' He smiled again and became aggrieved. 'It's my ass that's on the griddle. And I don't even know what it's about.'

Morrow said, 'If anyone's ass is on the griddle, it's mine.'

'I'm the one who will have to clean up here,' the Ambassador reminded him. 'It's going to be hell on wheels. They've got the car identified.'

'The car was stolen,' Morrow said. 'That's all they'll get out of Barbara. I've warned her.'

'How the hell did he get through that territory?'

'He worked it out,' Morrow said. 'He worked it out, and took a chance. He hit them in the south-east corner, in the one place the odds were even.'

Kramer hardened his mouth, shot a glance at his chief. The Ambassador was deep in his own thoughts.

'Our position with the Arabs is difficult enough. I'm walking on egg shells here. They could make a big production of this. Build it up into some kind of propaganda.'

'We've got a story, Ernest,' Morrow said. 'We stick to the story. He had a nervous breakdown. He was recently in London seeking treatment. I can arrange evidence from that end. If you want, I'll have him goddamn certified.'

'Max.' The Ambassador leaned forward pointing a finger. 'I don't know what kind of operation you've been running, and maybe it's better that way. But if I have to step up on the mat with a thin story like this, I'm going to want it confirmed by State.'

Morrow nodded his understanding.

'Agreed, Ernest.' He turned to Kramer. 'Did you get confirmation on my flight?'

'Four-thirty,' Kramer said.

'Ernest, until you hear from State, you'll have to stall.'

The Ambassador sighed.

'Yes. I can do that.'

Morrow got up.

'That's it then.'

In his room Max Morrow shakily poured a drink and took it to the window. He had no doubt that the Israelis would believe Lawrence. They would have been watching the Russians in the oil states, trying to put it all together. A cold and clammy fear, almost panic, shook his breath and his body. He thought of the man with the black patch on his eye, the thin, implacable nose twisted like a blade on his face.

Would Dayan strike?

Jesus, Morrow thought, sweet Jesus. The cold on his body changed into sweat. If Dayan should strike first . . .

The world erupted in Max Morrow's head. If Dayan struck, the Arabs would bury the oil in a frenzy of destruction. They would blow the wells, blow the ports, blow the pipelines everywhere. Western civilization would haemorrhage to death in a great black bleeding on the sands.

He shut his eyes and screwed his face for his own terrible responsibility. One bullet. He could have stopped it all with one bullet.

'Politic it,' he pleaded aloud, his eyes shut. 'For the love of Jesus, politic it. Pull back, get out of the Sinai. Promise anything, but promise.'

If the Israelis politicked it, if they would only keep their heads. All it would need would be an announcement. Just one announcement could defuse the bomb. When you've got a man right up on his toes, like the Arabs, strung agonizingly tight, if you can rock him back, back on his heels, something goes out of his mind and body.

'Time,' Morrow pleaded again. 'For Jesus's sake give us time.' Time to flannel, time to deal, time to save everyone's face.

He thought of Lawrence slamming through, the Bentley lit like a Christmas tree, as the guerillas had told it. They would puzzle that for a long time. They must have thought they were firing rubber bullets. Morrow wondered if he would have thought to light the armoured glass.

He had slammed his way through, and nobody could touch him. He hadn't been sworn. He was clean.

Morrow raised the glass.

'Here's to you, Character,' he said aloud. 'I'd never have believed you had the balls. Never have believed it.'

He went to the bed, sat there with his head in his hands.

In the chair facing the door Nicholas stiffened. Again his heart beat heavily, but deeper within him as though tired of too many summonings. He grasped the riveted handle of the sharp, pointed knife, stepped to the wall and waited.

The heavy footsteps passed. Nicholas heard the linoleum

181

squeak, could almost see the man turning. He flattened against the wall, jerked up the knife. The knob moved. The door partly opened.

'Doris?' a voice asked. The door slammed. And from farther along the passage. 'Doris? Where's Doris? She's wanted on the phone.'

The plodding steps again passed. Other feet went quickly, lightly by. Nicholas stayed against the wall, the knife dropped to his side.

The single window, covered by something like mosquito netting, had begun to mantle with dark. The quilted bed was shadowed. Shadows had begun to collect on the chairs. The little kitchen, half closed by the lacquered screen, had blackened. Nicholas went back to the chair, laid the knife on a table.

An affection for this shelter moved him. Exhaustion and gratitude shook him that it should have been put in his way. He felt a great need to stretch out on the clean bright bed and close his eyes.

Just a little longer, he told himself. Just a little more of darkening.

'Well ... hello!'

The rasp of the door, the sudden light on his closed eyelids, burst together on his mind. The young woman stared uncertainly at him, one hand on the light switch, the other about a shopping bag.

Nicholas fought for composure, and tried to smile. 'Hello,' he said. There were no other words in his head, only grey, spinning shapes.

She glanced about her, not moving.

'Who let you in?'

'I'm afraid ... I let myself in. You see ...' he said, and stopped helplessly.

She advanced a little, puzzled, very uncertain.

'Have we met before? That is ... I mean ...' She seemed careful in her confusion, as though not wanting to give offence.

'No.' Nicholas shook his head.

She studied him, looked back to the open door.

'It's just that you seem familiar. One doesn't always remember. That is,' she said quickly, 'you don't remember everyone, do you?'

'I'm sorry,' Nicholas began. 'You see ...'

'Did Harry send you?'

It was all so hopeless. He could have pushed past her, run down the stone stairs.

'Yes,' Nicholas said, grasping, 'Harry.'

She nodded.

'He didn't tell me. Perhaps he left a message. I've been out,' she said unnecessarily and looked again to the door.

'What's your name, then?'

'Nicholas. Nicholas Arden.'

'It's a nice name,' she said. 'I'm Connie. But Harry will have told you that.' She smiled a little. 'Sit down. I'll just put these things away.'

A light went on in the kitchen. She smiled again as she re-entered, took off the furry woollen top coat at a curtained corner and hung it here. The short woollen dress clung to her figure. She was slim, almost thin, small and neat, her eyes hollowed.

'You've not sat down,' she said.

'You're very kind.' It was so unreal. Nicholas was distracted by the open door, the shock he had got when she entered. I must have dozed, he thought. How could I have dozed? And felt claimed by the unaccountable intimacy she seemed to offer, his unfinished sentences that left everything suspended.

'Are you in . . . a hurry?'

'No,' he said. 'No. I'm not in a hurry.'

'I don't mind,' she said. 'You know? If you're in a hurry? Have you been waiting long?'

'No,' he answered uselessly.

She smoothed the woollen dress.

'Would you like a drink then? I've got beer and whisky.'

It had something to do with Harry. Who was Harry?

'You're very kind,' Nicholas said. 'Yes, I would like a whisky.'

'Kind?' she said, and wondered. 'You said that before.'

'I only mean . . .' Again the words hung, uncompleted.

'I like men with manners,' the girl said. 'It makes a difference, doesn't it? I have no soda. Will water do?'

Quickly she crossed to the door and pushed it closed.

'There,' she said, as though completing a contract. 'It's cold outside. There's snow expected.'

'It's warm in here,' Nicholas said. The words seemed to come from someone else.

'I'm lucky.' She crossed to the kitchen again. 'The building is heated. It has to be. You know, for the girls.'

He heard her there, moving things.

'Do you know any of the girls?'

'No. No, I don't.'

'I used to work with some of them. That's why I don't lock the door. Sometimes they come in and take a nap.'

She put down the tray with a bottle and glasses, a small jug of water.

'How in the world,' she asked, 'did that get there?' and blinked at the sharp, pointed knife, as though waiting on it to answer. 'Funny,' she said. 'Excuse me,' and took the knife to the kitchen.

The awakening night life of the streets rumbled and sounded in the walls, the way the engines of a big ship can be felt pulsing everywhere one touches.

'You've not poured yourself a drink,' she said. 'Say when.'

The spirit expanded in Nicholas in a great, hot glow, flushing his mind and body. She watched him, topped his glass when he put it down.

'You look better,' she said. 'You needed that, didn't you?'

'Better?'

'Yes. You looked, you know, one degree under?' Her voice lifted on the interrogative.

'Did I?'

'Yes,' she said gravely, and sipped at her drink. 'I didn't use to like whisky. I used to drink beer. But after . . . after . . . it makes me sick now.'

She began to search in her purse. Nicholas saw how pretty she was. The small face was oval, dimpled on the chin. With her head bent, the hollows of her eyes deepened, dark under the painted brows.

Hurriedly, he filled the silence.

'After?'

She found her cigarettes and offered him one. He shook his head.

'Do you mind scars?' she asked, half hesitating. And then in a kind of defiance, 'I've got a scar.'

Nicholas could see no scar on the small, watchful face.

'I've had an operation,' she said. 'You know, a hysterectomy. I've got a big scar.'

'I'm sorry,' he said and did feel sorry, in ways he could not define.

'I used to work here,' the girl said quickly. 'I used to do an act

184

in a cage. But after . . . after all that . . . well, you can't work with a scar, can you? It was too big to cover with cosmetics. You know what I mean?'

Nicholas remembered the girl he had glimpsed in the cage downstairs, hanging by her arms. It seemed unbearable to him that this should have been her act.

'Do you mind talking?' she asked. 'Harry says I talk too much. Some men don't like it.'

'No. I would like you to talk,' Nicholas said, and wrenched at all the other shouting in his mind.

'Talk about you,' she said, in a manner that disturbed him. It was too eager, too childish.

'There isn't much to say.' He thought what if I told her the truth? That I blundered in here to get away from dark men trying to kill me?

'What do you do, then? You know, for a living?'

'I'm a translator.'

She drew on the cigarette and tipped her head.

'Languages,' he said, to help her. 'I translate one language into another.'

And sometimes I interpret, he thought. I interpret important business discussions about water conservation. I work for an Arab with a slashed face and report to a liar in Room 27.

'Languages,' the girl said. 'You must be very clever. I was stupid at school. Backward, the teachers said. When I had to answer questions, everything, you know . . .' She waved her hand. 'Everything just turned into a big barrel of milk, with me at the bottom. She smiled. 'I've got a friend who's clever.'

Footsteps echoed in the corridor. Nicholas stiffened and waited.

'What does your friend do?'

'He's a dentist, at Highgate. He does all my teeth for nothing. He says that if I look after them I'll never need a plate. My Mum's had a plate for as long as I can remember.'

Again the footsteps went away. The girl had been saying something about her mother.

'Where does your mother live?' Nicholas asked.

'She's got rooms in Islington. She's on the pension now. She looks after my baby. I've got a baby.'

Nicholas thought again of the cage. He understood her now. She was a victim, as he had been a victim. As he had become a victim again.

'This friend. Is he a good friend?' He wanted very much that she should have a friend.

'He is, rather.' She frowned. 'He comes to see me every Sunday. We go to lunch. You know? Somewhere posh. We have wine. Brandy if I want it. Then we come back here. He's a bit queer in some ways,' she said.

She put out the cigarette, lit another. 'I'm not supposed to ask,' she said. 'Harry gets at me about it. But I've got this curiosity. Are you married?'

'Yes,' Nicholas said.

'Family?'

'A little boy.'

'Oh, well,' she said, 'that's life, isn't it?'

It was quite black now, behind the mosquito net curtain. Had Kemal's men searched in the club for him? Would they have waited, hidden in the street? The whisky had doped the nerves and emptiness in his stomach.

'That's another thing I'm not supposed to do,' the girl said, and swayed a little, pouring into the glasses.

Nicholas asked, 'What's that?'

'Get tight. I get tight very quickly. Harry doesn't like it. But you've got to get tight sometimes. It makes things easier. You know? Sometimes I get ... smashed. Then it's like it's happening to someone else. I can hardly remember anything, afterwards.'

She tilted her head, worrying, trying to capture a thought that had escaped. 'I don't mean it like that with you. I wouldn't want you to think that.' She put her hand on his knee. 'I'd better lock the door. Where's the key? You know, the girls?'

When she came back she pulled up the short skirt high on her thighs, stretched her legs and tipped her head. 'It's getting late.' she said, to remind him. 'Harry didn't tell me. I mean ... are you ... do you want to stay the night?'

Nicholas thought of the streets. She couldn't conceive of the gift she was offering him.

'I haven't much money,' he said, and regretted the stupidity of the admission.

'Money?' the girl blinked. 'Didn't Harry take the money?'

'No,' Nicholas said. 'He was in ... a hurry.'

'That will be the day,' the girl said loudly, 'when Harry's in that much of a hurry.' She changed, sceptical and cautious. 'You know? There's something a bit funny about this.' Then tipped her head and thought. 'You didn't have to tell me, did you? You didn't have to tell me you hadn't paid Harry.'

Nicholas waited.

'The joke would have been on me, wouldn't it?' She got up and sat on his lap. 'Doing it for nothing?' She felt very light and fragile. Her fingers touched his cheek. 'You've got lovely skin,' she said. 'Soft. Your hair, too. I like soft black hair. How much money have you got, Nicholas?'

'Eight pounds. Perhaps ten.'

'Will you take me out to dinner?'

'I don't want to go out,' he said quickly. And then, 'You see I left my coat on a bus.'

'Lost it, did you?' she sighed. 'But all night. You know what I mean?' She drew on the cigarette. 'Harry doesn't have to know,' I suppose. It could have been for a short time.' She continued to think. 'Fuck it, anyway,' she said, with simple, shocking finality. 'I feel blue and I like you. That's the main thing, isn't it? We can bring in something to eat from outside.'

He did not hear her at the door until she kicked it and called. He let her in. Her face was pinched.

'Fried rice,' she said, 'chow mein and sweet and sour chicken.' She shook her head. 'It's snowing. Would you believe? I bought a bottle of wine.'

In the kitchen she gave him a corkscrew.

'We should eat quickly before it gets cold.'

Carefully, Nicholas asked, 'Did you see anyone, outside?'

She took off her coat.

'What kind of anyone?'

'Dark men. Arabs. I noticed them when I came in. They were wearing tan raincoats.'

She stopped and looked affronted.

'You don't think that I'd have anything to do with darkies, do you? Is that what you're getting at? If it is, I don't like it.'

'Of course not,' he said. 'They just seemed to be looking for someone. It doesn't matter.'

She sniffed and hung up her coat. Then rubbed her hands briskly.

'Hurry up. Get the cork out.'

They ate on the little table. A radio played in the kitchen. She watched him.

'Hungry, weren't you?'

187

'Yes. A little.'

'Eat up, then. John, that's the Chinaman, always gives me extra portions. Once he gave me a tin of lychee nuts for nothing.'

The food and drink, the pop music the girl had tuned to, seemed to Nicholas like a single absorption in his body. Waves of weariness washed at him.

'Hey,' she said, 'Nicholas.'

He started.

'Have another drink. I'm tight.' She began to hum. 'When do you want to do it?'

She looked blurry to him. The room was blurry, unsteady.

'I'm going to finish this drink,' she said, 'and that's it. Hey, you won't tell Harry, will you?'

'Harry?' He had almost forgotten Harry.

'That you stayed all night and I got smashed. You only had a short time, remember.'

'Don't worry,' Nicholas said, and the unreality clapped again in his head. Kemal appeared between them. There is much to be reclaimed, Brother. Cairncross looked disapprovingly about the room.

'Nice Nicholas,' she said, went unsteadily to the bed and took something wispy from under the pillow. She held it up.

'I'll just wear this. All right?'

She folded the quilt, laid it aside, turned away to undress. She didn't want him to see the scar.

'Come and do it, Nicholas,' she called, her voice suddenly thick.

He watched her and waited. Heard the sudden rasp of breathing and went to the bed. She slept, one thin arm dropped outside the covers. He had not noticed how long her lashes were.

On the sofa, Nicholas covered himself with the quilt. Exhaustion engulfed him. He swallowed against the clot in his throat, then everything extinguished.

Once in the night he started up, his heart painfully thudding, lost in the dark. He searched for something to identify, ran his hand along the back of the sofa, all his body trembling. He reached out and felt the table, knocked over a glass, saw the netted window and began to remember.

There would be this day to get through. One night more. He wondered if other dark men had waited for him at the house. And if Hardy had reported to Cairncross that he had lost Nicholas Arden.

They would all be searching for him now. He had beaten Kemal, beaten Cairncross, beaten Kemal's dark men.

He couldn't attempt the Embassy again. Kemal's men wouldn't risk another failure. They would kill him there in the close. He couldn't return to the house. Cairncross's men would take him. There was this day to get through. One night more.

He had to survive, as once before he had survived. When the Israeli Embassy reopened, he would get to a telephone. Somehow he would make them believe. Somehow he would make them come to him.

Nicholas opened his eyes on sunlight, laying like a bright mat before the window. The rumpled head in the bed was turned away. He uncapped the old translating pen, unfolded one of Kemal's yellow sheets.

Connie,
Thank you for everything. I will never forget your kindness. Good luck.

He signed his name, paused, and added a cross as one does for children. Then he went softly to the kitchen, edged open the drawer and lifted the knife.

Outside, the street was hushed, empty with Sunday morning. Watertrucks, goggling dull yellow headlights, had flushed the interminable trash of the night off the narrow road, sailing it hectically along the gutters into the maws of the storm drains. In the clear cold the water lay like dark paint on the asphalt.

The bulging old woman in the rusty dress had trouble with her feet. She wore carpet slippers, and shuffled. In the doorway she searched among the keys in her apron pocket, carried her mop and plastic bucket down to the small table and the rucked stuff of the curtain.

Nicholas balanced the knife on his palm and tried to reject it. Then he pushed it into his waistband and closed the coat over the riveted wooden handle. He looked back once, saw the girl stir. Carefully he turned the door key.

He was almost outside, half in, half out, of the narrow linoleumed passage. The shape that lifted Nicholas with its shoulder, hurling him backwards, across the table with the note on yellow paper, had only been a glimpsed, rushing blur. The girl in the bed started upright. A cry choked from under the hand at her mouth.

Nicholas tried to rise from the smashed glass and wood. His lips moved, but made no words. He saw only the long barrel of the gun, the tan raincoat behind it.

'Salam-alekum,' the Arab said softly.

Nicholas had one beseeching hand held out when the silenced weapon ripped him.

The girl screamed, a long thin thread, drawn like spun glass. The second Arab quickly stepped towards her. His gun plopped like a tongue clucking. On her small pale form the nightdress stained with splashes.

The big Arab jerked his head. The door closed on the girl and the man in the middle.

In Room 27 Cairncross replaced his tea cup and bent for the red telephone buzzing in its drawer.

'Yes, Omega.'

He listened, his eyes expanding.

'Good Lord,' he said. 'The United Nations has been notified? The Israelis are pulling back from the Canal? Yes, Omega. Thank you.'

'Good Lord,' he said again and got up to trot about the room. Then he went to his desk and dialled a number.

'Hardy? Cairncross. Consider yourself fortunate. The alert on Nicholas Arden is cancelled.'